Books by Shirleen Davies

Historical Western Romance Series

MacLarens of Fire Mountain

Tougher than the Rest, Book One
Faster than the Rest, Book Two
Harder than the Rest, Book Three
Stronger than the Rest, Book Four
Deadlier than the Rest, Book Five
Wilder than the Rest, Book Six

Redemption Mountain

Redemption's Edge, Book One
Wildfire Creek, Book Two
Sunrise Ridge, Book Three
Dixie Moon, Book Four
Survivor Pass, Book Five, Releasing 2016

MacLarens of Boundary Mountain

Colin's Quest, Book One,
Brodie's Gamble, Book Two, Releasing 2016

<u>*Contemporary Romance Series*</u>

MacLarens of Fire Mountain

Second Summer, Book One
Hard Landing, Book Two
One More Day, Book Three
All Your Nights, Book Four
Always Love You, Book Five
Hearts Don't Lie, Book Six
No Getting Over You, Book Seven, Releasing 2015

Peregrine Bay

Reclaiming Love, Book One, A Novella
Our Kind of Love, Book Two, Releasing 2016

Sign up to learn about my New Releases:
www.shirleendavies.com/contact-me.html

Colin's Quest

MacLarens of Boundary Mountain

Historical Western Romance Series

SHIRLEEN DAVIES

Book One in the MacLarens of Boundary Mountain

Historical Western Romance Series

I care about quality, so if you find something in error, please contact me via email at shirleen@shirleendavies.com.

Description

Colin's Quest, Book One, MacLarens of Boundary Mountain Historical Western Romance Series

"The author has a talent for bringing the historical west to life, realistically and vividly, and doesn't shy away from some of the harder aspects of frontier life, even though it's fiction. Recommended to readers who like sweeping western historical romances that are grounded with memorable, likeable characters and a strong sense of place."

For An Undying Love...

When Colin MacLaren headed west on a wagon train, he hoped to find adventure and perhaps a little danger in untamed California. He never expected to meet the girl he would love forever. He also never expected her to be the daughter of his family's age-old enemy, but Sarah was a MacGregor and the anger he anticipated soon became a reality. Her father would not be swayed, vehemently refusing to allow marriage to a MacLaren.

Time Has No Effect...

Forced apart for five years, Sarah never forgot Colin—nor did she give up on his promise to come for her. Carrying the brooch he gave her as proof of their secret betrothal, she scans the trail from California, waiting for Colin to claim her. Unfortunately, her father has other plans.

And Enemies Hold No Power.

Nothing can stop Colin from locating Sarah. Not outlaws, runaways, or miles of difficult trails. However, reuniting is only the beginning. Together they must find the courage to fight the men who would keep them apart—and conquer the challenge of uniting two independent hearts.

Visit my website for a list of characters for each series.
http://www.shirleendavies.com/character-list.html

Dedication

This book is dedicated to all the members of my Street Team.
You are an awesome group and your support means a great deal to me.
Thanks so much!

Acknowledgements

Thanks also to my editor, Kim Young, proofreader, Alicia Carmical, and all of my beta readers. Your insights and suggestions are greatly appreciated.

As always, many thanks to my wonderful resources, including Diane Lebow, who has been a whiz at guiding my social media endeavors, my cover designer, Kim Killion, and Joseph Murray who is a whiz at formatting my books for both print and electronic versions.

Colin's Quest

Prologue

Scotland

November 1854

"Kyla, we must keep the bairns together." Angus MacLaren's booming voice rang above the chaos of those boarding the steamship SS Glasgow. At well over six feet tall, he towered above most of the passengers who shoved forward, waiting for permission to board.

Winds whipped around the large crowd as they waited for the captain to make the boarding announcement for those holding berths on the steerage or tween deck area of the steamship. Angus guessed well over two hundred would be living in close quarters during the trip across the Atlantic.

The savage storm, which they'd hoped to avoid, broke loose as the passengers huddled together, unsuccessfully trying to keep their meager personal belongings from soaking through. As the rain pounded down, everyone surged forward. Being trampled became a serious concern as Angus and his wife tried to keep their boys together while staying close to the three other MacLaren families.

"I have them, Angus. Do not separate yourself from us." Kyla gripped Camden's hand as Colin and

Blaine tugged at her dress, and Angus pressed himself to her back.

Finally, the announcement came.

"Angus and Kyla MacLaren, and children, Colin, Blaine, and Camden."

"Aye."

"Gillis and Audrey MacLaren, and children, Quinn, Heather, Bram, and Thane."

"Aye."

"Ewan and Lorna MacLaren, and children, Brodie, Jinny, and Fletcher."

"Aye."

"Ian and Gail MacLaren, and children, Sean and Bridget."

"Aye."

The attendant looked at the list once more. "Is that all the MacLarens?"

"Aye. We're all here," Gillis confirmed.

"Stay close, lads." Angus glanced toward his brothers, Gillis, Ewan, and Ian, as the mass of humanity surged ahead, rendering them unable to stop or step aside. Four of the MacLaren brothers and their families had spent years saving for the voyage to America, then another year waiting for enough space on the steamer to accommodate all twenty of them.

Following directions, they took steep, narrow ladders to what would become a cargo hold on the return trip to England. For the voyage to America, however, bunk beds, holding up to five passengers each, had been erected in rows of two from fore to aft.

Angus's wide shoulders scraped the sides as he took the steps down. Landing on the wooden deck, he stood, thankful he had a few inches to spare. Glancing amidships, he spotted what he wanted—four bunks together.

"Colin, Blain, come with me." Doing his best not to trample others, he turned sideways, making his way through a space not more than eighteen inches wide, tossing his bag ahead of him to land on one of the bunks. The boys followed his lead, several other MacLarens doing the same.

"Good of you, Angus." Gillis clasped his older brother on the back as all four families secured their space.

Angus glanced at his family, thanking God they'd made it this far. Four brothers, their wives, and their children were all taking a huge risk by leaving Scotland behind to forge what they prayed would be better lives in a new land.

"Da, wake up." Colin shook his father. Feeling the ship heave one way, then another, as massive waves slammed against the sides, Angus's eyes opened a crack, then widened at the jolt of the water's impact.

"Where's your Ma?" Angus's voice was full of unease as he pushed up, his head whipping around to count the number of MacLarens clustered together. He accounted for everyone except two—his wife, Kyla, and youngest son, Camden.

Gripping Colin by the shoulders, he held him close. "Where are your ma and Camden?"

"I...uh..." Colin's head twisted as his gaze roamed the tween deck. "I don't know, Da."

"Stay with your uncles." It was all the warning Colin got before his father pushed him toward Gillis and dashed up the ladder, unaware Colin had ignored his order and followed him.

"You can't be up here." The deckhand grabbed Angus's arm, his voice barely understandable over the roar of the crashing waves. "Get below where it's safe—both of you."

Angus wrenched out of the man's grip and whipped around, noticing Colin a few feet away, gripping the railing with both hands. Anger now added to the cold ball of fear building in his stomach. He didn't have time to deal with a disobedient son.

"My wife and son are missing," Angus roared, shoving the man aside. "Kyla! Camden!" Grabbing whatever he could to stay on his feet, he made his way aft, keeping watch over his shoulder at Colin.

Spotting no sign of them, he turned aft, grasping Colin's arm as the ship shifted, tipping toward starboard. Pulling Colin down with him, he landed on his back, failing to find anything that would stop his body from sliding toward the side. Seeing panic in his son's eyes, Angus calmed his features.

"Don't be afraid, laddie. We'll get out of this." Choking on water, Angus tried to stand at the same time another huge wave hit the port side. Water gushed onto the deck, lifting both of them above the level of the rail. "Let go of me!" Angus yelled as the momentum carried him away from Colin.

"Da!" Colin clung to the rail, wrapping both arms around it, peering overboard and around the deck. His father was nowhere in sight. "Help!" His scream died on his lips as strong arms pulled him away.

"Get him below. Now."

Kicking and squirming, trying to pull away, he found himself shoved down the steep ladder, landing with a thud on the tween deck's floor. Colin swiped at tears streaming down his face.

"Where are they?" His uncle Gillis knelt beside him.

Lifting a face full of anguish, Colin closed his eyes tight, then shook his head. "He—"

"And don't think of coming back up until the storm has passed." The angry voice preceded Angus, who landed in a heap at the bottom of the ladder, rolling to his hands and knees, coughing up water.

"Da!" Colin wrapped his arms around his father's neck, pulling tight.

"Loosen up, laddie. You may choke him." Gillis positioned himself on one side of Angus, Ewan on the other, both lifting him to his feet.

"I couldn't find them." The pain in Angus's voice ripped through his brothers. He turned to climb back up when two sets of hands pulled him back.

"You won't be going up there now. When the storm passes, we'll help you search." Ewan clasped Angus on the shoulder, giving him a grim nod.

An hour passed before the storm moved on and the ship quieted. Angus, joined by Colin and his younger brother, Blaine, refused to move from the base of the ladder. The rest of the MacLarens sat on the bunks, their faces full of grief, not accepting the fate of Kyla and Camden.

"I've waited long enough." Pushing to his feet, Angus grabbed the rails of the ladder, taking a step up as Gillis stood behind him, peering toward the opening above.

"Angus, look." He pointed overhead seconds before a long skirt began to descend, followed by a small boy.

Angus's throat closed at the sight of Kyla and Camden. Holding his arms wide, he wrapped them both in a relieved embrace, Colin and Blaine joining them. Other than being soaked, they appeared to be unharmed.

"Where have you been?" Angus couldn't keep the relief out of his voice.

Settling a hand on his arm, Kyla looked up into his tormented face. "A crew member took us below deck the moment the storm began, then disappeared. No one else knew where we were."

Wrapping her in his arms, Angus let out a shaky sigh. "Promise you'll never put yourself in danger like that again."

"Only if you swear to me that once we reach Philadelphia, we'll never move again."

"I give you my word, Kyla. Our travels will end as soon as we set foot in America."

Chapter One

Independence, Missouri, 1859
Five years later...

"Colin, Blaine, Camden." Angus cupped his hands around his mouth as he called to his three sons. Colin responded first, jumping down from the back of the prairie schooner and running up to his father.

"Yes, Da."

"The wagon master says we'll be ready to leave within the hour. Let your uncles know." Angus brushed his dirt-encrusted hands down his pants before wiping an arm across his forehead.

"I'll do it now." At eighteen, Colin had grown into a handsome young man. Tall and strong, his dark auburn hair and green eyes made him a favorite of the young girls, who whispered and giggled whenever he approached. Yet he seemed oblivious to their interest. Well-read, he'd focused on nothing except learning and helping the family build their farm. Other than his cousins, his social life consisted of one or two local boys, even though their time together was infrequent.

Stopping at each of the six MacLaren wagons, he spoke to his uncles and aunts, relaying the message, and getting an earful of how they did or didn't want to make the journey. He'd lend a sympathetic ear, shrug, then move on.

They'd made the painful decision to leave the family farm east of Philadelphia when it became clear they'd never make enough to do more than survive. The four brothers had voted to move west. It had been a costly choice for Angus. He and Kyla had fought bitterly over the decision. She accused him of breaking his promise to never move again, but he implored her to understand their situation. The brothers wanted more for their families than just survival. Leaving a legacy to their children and grandchildren came second only to providing shelter and food. They wanted to fulfill the dreams each held when they made the decision to leave everything behind in Scotland to start new lives.

The brothers sold all they owned, bought heavy Conestoga wagons, popular in the east, and traveled to Independence, from where hundreds of settlers left each year as part of the growing stream of wagon trains. Angus had secured the name of one of the best wagon masters, reserving spots in a train leaving Missouri in late spring.

Their meeting with the wagon master gave the brothers their first setback. They listened as the man told them their wagons would need to be replaced with lighter and more maneuverable Prairie Schooners. The change also allowed them to use fewer horses or oxen—a major advantage over the Conestoga. They'd been told at least half of their personal belongings had to be sold or left behind. He refused to take them otherwise. Also, the supplies they'd brought weren't adequate for the long journey. Food items needed to be repacked to last longer, such as storing bacon in barrels of bran. Tools, buckskins, spare axels, coils of rope, and additional weapons needed to be purchased. Each wagon had to be waterproofed using linseed oil on the canvas.

"Hey, Colin. You must come with us." His brother Blaine, two years younger but almost as tall, shot him a wide grin. Standing next to him, Quinn and Brodie, two of the older cousins, tried to hide smiles.

"Ah, so what have you lads gotten yourself into now?" The four were the closest in age and had always been tight. Their bond had grown stronger during the weeks at sea and over the last five years. They were almost inseparable.

"A family, much like ours, at the back. They have four wagons and another for supplies." Quinn shoved his hands in his pockets and studied his feet.

"And?" Colin's brows knitted together. Unlike Colin, fifteen-year-old Quinn thrived on the attention the girls bestowed on him. As tall and handsome as Colin, he'd already experienced the favors a local farm girl offered before they'd sold out and moved.

"Well, they have mostly girls...." Quinn let his voice trail off as his father, Gillis, approached.

"What are you boys up to now? No good, I'm certain. Get on with you. We'll be pulling out soon." Gillis crossed his arms, hiding a smirk. He knew perfectly well what his oldest son had seen and shared with the cousins. He also knew something the boys didn't. The family traveling at the back consisted of members of the clan MacGregor. In the old country, the MacLarens and MacGregors held no love for each other, their feud legendary over more than two centuries. The MacLarens no longer cared about old insults and misunderstandings, but the MacGregors had never been so forgiving. He'd speak to Angus, Ewan, and Ian. The four would decide how to approach the MacGregors to make certain they had no trouble during the trip. They'd left much behind in Scotland, including blood wars better left to past generations.

The boys had done as Gillis asked, except they'd made a slight detour, passing the line of waiting wagons on their way to the end.

"I've got work to finish, Quinn. I've no time for your antics today." Colin stopped, shooting his cousin an exasperated look. Blaine and Brodie stood aside, wise enough to keep their thoughts to themselves. "There will be lots of time to meet the others after we leave."

"A few more minutes, Colin. Two at most. Believe me, you won't be unhappy." Quinn turned his back on Colin and kept walking.

Colin let out a sigh, but followed. "Ach, he's going to lead us all astray someday," he muttered, shaking his head at his cousin's propensity for causing havoc.

"There." Quinn hid next to a wagon, pointing to the one behind it.

Colin followed Quinn's gaze. What he saw caused his breath to hitch, and as he'd tell others later, his heart to stop. Not twenty feet away stood the most beautiful girl he'd ever seen, laughing and gesturing with her hands as the other girls around her giggled.

His jaw dropped open as he watched tendrils of golden brown hair escape the tight bun to fly around her face. She brushed them away, her movements quick, yet graceful. Even from here, he could see a smattering of freckles across her nose and cheeks. And her smile...he'd never seen anything more radiant.

He couldn't stop staring, couldn't move if he wanted to, feeling as if he'd been nailed to the ground. Then she turned, saw him watching her, and froze. The brightest blue eyes he'd ever seen stared back. If it were possible for one's heart to stop and keep on living, he was an example.

Turning toward him, she took a few steps closer, never dropping her gaze.

"Sarah, I need your help in the wagon." An older woman, Colin guessed to be her mother, came up beside her. Noting the direction of Sarah's attention, she spotted Colin, sending him a scowl. "Off with you, lass. You've wasted enough time already." She grabbed Sarah by the arm and pulled her along.

Just before Sarah disappeared from view, she turned her head, sending him the brightest, most glorious smile he'd ever seen. At that moment, Colin saw his future as clearly as if it had already happened. Sarah would be his.

The first week on the trail after leaving Independence proved uneventful. Good weather kept the wagons moving at a steady pace. The MacLarens used their oxen to pull the heavier wagons and horses for the others. The men walked alongside, prodding the animals and clearing the trail when necessary. The women alternated between walking with the men and riding in the wagons. All except the youngest. Seven of the children were five and under, unable to keep up for longer than a few minutes. Instead, the older girls kept them inside the wagons, playing games and reading most of each day.

The older boys helped the men keep the wagons moving, while the younger ones tended the small herd of cows they used for milk. Everyone had a job, and within days, a routine settled over each member of the MacLaren clan.

Their first stop would be Fort Kearny. Built in the late 1840s, the wagon master said it wasn't much to see. What they most looked forward to was Dobytown. Established close to the fort, it had become a hub for westbound settlers, those in search of gold, gamblers, and assorted outlaws.

The wagon master had called a meeting the night before they arrived to prepare them for what to expect.

"I'm advising just the men travel into town, while the women and children stay behind."

"Why?" Ewan asked, knowing how much his wife had looked forward to a touch of civilization.

"It's a rough town without much law. The last time I came through, there were more saloons and brothels than stores catering to the ladies. 'Course, it's up to you."

After much discussion, the MacLarens decided to send the four men in for supplies, leaving the older boys in charge of keeping the others safe. The MacGregors and most of the others did the same, except for Dougal's wife, Robena, who refused to stay behind.

"Be back before dark," the wagon master cautioned as the group either rode horses or walked the half-mile into Dobytown.

"What do you say we walk around camp?" Quinn suggested to Colin, Brodie, and Blaine after the men left. "It's time we got to know our neighbors."

They all knew what Quinn meant by neighbors. The wagons contained a good number of boys and girls around their age. With all the work each day, they'd had little time to visit.

"You three go. I'll stay with the women and children." Colin's acute sense of responsibility kept him from much of the activities considered normal for most boys.

"Nae, you'll do no such thing, Colin MacLaren."

He whipped around, surprised to see his mother and twin sisters a few feet away.

"But Da said we should stay close to you."

"Look around. There's nowhere to go that you can't see the wagons. It's barren land as far as you can see. Who's going to bother us?" Kyla strolled up to him. "Go. Meet some of our neighbors while you have some time."

Quinn cuffed him on the back of the head. "Let's go, Colin, before your ma changes her mind." He flashed Kyla a brilliant smile, grabbed Colin's arm, and pulled him along. "What say we start at the back and go forward?"

The others nodded, following behind Quinn to the last wagon where several of the younger MacGregor children sat, their faces somber.

"What do we have here?" Quinn jumped inside, the heat oppressive. Seeing their sweat-soaked clothes and faces, he knew none could be older than nine. "Ach, you lads should be outside where there's a breeze. Come on now."

The older ones jumped down while he handed the younger boys to Colin.

"Where are the lassies?" Colin knew there were at least three.

The oldest stepped forward, his chin tilted up. "They're over there." He pointed toward a group of low bushes fifty yards away. "We didn't want to go." His voice held a hint of disgust.

"And why not?" Colin's eyes widened when he saw Sarah with the group of girls.

"She's a girl."

"Ah, I see now. Is she your sister?"

"Nae. There are only girls in Uncle Dougal's family. She's my cousin."

Colin turned his gaze back to Sarah. She threw her head back, laughing, then looked at the wagon to see him staring at her. Standing, she brushed leaves and twigs from her skirt as she walked toward him.

"Hello, Colin MacLaren." Her smile faltered when he continued to stare without responding. "Are you well?"

"Colin, the girl asked you a question." Blaine stood next to him, nudging his arm.

"Uh...aye, I am quite well. How did you know my name?" He didn't recall telling her.

"I asked, of course." She rolled her eyes as if it were the silliest question she'd ever heard.

"Come on, Colin. Let's go," Brodie coaxed as the other three started toward the front wagon.

"You go on. I'll catch up with you," he called over his shoulder, not taking his gaze from Sarah. "So you asked about me, did you?" He felt inordinately pleased her curiosity about him matched his.

Shrugging, she lowered her head, catching her lower lip between her teeth.

He took a step closer, wanting to coax a smile from her. "I've wondered about you, too."

Sarah's head shot up, her eyes wide as a smile played across her face. "You have?"

Nodding, he took the few steps to the wagon, leaning against it as he shoved his hands in his pockets. "Aye."

Taking a few steps forward, she clasped her hands together. "What did you wonder about me?"

"Well...how old are you?"

"I'll be seventeen in a month. How old are you?"

"Eighteen," he answered, straightening.

"Are you going to Oregon?" She held her breath, praying they would be going to the same place.

"Is that where you're going?"

She nodded, waiting.

He pursed his lips, already thinking of the distance between them. "My family is traveling to California. Da bought land from a family at our church. One of their relatives died, leaving them his ranch in California. They'd visited him once, but had no desire to move west."

Sarah moved next to him and leaned a shoulder against the wagon. "Tell me about it."

Colin had memorized every detail the family had given them until he could picture the land in his head.

"The land sits against the Boundary Mountain Range, which separates the Utah Territory from California. Several hundred acres make up Circle M Ranch. That's what Da and my uncles are calling it."

His voice fell into the Scottish brogue of his homeland as he spoke. Sarah relaxed, comforted by the familiar sound.

"There's at least one river and many streams. Miles of trees, and pastureland so rich, any animal will thrive and all vegetables will grow. And wildlife so plentiful we'll have as much meat as we need each winter."

"It sounds wonderful, Colin."

"Aye, it does."

"Colin, you'd best come now. Da and all the other men are returning." Blaine glanced at Sarah, then back at Colin, making certain his brother caught his meaning.

"It was good to see you, Colin MacLaren." Sarah's beautiful eyes bore into his and he knew she felt the same connection he did.

"I will see you again, Sarah MacGregor."

"We need to leave now, Colin. We can't wait any longer." Blaine grabbed his arm, pulling him along. Sarah climbed back into the wagon, glancing over her shoulder before disappearing inside.

"We're going through the supplies too quickly, Angus. We'll never have enough to make it the next four months if we don't conserve." Kyla worried her bottom lip. They'd been on the trail almost three months. She'd been as careful as possible, using the least amount of flour, sugar, and lard possible for two adults, three growing boys, and two small girls. The drop in what they started out with scared her.

The wagons had pulled to a stop, taking a break from the sweltering summer heat. They were almost to Fort Bridger, where Angus and the others planned to replenish their supplies.

"We shouldn't be this low." Kyla swept a strand of hair from her face, then blotted her forehead with a handkerchief. Arguing from several yards away caught her attention. Their twin girls, Chrissy and Alana, had been born a year after they landed in America. At four, they got along better than most sisters, but they did have their moments.

Angus wrapped his arms around her, pulling her close. "We'll be fine with what we have, lass." He glanced at the twins, who now sat on the ground, playing with their dolls and giggling. "If needed, we'll cut back further until we reach Fort Bridger. You worry too much."

Nestling into the comfort of his chest, she let out a deep sigh. "I'm becoming my ma."

Angus laughed, pulling back to place a kiss on her forehead. "Nae. It would never be so." Her mother had turned into a tyrant as she aged, alienating her husband and children. Kyla had sworn she'd never become her.

They'd settled their differences about the journey, Kyla acknowledging the brothers' reasons for pulling up roots to go west. All four men had big dreams. She wouldn't be the one to deny Angus his part of it.

"Come. We'll take the lassies for a walk before going back on the trail." Angus tugged at her hand, getting no protest.

They hadn't gone far when the sight of Colin speaking with a young woman had them stopping.

"Who is she, Angus?"

"MacGregor's daughter, Sarah. They talk whenever the wagons stop and she can get away from her da and ma." Angus felt bad for his oldest son. He already knew there'd be no future between a MacLaren and a MacGregor—Dougal MacGregor would make certain of it.

"How do you know this?"

"With so many MacLarens, nothing goes unnoticed for long. They spend as much free time together as they can." He let out a deep breath. "I'm afraid they have no future, but I can't bring myself to warn him away."

"Like my da tried to warn *you* off?" she teased, forever glad Angus had stood his ground.

"And look what good it did." He squeezed her hand, placing a kiss on her cheek.

"Sarah!" Chrissy MacLaren squealed before she and Alana ran toward their brother. Colin leaned down, scooping Alana up while Sarah crouched down next to Chrissy.

"What are you wee bairns doing about?" Colin asked, tickling Alana, provoking a stream of giggles.

The girls pointed in the direction of Colin's parents.

Setting Alana down, his cheeks warmed at the knowing look on his parents' faces.

"I should go." Sarah took a step away before Colin's hand took hers, pulling her close.

"No. It's time you met them."

Kyla smiled at Colin, then shifted her gaze to Sarah. "Angus tells me you're Sarah, Dougal MacGregor's daughter."

Moving closer to Colin, Sarah nodded. Her father hated the friendship she had started with Colin, even threatening to keep her in the wagon day and night until they reached their destination. Her mother had intervened, telling him she and Colin were too young for them to worry over. Sarah disagreed, but kept her thoughts to herself. At least for now, she and Colin were allowed to talk as long as she stayed within sight of the family wagons.

Kyla's sharp gaze missed nothing. They were young, but their feelings for each other were plain to see. A knot formed in her stomach, knowing the pain awaiting her son. Dougal would never agree to a union with a MacLaren.

"Sarah, this is my ma and da." Colin tried to ease her anxiety. Although he'd assured her his family hadn't brought old clan hatreds to America, she hadn't been able to accept it. Her da lived and breathed the past, even when he'd made the decision to start over in a new land.

"Hello. It's nice to meet you, Mr. and Mrs. MacLaren." Blushing, she leaned toward Colin.

Angus spotted movement near Sarah's wagon, knowing someone watched. "We need to get ready to leave, Colin. Say your goodbyes." With that, he and Kyla turned back toward their own wagon.

Colin's mouth tilted upward as he looked at her. "We'll meet after supper."

"Aye." She glanced over her shoulder, sensing her ma's eyes on her. "I have to go." Picking up her skirt, she ran back to the wagon.

Colin strode away, confused by the onslaught of emotions he felt each time they were together. No one had to tell him they weren't ready to marry. He'd almost gotten into fisticuffs with Quinn when he'd joked about Colin offering a handfast with Sarah, a dying custom in their homeland. He'd told Quinn they would wed, nothing less. Afterwards, Quinn had stayed quiet, keeping his distance when Colin and Sarah were together.

Before the trip ended, he'd offer for her hand, knowing they'd have to wait before they married. He prayed Dougal MacGregor would agree to Sarah accompanying the MacLarens to their land in California, with his da and ma as chaperones, until they'd grown the ranch enough to support more family. Quinn thought he was daft to expect MacGregor to put Sarah's wishes above his own. Colin knew Quinn might be right, but the knowledge wouldn't deter him. He might be young, but he knew his mind. And he knew who he wanted.

Chapter Two

"You will keep away from the MacLaren boy or I will tie you in the wagon until we reach Fort Hall." Hands fisted on hips, face red with anger, Dougal MacGregor glared down at Sarah sitting outside the wagon, hands clasped in her lap. He'd seen them together again at their last stop, holding hands and laughing as they walked away from the wagons. He knew what came next. "I've stated many times that I will not approve any marriage until you are older. You'll not be marrying at seventeen, maybe not until you're twenty-one. That is my decision, and you will abide by it. As God is my witness, I'd marry you to a Frenchman before letting a MacLaren have you."

Sarah's young heart twisted, believing her father would do as he said. He ruled the family with a firm hand, giving little thought to the pain he created by his hostile actions.

She knew part of his bitterness came from having three daughters and no sons. Sarah hadn't realized what a disappointment the first two girls had been to him until her third sister was born. She'd been old enough to witness his anguish, the way he blamed his wife, forbidding her from ever bearing another child. Sarah knew how babies were created and suspected the only way it could be avoided was for her parents to never share a bed.

"Do you understand me, Sarah?" His voice contained the fury still seething through him. "You will not see or speak to the MacLaren boy again."

"Dougal—"

"Quiet, Robena. I'll not have you interfering. This time, your daughter has gone too far." He waved her away. "Go be with the other women." Expecting his order to be obeyed, he turned toward Sarah, his eyes hard and unrelenting. "I asked you a question. Do you understand you're never to see the MacLaren boy again?"

Her throat clogged with tears she refused to shed, Sarah could only nod, although her heart said otherwise. They had less than a month before reaching Fort Hall. Her family would continue north on the Oregon Trail, while Colin's would head south toward California. The split in the wagon train meant they might never see each other again, a thought she could barely comprehend.

Although Sarah knew her father's threat was as real as the sweltering summer heat, she *would* see Colin again—if only to say goodbye.

Colin stared at the moon, knowing it had to be past midnight. Sarah hadn't come or sent word through her sister, Geneen, the one person she could trust. She'd missed their meeting four nights in a row, and had barely stepped outside their wagon at any of the stops. Every instinct he had told him to confront MacGregor, confess his love for Sarah, and accept the consequences.

At the sound of leaves crunching underfoot, he turned, seeing his father come up behind him, clasping a shoulder and squeezing.

"It's time to bed down, Colin."

Colin's chest squeezed as he turned pain-filled eyes to his father. "I love her, Da."

"I know, lad." Angus thought a moment, choosing his words carefully. "Come. Walk with me." They took a deer path along a small hill, using the full moon for light. When they were a hundred yards from camp, Angus broke the silence. "You're almost a man, Colin, and I'm certain you know your heart. My question is, what do you intend to do about your feelings?"

"I'll ask MacGregor for her hand." Colin explained his plan to have Sarah continue to California with them until they were old enough to obtain Dougal's approval to marry. Sarah had explained he wouldn't give approval to marry anyone until she'd turned twenty-one. Colin didn't care if he waited two years or ten, Sarah was the woman he wanted. Angus listened, his face a mask. "Will you support me on this, Da?"

He thought over his son's words, knowing they had less than three weeks to arrange a betrothal with Dougal. "Are you certain Sarah feels the same?"

"Yes. As God is my witness, we share the same love."

"Then we will speak with your Ma. She and Robena MacGregor have become friends. It isn't much, but any help with MacGregor will be accepted."

"Pull the wagons as close as you can and tighten down the canvases," the wagon master shouted as the sudden summer storm pounded them with drops the size of small stones.

Lightning speared from the sky in every direction, hitting the ground a few hundred yards all around. Even the stalwart oxen bristled at the flashes and subsequent thunder. Cows, so carefully tended throughout the journey, panicked, stampeding in fear as the wind and rain increased.

"Let them go," Angus yelled to the younger boys tending the animals, motioning them back to the wagons. "We'll find them when this passes."

Canvas covers on several wagons tore away, slapping as the wind turned into a gale, sweeping rain through the open wagons, soaking all within. The ground turned into a muddy mess within minutes, sucking the boots right off the men's feet as they scrambled to secure their families and belongings.

A crack of thunder followed by a loud scream had Colin shifting to stare toward Sarah's wagon. The canvas had nearly ripped off, the ropes whipping around, creating a danger to the women inside. Abandoning the work he'd been doing, he rushed to their wagon, grabbed Sarah around the waist and lifted her off the wagon, then gripped her shoulders to stare into her eyes.

"Take your mother and sisters and get in our wagon. You'll be safe there."

She grabbed her youngest sister's hand and started to run, seeing Geneen and their mother follow the moment Colin set them on the ground. Kyla reached out her hands, helping them into the MacLaren wagon.

Colin stood at the back, sending Sarah a reassuring glance. With a quick nod, he returned to securing their own wagons before helping Angus with the animals.

The storm hovered above them for what seemed like hours. Wheels shifted, sinking into the soaked ground, causing wagons to tip precariously. Men rushed to haul the wagons upright, securing them with ropes and stakes, which quickly gave way in the water-logged ground.

Through it all, Colin had yet to see one sign of Dougal or the other MacGregor men. Not once did anyone come back to check on the women and children. He suspected they chased panicked cows and horses. Colin's gut clenched in disgust at men who'd let their families fend for themselves in such a raging storm while chasing animals easily found when the rain passed.

"Colin, we've done all we can for now. Blaine and Camden are in the wagon. Join them, make certain everyone is all right. I'm going to check on Gillis and the others." Angus pulled his drenched coat around him, trying to keep his boots from sticking in the deep mud as he made his way to his brothers' wagons.

"I'll go with you," Colin called after him. All he got was a raised hand, warning him off. Wiping rain from his face, he grabbed hold of the wagon frame and pulled himself inside, staring into a sea of tired and strained faces. Without thought, his gaze searched for Sarah, finding her sitting at the front with his mother.

"You stay put," Kyla said to Sarah. "I need to check on the girls." She rose, nodding at Colin to take her place as she moved in the cramped space, finding a seat next to the twins.

Colin lowered himself next to Sarah, letting their thighs touch as he ran his hands through his hair, squeezing out the moisture. Lowering his hands, he turned toward her, his heart swelling at the look of adoration in her eyes.

"I've missed you," he whispered so no one else could hear, grasping her hand in his. "We have to talk."

"I know, but how? Da doesn't let me get more than a few feet away from the wagon." She threaded her fingers through his and squeezed.

"Everyone will be busy for the next two days, cleaning up after the storm, searching for lost animals, and repairing wagons. Your da can't watch you every minute. We'll find a way." He leaned toward her, wishing he could brush his lips across hers. He'd kissed her for a brief moment once and couldn't forget the taste of her. He had no intention of ever forgetting.

"Robena, Sarah, are you in there?"

Sarah's frightened eyes locked on Colin at the sound of her father's voice. Without thought, he leaned over and placed a kiss on her cheek before launching himself out the front of the wagon as the back flap flew open.

Dougal's dark gaze raked over those inside, searching for one face but not seeing it. "Robena, it's time to return to our wagon," he barked out. When she didn't move right away, he leaned further inside, glaring at her. "*Now*, wife."

By the time the MacGregors climbed from the wagon, Colin had made his way over to his father and uncles, keeping watch as Sarah approached on her way to their wagon. Dipping his head, he shifted enough to let his side touch hers as she passed by.

"MacGregor," Angus called after him.

Dougal turned, fisted hands on his waist. "What is it you want, MacLaren?"

"Let your family stay in our wagon. You have two days of repair to get yours back in shape."

"Where my family sleeps is no business of yours."

"There's no reason for them to sleep without cover when we have room for them," Angus tried again.

"Ach, you're as thick as a chapel stone, MacLaren. I said no. We don't want or need your charity."

Ewan came up beside Angus, shaking his head as Dougal stormed away. "The man has no thoughts of anyone except himself. At least you offered."

"As if it did any good." Angus cast a look at Colin, already knowing the outcome of any discussion about Sarah with her father. His heart ached for his son. There would be no future for those two.

The next two days passed in slow frustration for all the settlers. Few wagons were spared and most families lost some of their supplies. As Colin predicted, he and Sarah had been able to talk when the MacGregor men left in search of the rest of their small herd of cattle.

Grabbing her hand, he drew her past the wagons and into the privacy of a stand of pines. He wasted none of the few precious moments they had.

"I'm going to ask your da for permission to marry you, Sarah."

Her hands covered her mouth, her eyes going wide, then closing as tears threatened.

Misinterpreting her reaction, Colin wrapped an arm around her shoulders. "You do love me, don't you, Sarah?"

Nodding, she let the tears run down her cheeks as arms circled his neck. "Yes, I love you. More than you know."

Hugging her close, he lowered his head to her ear. "I love you, Sarah, and want to spend my life with you." Brushing a kiss across her lips, he leaned back to look at her. "This is what Da and I plan to do."

Two weeks passed since the storm's damage had been repaired and the wagons resumed their journey. Colin had spotted Sarah a few times, but knew the trouble it would cause if he approached her.

He derived comfort from knowing they'd said all they could about their future the night after the storm. All they could do now was communicate through messages passed through Geneen. MacGregor had reaffirmed his order forbidding Sarah from ever speaking to or seeing Colin again. As before, he'd confined her to the wagon, allowing her outside only for personal needs and to help her ma prepare meals.

"She cares about you deeply, Colin. Do not doubt it." Geneen had taken her own risks getting word to him. "Sarah is miserable. I wish there was something I could do."

"You are doing enough. There is no purpose in bringing your da's wrath down on you also."

"We reach Fort Hall in four days. What will you do?" At sixteen, Geneen seemed old for her years, holding wisdom many adults would welcome.

"My da and I will meet with yours. I will ask for her hand."

Geneen's eyes grew wide. "Do you have any idea what you're asking?" She gripped his arm tight, surprised Sarah had not told her of their plan. "He'll never allow her to marry any MacLaren. Not while there is a breath in his body. Da cannot get over old feuds, no matter how far from the old country we travel. He's a bitter man, full of hate." She glanced around, reassuring herself they were alone. "You must take her and run. If you love her, you'll leave and not look back."

"You're asking me to steal her away, leave our families, and take our chances alone?"

"Nae. I'm saying the both of you should go while you can. Hide, then meet your family somewhere between Fort Hall and California."

"That's a fool's journey, Geneen. I've no experience on the trail alone. My mistakes could get us killed."

"Aye, but you have three days to prepare and talk with your da. Surely he'll help you."

Trying to think, he paced a few feet away. He'd thought the same more than once, discarding the idea each time, knowing MacGregor would send men after them, accuse Colin of kidnapping. No matter Sarah's denials, he'd find a way to punish both of them, possibly sending Colin to prison. There'd be little his family could do.

Turning toward Geneen, he shook his head. "I cannot ask my family to aid me in such an effort. Nae, we will speak to your father as men and come to a reasonable understanding so Sarah and I can marry. I don't want to ask her to start a life by running from her family, perhaps never seeing you again."

Geneen caught her lower lip, then shook her head slowly. "He'll never agree to a union—not between you and Sarah. All we can do now is pray that God will soften his heart so when you and your da state your case, he might listen."

Offering her a weary smile, he nodded. "Then we will pray."

"Are you ready, lad?"

"Aye, as ready as I can be."

They'd waited until the last night on the trail. Tomorrow morning the wagons would enter Fort Hall, a major stopping point for emigrants along the Snake River. From there, the MacGregors would travel west, then north, following the trail through Oregon to the Willamette Valley. The MacLarens would journey southwest to their destination at the base of Boundary Mountain.

Colin turned to Angus and let out a steadying breath. "Let's go."

The MacGregors sat around a fire, finishing their evening meal. Unlike the MacLaren camp, where laughter and constant conversation filled the time, this camp was solemn, oppressive. A sense of foreboding crept through Colin as they walked straight up to Dougal.

Without acknowledging them, Dougal washed down his food with coffee and set his cup aside.

"You've wasted your time, MacLaren."

"But you've yet to hear why we've come," Angus replied, frustration at the man's lack of respect burning a hole in his gut.

"I know why you're here and my daughter will never marry your boy. I'll send her to a convent before I'd let that happen."

A collective gasp from Dougal's wife and Sarah had no impact on him.

"Mr. MacGregor, let me—"

Standing in one abrupt move, Dougal whirled on Colin, their chests touching. To his credit, Colin stood firm, glaring into the older man's eyes.

His face red, eyes bulging, he repeated his message. "You'll not have my daughter. It makes no difference if you offer all you and your family own. She'll never be yours."

Colin took his gaze off Dougal long enough to glance at Sarah, tears streaming down her face as her mother wrapped an arm around her shoulders. Anger swelled within him. He should be the one comforting Sarah, telling her to forget what her da said and believe they still had a future. Sarah had to understand he'd never give up on them—not ever.

Angus stepped forward, trying to ease the tension. "Perhaps if we calm down—"

This time Dougal's wrath turned on Angus. "Take your kin and leave." He jutted his chin toward Colin, unmistakable hatred blazing from bloodshot eyes. "We'll speak of this no more."

"But, Da..." Sarah tore herself from her mother's embrace and ran toward Dougal. "Please, Da, just listen to him." She got to a foot from him before his massive arm swung out, knocking her to the ground.

Colin could take no more. Launching himself onto Dougal's back, he grabbed the man's arms, wrenching them backward, pulling him away from Sarah.

"You'll not hurt her," Colin yelled, his voice containing all the pent up fury he felt for the vile man.

Dougal whirled, throwing Colin from his back, then turned toward his wife. "Take her to the wagon," he ordered, shooting a gaze at Sarah. He spun back toward Colin who charged, ramming his head into Dougal's stomach.

The man stumbled backward, falling over a log before landing with a thud. "I'll kill you," he bellowed before storming toward Colin.

As if prearranged, the three oldest MacLaren men and their sons appeared from out of the darkness, standing behind Colin.

"You fight one of us, you fight us all, MacGregor. Make your decision carefully," Angus warned, inserting himself in front of Colin.

Even with his one brother and cousin, Dougal knew they were no match for the four brothers and oldest sons. Although he wanted nothing more than to teach the MacLarens a lesson, he couldn't afford to get hurt before finishing their journey to Oregon.

Dougal stepped up to him. "You take your boy and go. Do not let him near me or mine again. I won't be responsible for what happens to him if you do."

Angus's eyes narrowed on him before nodding, then turning to Colin.

"It's over, lad. Let's go." He took his son's arm.

"Da...I can't—"

Angus yanked Colin to him, sending him a stern look. "You will do as I say and leave. It's done." Pushing his son ahead of him, Angus followed, his body shaking with anger at MacGregor and grief for his son.

They'd made it no more than twenty feet when Sarah's anguished cry carried through the night.

"Colin!" His name echoed through the camp, then her voice grew silent.

Angus tightened his grip on Colin, Gillis and Ewan using their bodies to keep him from moving away. His eyes focused ahead, Angus forced himself not to look at his son, already knowing what he'd see.

Nodding to his brothers as they reached their wagons, Angus guided Colin ahead, detouring toward an outcropping of rocks, then let go of his arm.

"You will not go near the MacGregor's camp again, do you understand?"

Colin's tormented face nearly brought Angus to his knees, but he wouldn't relent. Colin's life might depend on him agreeing to let Sarah go.

"Colin, did you hear me, lad?"

Swallowing the bitterness he felt, Colin nodded before fastening a determined look on Angus. "I will stay away from her...for now. But I will never let Sarah go. One day, she will be mine, Da. I swear before God she will."

In a somber mood, the MacLarens entered Fort Hall the following morning. The events of the night before had affected all of them, and besides Colin, perhaps none more than the oldest MacLaren. They spoke little of it, yet all had experienced the same youthful love, accepting it as part of what their ancestors called the MacLaren curse. When MacLaren men found love, they gave their heart for life. It had happened to their father, then to Angus, Gillis, Ewan, and Ian. Although they'd joked about it over the years, acknowledging it to be more a fairy tale than fate, it appeared there'd be no changing the MacLaren legacy.

"I need to see her once more, Da. I can't let her go without saying goodbye."

Angus knew this conversation would come. He'd spoken to Kyla about it, already deciding what would be done. Reaching into his pocket, he pulled out a small object, wrapped in almost threadbare material, and handed it to Colin.

His brows knitting together, Colin looked down on it in confusion. "What is it?" He let Angus slip it into his hand.

"It belonged to my ma, your gram. When she died, her wish was that this go to the oldest MacLaren grandson, then passed on to his wife. It is yours, Colin. You can choose the lass you give it to."

Colin's hands shook as he let the object slide from the fabric. His gaze shot to Angus, then back down to the most beautiful brooch he'd ever seen. Made of silver, the oval brooch, open in the center, had crosshatched hand engraving on the face, three Citrine stones on the top were set in an ornate silver wing, with one stone set on the bottom. He held it in his palm, already envisioning Sarah wearing it.

"My da gave it to her when they married," Angus continued. "Be warned. When you give it, your heart will go with it."

"It's already hers, Da. There'll be no other wife for me."

Angus clasped his shoulder. "Then we'll find a way for you to see Sarah before we leave."

Getting Colin and Sarah alone had been easier than anyone thought. The MacGregor men had left in the early evening for a round of drinking, leaving the women and children alone. Stumbling into camp before midnight, each collapsed, falling into a deep, undisturbed sleep.

"Now, Sarah, while everyone is asleep. There will be no one to catch you together." Geneen tugged at her sister's arm. "He's waiting for you next to the general store." She pointed up the street.

Seeing Colin's lean form, Sarah broke away and ran to him, hurling herself into his arms.

"Ach, lassie, it's a wonder I caught you." Colin chuckled, burying his face in her hair, breathing in her unique scent, wanting to make it last so he'd never forget it. Squeezing his eyes tight on the thought, he pulled back, offering her a warm smile. "I love you, Sarah. I'll never let you go."

"But, Colin..."

He lifted a finger to her lips. "Shush now, lassie. You must believe. When we're older, I'll come for you, claim you as my wife, and bring you home. Will you leave with me when that happens?"

Her eyes filled with tears as she nodded. "Aye, Colin. I'll wait forever for you."

"And marry me?"

"Aye, no other."

Sliding his hand into a pocket, he pulled out the brooch. "This belonged to my gram. Now, it's yours. It's my promise to you, Sarah. Do not misunderstand. We are betrothed as surely as any two people can be. I will come for you as soon as I can and we'll marry. Never doubt it for a minute." He took her hand in his, laying the brooch in her palm.

She clutched it to her heart, her body shaking. "Take me with you, Colin. Please. Don't leave me." Tears streamed down her face as her eyes implored him not to go.

It took all the strength within him not to grab her hand and run. "We cannot be together now, lassie, but we will be one day. I swear it to you. Just don't forget me, Sarah."

Her eyes blazed in confusion. "Forget you, Colin MacLaren? Not as long as I have a breath left in me." She tried her best to smile.

He held her as long as he could before letting his arms drop and stepping back.

"Go now, Sarah, before you're missed. Know this. I'll never love another."

"Nor will I, Colin." Gripping the brooch tight in her hand, she reached up to place one last kiss on his lips, then turned and ran. Taking one more glance behind her, she climbed into the wagon and disappeared.

When Colin woke the next morning, the MacGregor wagons were gone, leaving a deep, open wound in his heart. Setting his jaw, he steeled himself for the promise he made. He'd build a life in California with his family, then travel north to find her. No matter how long it took, he'd never give up. It was as he said. He'd never let her go and never love another.

Chapter Three

Conviction, California, 1864
Five years later...

"One more, Colin," Quinn urged, lifting his hand to order another round of whiskey. The two of them had ridden into town with Blaine and Brodie to celebrate Colin's twenty-third birthday. All the MacLarens would celebrate tomorrow at their normal Sunday meal, but tonight, the young men were dedicated to losing themselves in whiskey, mischief, and women.

"Look there, Colin. Your birthday present is walking down the stairs." Quinn nodded toward a curvy lass with deep red hair and full, pouty lips. "It appears Gwen is coming this way." Slapping Colin on the back, he winked at Brodie and Blaine. The three had already paid her to help him celebrate in style. The question they all shared was would he accept.

Colin grinned, knowing he'd not partake of his present from Quinn and Brodie. They knew he had his mind on only one woman, and it wasn't Gwen.

"Good evening, boys." She looped a hand through Colin's arm, leaning close.

"Evenin', Gwen. You look quite charming tonight." Colin brushed a kiss across her temple, breathing in the thick perfume she preferred, perhaps from the bottle he'd given her at Christmas. He'd been with one woman for just one night. He, Quinn, and Brodie had celebrated his nineteenth birthday in this same saloon, which ended with him in Gwen's bed upstairs—courtesy of his cousins.

"Ach, you MacLarens. You think your good looks and charm are all you need to coax a woman into bed," she chuckled.

"Not so, Gwen. We aren't eejits, although you may think so some nights. It also takes a fair amount of coin to get what we want." Colin pulled her to him. A few years before, she'd come from the old country, following her lover from New York to San Francisco. After he died in a bar fight, she traveled east to the town of Conviction, looking for a fresh start.

Older than Colin by a few years, she'd taken a liking to him, understanding when he confessed his inexperience with women. He'd been drinking with his cousins most of the night. Still, he'd been sober enough to know what he wanted—to learn what he needed to make it good for Sarah when he went for her. Gwen agreed. In return, he'd always been a gentleman. Although they'd been together just the one night, she always smiled when she thought of it. He'd been so serious in his determination to learn.

No passion, no emotion. It had been a teacher and student relationship—nothing more.

"Quinn and the boys tell me you're celebrating tonight. Another birthday, is it?"

"Aye. I'm twenty-three." He gave her a meaningful smile. Only Gwen and those with him tonight knew the true significance of this day. By the end of the following week, the entire MacLaren clan would know. Tonight, however, was about celebrating. "A drink for Gwen," he shouted over the noise at the bar, taking the full glass the bartender handed him.

Most nights the cousins played cards, sang along to tunes from the tinny piano, and relaxed. After six days of hard work on Circle M Ranch, all they wanted could be found in Buckie's Castle, the only saloon in Conviction.

Within an hour, they'd consumed another bottle of whiskey and sang until their throats ached. Leaning on Gwen to prevent himself from falling over, Colin picked up the bottle of whiskey and shook it.

"Another bottle," he yelled before Gwen could stop him.

"I think you've had your fair share tonight, laddie. Why don't you come upstairs with me and sleep it off?"

His glazed eyes tried to focus as he scanned the room for Quinn, Brodie, and Blaine. "I can't find them, Gwen."

Chuckling, she pointed to a table where the three sat, passed out, each in a different pose.

"Ach, they never could hold their liquor," he slurred before slumping against the bar.

"Up with you, laddie." Motioning for help, she and three others soon had Colin upstairs, tucked into her bed. Looking down at his face, peaceful in sleep, she thought of his plans and how they'd spoken of them. She knew something of young love and hoped his quest would end better than hers.

Brushing dark auburn hair away from his forehead, she placed a kiss on his brow, praying his journey would be successful. She'd wished this for him. Strong, hardworking, and honest, Colin had matured into a strong leader, a young man others respected.

Drawing the covers under his chin, she walked toward the door, taking one more look at a boy who'd become a man, knowing he'd be gone when she returned in the morning.

"Good luck and Godspeed, Colin MacLaren," she whispered, silently closing the door behind her.

"Colin, take your brothers to the southern pasture and bring the cows closer." Angus looked at the sky, watching the clouds shift into a formation foretelling a coming storm.

"I'll need more than the three of us, Da." Colin slid the gloves he'd been wearing to repair a broken corral fence into a back pocket and followed his father's gaze. "I don't see any thunderheads."

"They'll be coming, trust me. Find Quinn, Brodie, Blaine, and Sean. If they're not enough, come back and get me and your uncles. We'll show you how it's done." Grinning, he returned to his own chores, knowing there'd be no chance the boys would ask for their help.

Colin found the others and rode south. The Circle M Ranch had grown over the past five years, adding more acreage as they prospered. Angus and his family lived in the main ranch house, which included a dining room large enough to hold thirty people. At the current rate, they'd outgrow the room in a short time. Three other homes stood within four hundred yards of the main house, each with several bedrooms, a large kitchen, and small barns. Two larger barns sat across from the main house, each with two corrals for breaking and training horses.

The group rode in silence toward the pasture where the small herd grazed. It had been two weeks since his birthday and Colin had yet to announce his decision to leave. Even so, all his thoughts were on finding Sarah and bringing her home.

"What are your plans?" Quinn asked, riding up next to him.

"I leave in a week, after we get the herds moved."

"Are you certain where she is?" Through contact with travelers coming south from Oregon, and friends who traveled north, he knew Colin had done his best to track her. He knew Dougal MacGregor planned to settle in the Willamette Valley, which covered a large area on the western side of Oregon.

"Nae. Somewhere in the Willamette Valley. I should've left years ago." Colin shifted in the saddle. Since turning twenty, he'd had this argument with himself several times. However, Sarah would've only been nineteen at the time, and he remembered Dougal's decision not to let her leave until she turned twenty-one. So he'd hesitated, wanting to show some respect to the man he loathed, and needing to build the ranch into something she'd be proud of. It had now been five years, a long time to dream of one woman and a shared future. Perhaps she'd fallen in love with someone else, married, maybe even had children. He shook his head, pushing the thought aside, not letting himself second-guess his journey.

"I'm going with you."

"What?" Quinn's comment took Colin by surprise.

"I've made up my mind. You won't make the journey alone, not when I'm able to go. Da will understand. Heather rides as well as any man, and Bram is as large and strong as anyone," Quinn said, referring to his twenty-year-old sister and eighteen-year-old brother.

Colin chuckled, thinking of Heather, stunningly beautiful and willowy, and a fireball if he'd ever seen one. "Who'll protect her from all the suitors if you leave?" He didn't look at Quinn, knowing he'd break into laughter if he did.

"Hell, I'll probably have to pay someone to court her, although Ma would box my ears if she heard me say that."

Spotting the herd, they drove them north toward a large meadow not far from the ranch houses. Afterwards, Quinn leaned against a stall, watching as Colin groomed Chieftain. Not until he'd finished did Colin reply to Quinn's offer.

"I appreciate you wanting to go with me, but it's a journey I'll make alone. You're needed here."

"Did I give you the impression you had a choice? If so, I apologize. You'll not go by yourself, Colin. Accept it." Quinn marched off toward his family's house, leaving Colin to stare after him.

Colin had waited until the following Sunday, when the MacLaren clan congregated for the weekly family supper, to speak of his decision. He'd already told his parents, who supported him, offering any help they could. Quinn had also been given the blessing of his da and ma, although his ma had been less enthusiastic about her son traveling over five hundred miles from home. The time had now come to tell the rest of the family.

As usual, the conversations shifted at a quick pace, everyone trying to catch up with the events of the week. Colin waited, wanting to find the right time to convey his news, but getting a word in proved difficult.

"I have no interest in sewing, Ma. Besides, Da needs me out with Quinn and Bram. Right, Da?" Heather's eyes pleaded with him to save her from sitting around in a sewing circle with her aunts and cousins.

Gillis glanced at his wife, Audrey, noting her set expression. All the MacLaren women could ride and help with the cattle, but they also knew how to cook and sew, skills Heather avoided with a single-minded intensity.

"We'll talk about it at home, Heather."

"But, Da—"

He pierced her with an intense glare. "At home, lass."

Colin took the short silence as his chance to tell them of his decision. "I'll be leaving in two days to find Sarah." The quiet announcement caught his family unprepared.

"I'll be going with him," Quinn added before anyone had a chance to comment.

Brodie stared at his cousins, feeling a sense of betrayal they hadn't discussed it with him. The three, plus Blaine, had been inseparable for years. The four made up the oldest set of cousins and whatever one did, the other three followed. He cleared his throat, his voice overriding the other comments.

"How long will you be gone?" He kept his voice low, his expression hooded, not wanting anyone else to know the disappointment he felt at not being included.

"My guess is three months." Colin glanced at Brodie, knowing he'd made a mistake not talking to him before today. He hadn't planned on Quinn forcing his way into the journey, but when that happened, Brodie should've been the first person he spoke with, even before his da and ma.

Brodie tossed his napkin on the table and stood. "I have some chores to finish." Stalking from the house, he headed toward the larger of the two barns, disappearing inside. Picking up a shovel, he started mucking out a stall.

"I should have told you sooner." Colin walked up next to him, leaning against the top rail.

Brodie set the shovel aside, not sparing a glance at Colin as he closed the stall gate.

"I planned on going alone. When I told Quinn of my decision, he gave me no choice, said he was going to speak to Uncle Gillis about going with me." He cleared his throat. "I should've told you the same day."

"It's done." Brodie saddled his horse, Hunter, and secured the bridle. Swinging up in one fluid movement, he left out the back door without another glance at Colin.

"Ah, hell," Colin murmured.

"Where's Brodie?" Quinn walked up beside him.

"Took off. He's angry and I can't fault him for it. I should've told him." Scrubbing a hand over his face, Colin shook his head. "I'd better go after him, try to explain."

"Nae. We'll speak with Uncle Ewan. Brodie should be going with us."

"How can they get by without three of us? Two of us is one more than should be going, but Brodie, too? I've already spoken with Blaine. He understands Da needs him here."

"It's not our decision. All we can do is ask. You're right. He should have been told when you told me, but it's done now. Let's see if we can fix it." Quinn grabbed Colin's arm, pulling him out of the barn and toward the house where the rest of the family still sat at the table, eating dessert.

Ewan saw them approach, their gazes locked on him. Standing, he looked at his wife, who nodded. "We'll talk in the study," he said to Colin and Quinn. Closing the door behind them, Ewan turned toward his nephews. "We're a fortunate family, having lots of hands to help out, many capable of carrying a man's load."

Colin shot a glance at Quinn, both holding their breath.

"If you agree, it would be best if Brodie rode with you, assuming that's what he wants. It will be a long trip and I think all of us will feel better if it's the three of you. Besides, I can't imagine spending three months with Brodie if you two are nowhere around. What say you?"

"Aye. It would be better if he were with us." Colin smiled before letting out the breath he'd been holding.

"It's settled then."

The rest of the family had gone to bed, leaving Angus and Colin to discuss final preparations for the trip. They estimated it would take about twenty-five days to reach the south end of the Willamette Valley. The best route would be to retrace the trail that had brought them to California, then take the Applegate

Trail cutoff, following it all the way to their destination.

"What will you do once you reach the valley?"

Colin pinched the bridge of his nose. "Start talking to the ranchers and hope someone recognizes the MacGregor name. With three of us, we can split up to cover more ground."

"You'll need money." Opening the wall safe, he extracted a bag, tossing it on the desk. "Take that. Send me a message if you need more, bringing back what you don't use."

Picking it up, Colin looked inside, stunned by the amount. "It's too much."

"You don't know that. MacGregor may ask you to pay a dowry for Sarah. At least you'll have some negotiating power. It's the clan's money. Use it to bring Sarah home."

Colin took the bag, deciding he'd split it between the three of them so no one man would be carrying it all.

"Take this with you." Angus held out a piece of paper.

"What is it?" Colin opened the paper, seeing one name.

"There is a colony of Stewarts somewhere in the valley. We've been closely aligned with them for generations. I'm certain they'll do what they can to help you. If you find them, ask for William. Now, repeat again the route you'll take."

Angus didn't let Colin rest until they'd gone over the route so many times, it became ingrained in his memory. According to his da, Gillis and Ewan were doing the same with Quinn and Brodie. Several hours later, Angus felt satisfied he'd done all he could to prepare his son for the journey. All he could offer now were his prayers, hoping it would be enough.

As they finished packing the food and clothing into saddlebags, the three couldn't look at their mothers. If they did, they knew what they'd see. A combination of pride and fear. The pride they could handle, but the fear would be harder. They were the strongest women Colin, Quinn, and Brodie knew. Watching as their oldest sons left to follow a primitive emigrant trail, not knowing when they'd return, cut like a knife, although none would let even one tear fall.

Finishing, Colin gazed at his mother before taking the few steps toward her, wrapping her in a fierce hug. "I love you, Ma."

"Love you, too, Colin. You be safe, and if possible, let us know where you are." She gave him one more squeeze, then stepped aside, allowing the others to say their goodbyes. All was fine until his nine-year-old sisters, Chrissy and Alana, moved toward him. Their lower lips trembled and their eyes watered before throwing themselves into his waiting arms.

"Do you have to go, Colin?" Alana asked, her voice breaking.

"Aye, lassie. It's time I brought Sarah here to be my wife. You'd like that, wouldn't you?" Both nodded, hugging him with all their strength before he set them aside. "Now, you be brave for Ma and help her. She'll need both of you now more than ever."

Nodding, they clung to Kyla, who pulled them to her.

Quinn and Brodie were going through the same ritual several feet away. After several minutes, he tilted his head toward the horses, indicating the time had come to leave.

They took one last look at the people who meant everything to them, then reined their horses around. At first, they rode at a slow pace, none glancing back, not wanting to see the expression on their mothers' faces.

Approaching the fence line of the last corral, they looked at each other, pulled off their hats, and let loose with the fierce MacLaren war cry, "Creag an Tuirc," the Boar's Rock, before kicking their horses into a gallop and disappearing down the trail.

Chapter Four

River City, Willamette Valley, Oregon
"Sarah, are you ready?"

"Almost, Ma. Give me a few more minutes." Sarah finished tying a yellow ribbon in her hair, adjusted her bonnet, and took the stairs to the front door at a quick pace. Checking the mirror one more time, she dashed outside, climbing into the buggy next to Geneen and her youngest sister, Isla. She couldn't help the excitement she felt.

They were going into town to celebrate her twenty-second birthday and her father said he had a wonderful surprise for her. How she prayed it would be the new horse she'd been asking for since she first spotted the mare at the neighboring Bell ranch. She'd been riding the same old mare since before they arrived in Oregon. Although sweet and dependable, Sarah was more than ready for the challenge of a younger horse.

The one person she didn't want to see in town was Wes Bell, the son of the wealthy rancher. His requests to court her over the last year had become tiresome, even intimidating. She'd expressed her disinterest numerous times, recommending he find another woman to pursue. Wes had disregarded all her objections, instead increasing his efforts to court her. Sarah's frustration at his persistence had garnered the interest of her father, which made dealing with the younger rancher more difficult. Dougal MacGregor welcomed the advances of their neighbor, encouraging Sarah to consider his requests. She found it easier to ignore both men.

"This will be so much fun." Geneen reached over and squeezed her hand. A year younger than Sarah, she looked forward to celebrating her sister's birthday and their father's gift.

"I hope my surprise is the mare I've been wanting." Sarah's face lit up at the thought. Without thinking, she reached a hand into her reticule, fingering the silver and Citrine brooch she was never without. When she turned nineteen, she'd prayed Colin would come for her. Her prayers weren't answered, although she never lost hope. In her heart, she had no doubt he'd arrive someday, unannounced, and take her to California with him.

"I shouldn't be telling you this, but Da rode to the Bell Ranch last week."

"Really?" Sarah's heart rate picked up, sensing she might indeed be given the mare.

"Aye. Even though I begged, Ma wouldn't tell me why he rode over there. It has to be the horse, don't you think?"

"Oh, I hope so."

It didn't take long to reach the outskirts of town. Their father had ridden in ahead of them, saying he had to prepare for her surprise. As the buggy stopped in front of the restaurant where they'd be celebrating, Sarah looked around, anxious to see if she could spot her present.

"Are you planning to get down, Sarah?" Her mother, her face a mask, waited near the restaurant steps with Isla.

Taking one more look around, Sarah and Geneen followed her inside, seeing their father at a table in a private alcove near the back. Standing, he pulled her chair out so her back would be facing the entrance.

"I'm glad to see you wore your best dress, Sarah." Dougal took a sip of the whiskey already in front of him. He had yet to mention her birthday.

Touching the brim of her bonnet, Sarah glanced down at the dress she'd spent hours sewing, dreaming about wearing it for Colin one day. A few minutes later, the food arrived and supper passed in utter silence, her father not saying a word about her birthday.

"Da, when are you going to give Sarah the surprise you promised?" Geneen glanced at her sister, knowing she would never ask.

Casting a glance at the entrance, Dougal's face tightened. "Any minute now."

Something about his answer sent a chill through Sarah. Looking toward her mother, anxiety filled her at the pursed lips and icy expression on her face.

"Ah, there he is now."

He? Sarah thought as she turned to see Wesley Bell come up behind her.

"Wes, glad you could join us. Pull up a chair." Dougal shook the young man's hand, then cast a hard stare at Sarah, which she took to be a warning.

Geneen's response mirrored Sarah's. Her heart pounded at the sight of Wes, palms growing damp. Wiping them down the skirt of her dress, she sent him a suspicious smile, but his attention was locked on Sarah. Something felt terribly wrong.

"You know Sarah, of course, and my daughters, Geneen and Isla."

Wes sent them a bland smile. "Of course." His gaze shifted back to Sarah, his face breaking out in a broad smile. "I understand you're celebrating your birthday. Congratulations, and may I add how stunning you look tonight, Miss MacGregor."

Sarah's stomach tightened as she squirmed in her chair. Feeling sick, she nodded, not offering any other reply as he settled in his chair next to her. Feeling his leg touch hers, she moved away, putting as much distance between them as possible in such a tight space.

"Wes asked to join us tonight, Sarah, specifically asking to be allowed to sit next to you." Dougal ignored the shock on Sarah's face, not caring how uncomfortable she looked.

Both girls shot looks at their mother, but Robena kept her eyes focused on the vase of flowers in the middle of the table, offering no support. As awareness of their father's intentions shot through both of them, Geneen reached her hand toward Sarah, who grasped it tight.

"I'd hoped to arrive in time for supper, but a group of wayward cows took longer to round up than I'd thought." He let his appreciative gaze once again wander over Sarah, who flinched at his unconcealed attention.

"Well, you've made it for the important part." Dougal narrowed his gaze at Wes, nodding once.

Clearing his throat, Wes reached over and placed his hand over Sarah's, tightening his hold when she tried to snatch it away. A look almost of pity passed over his face, replaced by unquestionable resolve.

"Your father and I have spoken of you many times, Sarah. For a long time, you've known of my interest in you, as well as our fathers' desire to join our two ranches. Your father's concern, and mine, has always been for your happiness." Feeling her squirm under his unwavering gaze, he hurried to continue. "Yesterday, we came to an understanding."

No, no, no! her mind screamed as panic rose in her chest.

"I offered for your hand in marriage, and your father accepted."

Geneen's gasp matched the jolt she felt at Wes's words. Sending one more look toward her mother, her heart sank, realizing she'd known of her husband's dreadful action and did nothing to warn Sarah.

Shock vibrated through Sarah. Turning the chair over in her haste to stand, she wrenched her hand from his grip, taking several steps back, shaking her head. Glaring at her father, then sending a withering look toward Wes, she moved backward, her face contorted in disbelief.

Steeling herself while casting a contemptuous look at her father, Sarah forced her voice to sound calm. "Your request for my hand is noted, Mr. Bell. Unfortunately, I'm already betrothed."

She would have laughed at the look of horror on Wes's face, except at the same moment, her father threw his napkin on the table and stood, eyes bulging in anger.

"You will not dishonor me, Sarah. The request of MacLaren was refused, no matter your wishes. You will wed Wesley Bell and no other." His attempt at lowering his booming voice failed. It echoed throughout the restaurant, surprising the other patrons.

The only couple who showed any sympathy sat several tables away, their faces awash in understanding. Reverend and Mrs. Olford had always been wonderful to her and Geneen. Besides her sister, Sarah had shared her acceptance of Colin's proposal with two others, the Olfords, who promised to keep her secret.

Face burning, she lifted her chin in defiance. "Nae, Da. I will *never* marry Wes Bell or any man other than Colin MacLaren. It is a promise I made and it shall be kept." Lifting her skirt, she rushed from the restaurant, running down the street, oblivious to where she headed. All Sarah knew was her life in her father's house had ended with his deceitful, selfish decision to barter her off as if she were another of his cows. And she had no doubt a barter had been arranged.

Dougal MacGregor never gave away a scrap of wood without some form of recompense in return. He'd never give one of his daughters away without making certain he obtained significant payment.

"Sarah, wait."

Her breath coming in gulps, Sarah stopped, her hand resting on the side of a building, steadying her shaking limbs. Glancing over her shoulder, she dropped into a nearby bench as Geneen came to a halt beside her. Neither spoke a word for several moments as she took a seat next to Sarah, her own misery as intense as her sister's.

"I'll not be returning home."

Geneen nodded, already accepting a rift had been born that would take a miracle to close. She'd never heard Sarah speak to their da in such a way. The stunned silence around the table when she dashed from the restaurant caught everyone unawares—except Geneen. She'd known of the betrothal and Sarah's determination to keep her promise to Colin, as well as her hatred of their father's ways.

"I'll not go back, either." Geneen's calm voice should have reassured Sarah. Instead, it sent another wave of panic through her.

"Nae, Geneen. You cannot make my burden your own. Besides, I've no idea where I'll stay or how I'll live. We cannot both be in such a state."

"Sarah?" The soft voice of Mrs. Olford jolted them both. Standing, they faced the reverend and his wife.

"I apologize you had to witness that." Sarah clasped her hands in front of her.

"Nonsense, my dear. We've seen many family disagreements during our time in River City. I'm sure your father is trying to do what's best for you." She reached out, taking Sarah's hands in hers. "The Reverend Olford has already spoken to him and asked he give you time to consider Wes's proposal. For now, you'll be going home with us." Seeing confusion on Sarah's face, she smiled. "It didn't take much to guess you wouldn't want to ride back to the ranch tonight."

"Never."

"Excuse me?" Mrs. Olford asked.

Sarah lifted her chin, her lower lip trembling as she came to terms with what had to be done. "I'm never going back there. I made a promise and it will be kept, even if I lose my family." She fingered the brooch in her pocket, then made a quick decision to pull it out and secure it on her dress. From this day forward, she'd wear it proudly instead of hiding the proof of her promise.

"Sarah, dear, you don't know what you're saying. It's understandable you're upset about how your father and Wes confronted you. No matter how long he's been pursuing you, any woman would be offended by such a public announcement. However, if you turn your back on them, your father may never let you return. You and Geneen know your father to be one of the most stubborn men ever created."

"Now, Bessie, we don't want to judge her father." The reverend stepped forward, touching his wife's arm.

"Of course, you're right," Mrs. Olford agreed. "Geneen, it would be best if you returned to the restaurant while we take Sarah home. In a few days, I'm sure everyone will be calm enough to discuss Wes's offer in a more rational way."

"I'll ride into town tomorrow to visit you, Sarah, and bring your clothes." Leaning up, Geneen kissed her sister on the cheek. "All will be well. I'm certain of it."

Sarah's grim smile was all the response Geneen received as she left.

"Come, dear. We'll get you settled, then make tea. Tomorrow will be soon enough to decide what you want to do."

"Are you certain this is the trail, Colin?" Quinn rode Warrior, his five-year-old stallion, in circles, looking for the landmark Angus had told them about.

Colin didn't answer as he and Brodie did the same, trying to locate the rock with a whitewashed arrow.

"Here it is." Brodie slid from Hunter, walking his gelding toward a large boulder hidden by bushes. Pulling them aside revealed a white arrow, the word Oregon crudely written below. "Uncle Angus was right. What say we ride another hour, then camp?"

"We can get an early start tomorrow," Colin agreed, turning Chieftain northwest.

All on the same day, Colin, Quinn, Brodie, and Blaine had gotten their horses from a local rancher who'd decided to sell his small place and move to

Oregon to be closer to his daughter. Angus had negotiated a purchase for the land and animals. It had been a good outcome for everyone.

As the sun fell behind the mountains to the west, they sat around a fire, eating hardtack and jerky. Tomorrow, they'd take a day and hunt for game, hoping to replenish their supplies until they reached Mindell, the last town before reaching southern Oregon.

"Who's the girl you were talking to at church before we left?" Quinn glanced at Brodie as he tossed a few twigs on the fire.

"Which one?"

"The one I didn't recognize," Quinn smirked. "Dark hair, round face." He prided himself on knowing all the eligible young women in town. He had no plans to court or do anything else with a local girl, but he enjoyed flirting as much as any man.

"Louisa...Linda...Lillie...that's it. Lillie. Her family bought the old Miller place west of town. She's the same age as Jinny, so I introduced her." At eighteen, Brodie's younger sister had boys surrounding her wherever she went.

"I'm afraid you're going to have your hands full with her," Quinn said, standing to stretch. "How about some cards?" Pulling a deck from his saddlebag, he shuffled, then dealt.

"You hear from..." Brodie's words trailed off as Colin put a finger to his lips, his eyes shifting to his left. Brodie nodded, setting his cards down. "Long day in the saddle. Gotta stretch." Moving to a crouch, he rolled, pulling his gun the same instant as Colin and Quinn.

"Whoever's out there, come out now." Colin's hard voice rang through the quiet night, signaling the others to spread out. A rustling noise, then footfalls had Colin up and running, followed by Quinn and Brodie. It didn't take them long to spot and overtake the three fleeing forms, tackling them to the ground.

"What do you think you're doing sneaking up..." Colin's words died in his mouth as he turned the person over, long, golden hair spilling out of the hat. "What the hell?" he murmured, hearing the same bewildered curses from Quinn and Brodie when they discovered they'd wrestled two girls, and not boys, to the ground.

All hell broke loose as the three kicked and screamed, clawing at their captors, attempting to break free.

"Calm down. We aren't going to hurt you," Colin hissed at the hellion who shot him a furious gaze. He could feel her relax and loosened his hold, regretting it an instant later when she tried to knee him in the groin. "Dammit, stop that." Still straddling her, he grabbed her wrists, holding them above her head.

For the first time, he got a good look at her face. If it weren't for the dirt and foul temper, she'd be a pretty little thing.

"How you boys doing?" Colin asked Quinn and Brodie, giving her a warning glance as he hauled her to a standing position.

"She's a feisty one, but I have her," Quinn replied, cursing as the girl's foot connected with his shin.

"Stop scratching me," Brodie ground out as he hauled his captive up, pulling her arms behind her, then marching her toward the others. Wiping an arm across his brow, he studied the three girls. He guessed the oldest to be seventeen or eighteen. The others looked younger.

"What are you girls doing out here alone?" Brodie asked.

"None of your da—"

Colin yanked the oldest girl's arm before she could finish. "None of that, lassie. Now, answer his question."

Her eyes shooting daggers at him, she tried to break his hold, only to find herself yanked against his hard chest.

"That's enough. You'll not struggle any longer." Pulling her after him, Colin walked to Chieftain's saddle, grabbing his rope, then wrapping it around her wrists. Setting her beneath a tall pine, he did the same with her ankles, then stood, watching as Quinn and Brodie tied the other two. Separating the girls by several feet, the cousins huddled together, talking in soft voices.

"What are we going to do with three lassies, Colin?" Quinn swiped at the blood on his cheek where he'd been scratched. "I always thought if a lass scratched me it would be for a much different reason." His joke fell flat as they turned to watch the girls struggle with their restraints.

"Well, we can't take them with us." Colin watched the one he'd wrestled with, seeing her shoulders slump. "I wonder how long it's been since they've eaten."

"One way to find out." Brodie pulled hardtack from his saddlebag, walked over, and offered it to one of the girls.

She hesitated a moment before nodding.

Kneeling down, he held it to her mouth, then quickly pulled his hand back. "You bite me and there'll be hell to pay."

It took almost an hour of feeding them by hand before the girls shook off further food and quieted. They'd learned nothing about them, not even their names.

"What now?" At a loss, Quinn crossed his arms.

Colin ran a hand down his face. "We'll check the ropes one more time, then get some sleep. We can decide in the morning."

"Aye. Maybe they're fairies sent here to muddle our brains and they'll be gone by morning." Quinn continued to stare at them as if he thought they might actually disappear right before their eyes.

Colin laughed, slapping him on the back. "Aye, laddie. It might just be so."

Chapter Five

"The girl will *not* be disrespecting me so, Robena." Dougal paced in front of his desk, his hands fisted on his hips, cursing with each step.

"Calm yourself, Dougal. You'll not be going into town to bring her home today."

He stopped, his mouth agape as he stared at his wife. "And why is that?" he hissed out.

"It's been one day. You gave your word to Reverend Olford to let Sarah stay with them until you both have time to calm your tempers."

"She's a brazen lass, defying me the way she did. Her actions cannot go unpunished."

"Ach. Sarah is not a wee lassie you can scold for not behaving. She's a grown woman. You shouldn't have taken her birthday and turned it into a spectacle for all to see." Robena would never have talked to him like this in front of others. In public, she played the dutiful wife, accepting his commands. In private, however, she didn't hide her feelings, even though her pleas often had little impact on her husband.

"As long as she lives under my roof, she'll do what I say. I've made an agreement with Wes. I'll not go back on my word." Slamming out the door, she watched him storm to the barn.

She breathed out a relieved sigh. Robena knew her husband didn't see the flaws in his thinking. He never did. She wouldn't blame her daughter if she never returned home to live under the brutal thumb of her da.

"Ma?"

Robena turned at the sound of her youngest daughter's voice. At sixteen, Isla was quiet and studious, making her the opposite of twenty-one-year-old Geneen, who'd always been headstrong and would rather be out riding her horse than doing her lessons. Sarah fell somewhere in between. The oldest, she'd always enjoyed reading and had wanted to become a teacher—until Dougal informed her he had no money for extra schooling. Undeterred, she schooled herself, borrowing books, hiding them in her saddlebags. Like Geneen, she loved to ride and would often disappear for hours after completing her chores. Dougal considered her a good shot, learning to handle a rifle and shotgun as soon as they left the trail and founded their ranch near River City.

Now she'd left, and Robena had to wonder when she'd see her oldest child again.

"Are you certain it's what you want, Sarah?" Bessie Olford asked as they sat at the breakfast table after her husband had left. Four days had passed since her father's announcement of the agreement with Wesley, but Sarah's resolve not to return to her home hadn't faltered.

"Yes, Mrs. Olford. I couldn't be more certain. I'm determined to be out from under Da's rule."

"What of Wesley?"

"I have no interest in him. None. I'll wait as long as needed for Colin." She sighed, touching the brooch on her dress. "He'll not come here to find I've married another."

"You're certain the feelings you have aren't just a young girl's fantasy? If you decide on this path, make sure you're in love with him and not waiting out of a sense of obligation."

Sarah's face softened, recalling their last moments together. She'd loved him with all her heart then and those feelings had never wavered. "I love him, Mrs. Olford. I'm certain of that. Of course, if I do stay in town, I'll need to find work and a place to live."

Sipping her coffee, Bessie thought of how hard it would be for a single woman to find respectable work in River City. Though the town had grown to over two thousand people, it still offered few opportunities for women. Except...

"Would it be all right if I stayed a few more days?" Sarah didn't want to impose, yet she had no other options.

"Yes, yes. Of course, dear," Bessie answered, waving her hand in the air, her thoughts already shifting. "If you'll excuse me, I just remembered an errand for my husband."

Sarah's brows drew together in a combination of surprise and amusement at Bessie's quick departure. Washing the dishes left on the counter, she dashed upstairs, grabbing her bonnet and reticule. Checking herself in the mirror, she adjusted the brooch. She'd never had a chance to wear it in public before, afraid her father would guess its meaning. Now she could do what she'd promised Colin. Stepping outside, she lifted her face to a bright, cloudless sky and smiled.

She bit down on her lower lip. Her father would be beyond angry when he learned what she'd done, but Sarah couldn't bring herself to care. As she walked, a thought crossed her mind. Dashing across the main street, she entered the general store, waving to the owner as she headed straight toward the dresses.

An hour later, she emerged, arms laden with packages. She'd collected items needed for living on her own, including a few cooking supplies, which would be delivered to the reverend's home. Hearing a shout as she stepped into the street, Sarah turned as a rider barreled down on her.

"Watch out, Sarah!" Bessie's voice reached her in time to get her terrified body moving.

Her eyes wide in fear, she dropped her packages and jumped away, tripping over a step, landing on her behind.

"Are you all right, dear?" Bessie helped her to her feet, then whipped around, trying to find the maniac who'd almost run Sarah down. "I don't see the fool. Did you recognize him?"

Shaking her head, Sarah straightened her dress and bonnet, then stepped back on the street to collect her packages.

"Let me help you."

She glanced up at the sound of the unfamiliar voice, ready to reject his help, then stopped. Something about him looked familiar, but she couldn't quite place where she'd seen him.

"Um...thank you."

"That was a fool act. Did he hurt you?"

"No. I'm a little shaken. Nothing more."

"If you show me where you're going, I'll carry these packages for you." Not raspy, or deep and smooth, but somewhere in between.

Turning to look at him, she crossed her arms, head tilted. "Do I know you, sir?"

"In truth, yes, you do, although I doubt you'll remember. I'm Caleb Stewart. My family and I were on the same wagon train as you and your family."

Sarah's jaw dropped. "Oh my. Yes, I do remember you, Mr. Stewart. It's been so long and you have, well...you've..."

"Grown taller?" he prompted, a smile touching the corners of his mouth.

Laughing, she nodded. "Yes, you have." When she'd first met him, he'd been as thin as a bean pole. Now he had wide, muscled shoulders and strong hands. His dark blond hair touched his collar at the back. Although his hard, chiseled features weren't exactly handsome, his face held a certain warmth and sincerity, making him more than easy to look at.

Both turned at the sound of Bessie clearing her throat.

"Are you going to introduce me, Sarah?"

"Oh, I do apologize. Mr. Stewart, this is Mrs. Olford, our minister's wife. This is Caleb Stewart. We came west on the same wagon train."

"It's a pleasure to meet you, Mrs. Olford."

"Mr. Stewart. Are you planning to give Sarah back her packages?" Bessie's brow quirked upward.

"He's offered to carry them to the house for me, if that's all right with you."

Bessie glanced between the two, making a quick decision. "Of course, dear. And you'll stay for cake, Mr. Stewart. I'll not take no for an answer."

Cocking one eye open, Colin lay in his bedroll, hoping Quinn might be right and the girls would have disappeared during the night. Letting out a weary sigh, his gaze locked on the oldest of the three. She stared back at him, her anger no less evident than the night before. Sitting up, he rubbed his eyes, then stood.

"Quinn, Brodie, up with you." Strolling behind a bush several feet away, he took care of his business. Looking up at the early morning sky, he knew their plans to hunt might need to be changed until they figured out what to do with the girls.

"We need to decide what to do with them, Colin," Quinn said as Colin returned to the camp.

"I say we get ourselves ready, give them some food, then continue on our journey. We can't be sidetracked by three young lassies." Brodie rested his hands on his hips, glancing over his shoulder at the girls.

Colin agreed, but it didn't seem right to leave them out here without protection. "We can't leave them here alone. We need to find out where they're from and what happened."

Cursing under his breath, Brodie's eyes narrowed. "And what then? Do we take them home? Seems they either ran away or they have no home to go back to. Why else would they be out here alone?"

"Guess we won't know until we ask." Colin grabbed the water pouch, crouching in front of the oldest girl. "Have a drink, then you and I are going to talk."

Glaring at him, she took a sip of water. "I need some privacy."

Untying the rope around her ankles, he helped her stand, giving her time to get her wobbly legs to adjust. He guided her to a cluster of bushes.

"There." He made no move to leave.

"You can't stand there."

"And why not?" He crossed his arms, his eyes sparking in amusement.

"Fine. If you want to watch, go right ahead, but I need my hands free, unless you want to undress me, too."

He knew she taunted him, but she was also right. Stepping forward, he turned her around, loosening the rope on her wrists, then adjusting it so one end still held firm to her arm. The other end he held tight, like he would a lead line on a horse.

"All right. Go do your business."

By the time they walked back, Quinn and Brodie had finished doing the same with the other girls, with one difference—Brodie had learned their names.

"Coral, Opal, and Pearl." Brodie nodded from the oldest to youngest.

Colin stooped next to Coral, lifting her chin with a finger. "Where are your folks, Coral?"

Her eyes shot open in surprise, then closed. "Don't know."

He stifled a curse. "Where'd you come from?"

She looked up at him, her eyes pleading. "Don't send us back, mister. Please."

The fear in her eyes surprised him. She'd been so strong, so determined. Now he saw a scared young woman with nowhere to go.

"Don't send you back to where?"

"Crocker."

Colin, Quinn, and Brodie had ridden through the town of Crocker three days before, taking as little time as possible to do their business, then leave. It didn't seem like much to outsiders, maybe a hundred people and a few stores. Most saw it as a stop for settlers to replenish supplies rather than a place to lay down roots. And those perceptions were close but not completely accurate. The MacLarens knew what most others did who lived anywhere near the Nevada border town. Crocker was a haven for some of the worst criminals in the western United States.

"Why don't you want to go back?" Colin wondered why anyone would choose to raise their children near a town lacking any sense of right and wrong. In his mind, there could be only one reason— their kin were a part of the lawless element of Crocker.

Coral didn't answer.

He tried again. "Are these your sisters?"

She nodded. "Opal and Pearl."

"Will you run if I take off your ties?"

Jutting her chin out to him, he saw the spunk return to her face. "Yes."

Pinching the bridge of his nose, Colin stood. "I'm guessing you try everyone's patience," he murmured before motioning for Quinn and Brodie to follow him.

"They're sisters from Crocker."

"That answers why they ran. I sure as hell wouldn't stay there if I had another choice." Quinn settled fisted hands on his hips, staring at the girls. "It's three days behind us."

"Three days ride, then three days back to this spot. We'd lose almost a week." Brodie didn't like the idea of losing the time or leaving the girls in such a miserable town.

"They don't want to go back. They're running from someone, but Coral won't say who or why." Slamming his hands in his pockets, Colin looked at the sky. They were wasting time. "We're going to Mindell for supplies. We'll leave them at the church, pay the minister to keep them until we return."

"Please tell me you aren't suggesting we take them to the ranch with us." The idea didn't appeal to Quinn at all. He wanted them out of their lives, not more deeply ingrained in them.

"I'm hoping the minister can find a home for them so by the time we ride back through, they'll be settled."

"Colin, I never thought I'd say this, but you're daft. No one is going to take three sisters. The best we can hope for is they each find a family. Might be best to leave them with the law in Mindell. They can sort it out." Brodie wanted another answer, but he knew the choices were few.

Quinn scrubbed a hand down his face. "I understand you want to help them, Colin, but hell, they aren't our problem. I'll go along with taking them to Mindell and either leave them with the law or the church, but that's where it ends."

Colin and Brodie knew he was right. There was a reason for their trip, and it didn't include being responsible for three young girls.

"All right," Colin responded. "We're agreed then. They ride with us to Mindell. We'll start with the church and hope that's the end of it."

"Are you living around here, Mr. Stewart?" Bessie set a slice of cake in front of him, along with a cup of coffee.

"Please, Mrs. Olford. I'd appreciate it if you and Miss MacGregor would call me Caleb."

Bessie nodded as Sarah leaned forward.

"Then you'll have to call me Sarah."

His mouth curved up at the corners. "To answer your question, my family has a ranch a little bit north of here."

"How come we've never seen you in church?"

Caleb chuckled. "Oh, we go to church. Ma would have our hide if we didn't, but it's the one in Slade. We get most of our supplies and Pa conducts his business there. It's closer than riding to River City."

"What brings you here, Caleb?" Sarah picked at her slice of cake. The presence of a person who experienced the same hardships as her family during the trip west reminded her of Colin. Without thinking, her hand fingered the brooch. The feel of it always gave her comfort.

He leaned forward, resting his arms on the table. "It was time I headed out. I waited until my brothers and sisters were able to help our folks. If I didn't leave now, I worried I might end up staying in Slade the rest of my life." He pushed his empty plate away. The Stewarts had been in this country several years before the MacLarens made the journey. He'd always had a strong urge to see more of it. "I was born shortly before my family came to America. When they decided to move west, I wanted to stay behind, see more of the country. I couldn't then, but now..."

Sarah cocked her head. Most people she knew stayed close to where they were raised, preferring what they knew to the unknown.

"Where do you plan to go?" Sarah let go of the brooch, dropping her hand to her lap.

"I thought I'd work here for a spell, maybe through winter, then move on. The next town south is Mindell, but I'm not quite ready to start for it yet."

"Well, you speaking of finding work reminded me of my morning. In truth, I may have good news for both of you." Bessie had already made up her mind she liked Caleb. Maybe if he got a good job, he'd stay. They could use people such as him.

"What news, Mrs. Olford?"

"Well, I spoke with the head of our town council this morning. He confirmed our teacher is leaving and we'll need a replacement."

Sarah's heart beat so hard, she thought it would burst from her chest. "And what did he say?"

"He's asked to meet with you. I believe he might offer you the position."

No longer able to contain her excitement, Sarah jumped up, hugging Bessie. "I'll never be able to thank you enough, Mrs. Olford." She swung her gaze to Caleb. "It's always been my dream to teach. I can scarcely believe it."

"Now, Sarah, you still must meet with the men who will make the decision. Although, I do believe you have an excellent chance."

"When would they like to meet with me?"

"Tomorrow morning. They'd like you to be there right after breakfast."

Sarah's heart began to slow. Settling herself back in her chair, she took a large bite of cake, following it with a swallow of lukewarm coffee. Looking at Caleb, she smiled, then set down her fork.

"And what news might you have for Caleb?"

Bessie shifted in her seat, turning toward him. "You may not have heard of Fergus Bell, but he owns the largest ranch in River City. Hundreds of acres. He's always looking for men and made it a point to mention it to my husband, Reverend Olford, at last Sunday's service."

Sarah's enthusiasm dropped at the mention of Wesley Bell's father. Everyone knew Wes served as the foreman and would take over for his father one day. She hated the thought of Caleb working around him. She wouldn't, however, pass her concerns onto Caleb. He needed work and no one in the area paid better than the Bells.

"She's right, Caleb. The Bells always need good men and pay well. And it's not too far a ride from town."

"Sounds good. Tell me where it is and I'll ride out there tomorrow."

"We can do better than that. My husband and I are going out there tomorrow anyway. You can follow us." Bessie pushed from the table, picking up plates, waving off Sarah's offer to help. "Why don't you two young people take a walk? Sarah, you can show Caleb our town. Maybe he'll decide to make River City his home."

Chapter Six

Mindell, California

"You understand, I cannot promise you anything. We are a small congregation with few people and little money to feed three more mouths. Our children are gone, so my wife and I will take care of them until you return. If families haven't been found for the girls by then, they'll have to go back with you."

Tightening his grip on the brim of his hat, Colin cast a quick glance at his cousins, who flanked Coral, Opal, and Pearl. They'd convinced the girls to clean up as best they could, even though little could be done with their soiled clothes.

"Whatever you can do would be appreciated, Reverend. We won't be back through here for at least two months. Is that accceptable?"

"Yes, young man, as long as you promise to return. There's only so much I can do for them." He looked at his wife, who eyed the girls with the same wariness Colin had felt when he first saw them. The reverend turned toward her, indicating with a nod for her to show the girls inside.

"Come, girls." Without waiting, the older woman started inside, not noticing the three didn't follow.

"Go on with you, lassies." Quinn settled a hand on Coral's back, encouraging her to follow the woman.

"No. We're not staying." Coral moved away, crossing her arms, her face set. "We don't need their help."

Wrapping a hand around her arm, Quinn pulled her toward the house. "Sorry about that, ma'am. She's a little upset about us riding off." He glared down at Coral, daring her to speak.

"I quite understand." Stepping forward, she wrapped her arm around Coral's shoulder, directing her inside. "Come, dear. You other girls follow us and don't give these poor men any more trouble." This time, the woman's stern gaze moved the younger girls to action and they rushed to catch up.

Rummaging in a pocket, Colin pulled out money, holding it out to the reverend. "It's all I can spare."

"It'll be enough. You have a safe journey. Rest assured, we'll take good care of them."

Swinging up on Chieftain, a sense of unease filled Colin. The reverend and his wife appeared to be good people and were willing to take the girls in until their return from Oregon. In his mind, the worst situation would be they'd have to take the girls to Circle M Ranch and find homes in Conviction or nearby ranches.

Reining his horse around, Colin glanced over his shoulder, seeing Coral watching him out of a grime covered window. Spotting his gaze, she dropped the curtain. Something about the look in her eyes bothered him in a way he couldn't define.

"Let's go, lads. We've miles ahead of us." Brodie held Hunter steady next to Chieftain as Quinn joined them.

Shaking off the apprehension, Colin nodded. "On to Oregon, lads."

River City, Oregon

Bessie dropped the towel next to the sink, mumbling at the pounding on the door at such a late hour. Her husband had left hours before to be with a family whose father's illness had taken a bad turn. The doctor didn't expect the man to live through the night. She hoped whoever came calling didn't need her husband's help.

"Coming." Pulling the door open, she schooled her surprise at who stood outside. "Dougal MacGregor. What brings you here at such a late hour?" She didn't step aside, preferring he state his business, then leave.

"I've come for my daughter."

"Oh, you have, have you? Well, she's long in bed and I won't wake her. You should return at a decent hour so the two of you can talk." She crossed her arms, not budging.

"Step aside, Mrs. Olford. She's my daughter and I'll take her with me now."

She could see his jaw twitch as a red tone crept up his face. Neither dissuaded her. "She may be your daughter, but Sarah is also a grown woman, able to make her own decisions. You may not like it, but that is the way of it."

"I'll speak to your husband," he demanded, taking a menacing step forward.

"He's not at home, but he'll tell you the same. You may have a chance to change her mind if you return when you're both rested. It's all I can offer tonight, Mr. MacGregor."

"You're making a terrible mistake. Sarah doesn't know her own mind. Her place is with her family, not staying in town as if she has nowhere else to go."

Bessie hid her amusement at the extent to which MacGregor fooled himself. Her opinion of the man had changed over his years in River City. At first, she thought him to be simply arrogant and rude. Those impressions had turned. Now she believed his need to control every decision and action by those in his family was unnatural, coloring his judgment.

"Despite your objections, she is welcome here as long as it suits her. You, however, need to return at a respectable hour. Now, I have chores to finish. Goodnight to you, Mr. MacGregor." She closed the door before he could utter another word, although his cursing could be heard all the way into the kitchen.

"Thank you, Mrs. Olford. I'm sorry you had to deal with him." Sarah came down the stairs, a wrapper secured around her.

"Nonsense. The man is used to getting his way with bluster and bullying. Well, I'll have none of it. He can return tomorrow or another day, which is what any other person would do." She walked over to a settee, taking a seat on one end, patting the space next to her. "Now, tell me about Caleb Stewart."

Sarah smiled, taking a seat. "You already know he's working for Fergus Bell at the ranch. What else would you like to know?"

"What you think of him, of course. He's handsome, strong, and has a good brain. And I believe he may have an interest in you."

Sarah put a hand over her mouth, stifling a laugh. "Caleb is all you say, except he has no interest in me." Her humor died when she thought of what he'd told her. "I learned the true reason he left his family, and it had nothing to do with me."

"A rift with his father then?"

Even though Caleb hadn't asked her to keep his reason quiet, she felt a slight unease at sharing his sorrow. "All I'll say is he loved another and it didn't work out."

"Ah, the poor man. He left to forget." Taking Sarah's hand, she squeezed before letting go.

"Sometimes distance is the best cure for aches of the heart."

Sarah lifted her gaze to Bessie, wondering if her words held more than one meaning. Licking her dry lips, she thought a moment before speaking.

"You don't believe Colin will come for me, do you?"

Bessie had never met the man and didn't want to judge his actions, yet five years seemed a long time to hold off coming for the woman you loved.

"You're asking me a question I have no answer for, dear. I know you pray for him each day, and I pray for you. If our prayers are answered, then yes, I do believe your young man will come someday."

Sarah let out an audible breath. The same question greeted her when she awoke each day. Most mornings, she answered with a resounding yes, Colin would come for her. Other days, her optimism faltered.

"So, tell me, are you ready to start school?"

Sarah's meeting with the town council had gone well. She'd walked away with a job and a place to live, as soon as the house received needed repairs. The wage would allow her to be independent, and if she were careful, the means to start saving for her wedding to Colin.

"Next week. I've met with the previous teacher and looked at the books she used. Although there aren't many supplies, I'll manage." Sighing, she thought of all her books at home and what she could do if they were with her.

"What is it?"

"Nothing. I just wondered how I could get my books from home without Da knowing."

Bessie's mouth quirked up at the corners. She liked nothing more than a challenge. "Let me think about it a few days, dear. I'm certain we'll figure out a way."

"Deal me out, Wes. Your luck is too strong tonight." The ranch hand tossed down his cards and stood, providing an opening for Caleb to sit down.

He'd been at the Bell Ranch a few days. It hadn't taken him long to form opinions on many of the men, including Wes Bell. Within a day of being at the ranch, Caleb had heard about the betrothal announcement and how Sarah had turned it down. Although Wes didn't speak of it, Caleb knew the rejection must have stung.

"Deal me in." Caleb sat across from Wes, giving him a good view of the man's expressions and how he reacted to his cards.

They'd played several hands before one of the men mentioned the betrothal. "She is quite the beauty, Wes. Heard she's living in town, going to be the new school teacher."

Wes looked up, his eyes slits. "No wife of mine will work."

"You may have forgotten, but she turned you down in front of a roomful of witnesses."

"Given the way MacGregor handled it, any woman would have. The man's a fool. Once I'm able to speak with her in private, it won't be long before she accepts my proposal." Wes tossed his cards on the table, pinning the man with a hard stare. "Sarah MacGregor will be mine, and any man who says different will deal with me."

Caleb listened to the exchange, saw the doubt on several of the men's faces. Sarah had already confessed to him her love for Colin, showing him the brooch. He'd let her talk, already knowing of the incident on the journey west. It had almost escalated into a brawl between the MacGregors and MacLarens until Angus MacLaren pulled Colin away. Caleb had stood not twenty feet from them with many of the other settlers, watching the altercation and feeling sympathy for two young people who were close to his age. It seemed Dougal hadn't changed in all these years.

The man sitting next to Wes leaned toward him. "And your pa's wife? What will you do about her?"

Although spoken in a whisper, Caleb had clearly heard.

Without warning, Wes stood, tipping over the table, and lunged at the man he'd known for years, grown up with, and called a friend. Grabbing Walt by the throat and wrestling him to the ground, Wes pounded his fists into his face, not letting up until being pulled away.

"What the hell are you doing, Wes? You'll kill him." One of the older men shoved him against a wall.

"Let go of me," Wes growled, pushing away. He pointed to Walt who stood several feet away, his face swollen and bloody. "You and I will talk outside." Propelling him out the door, he turned to the others. "We're doing this alone."

Stumbling outside, Walt used an old bandanna to wipe the blood from his face. "What was that about? No one heard me 'cept you." He gingerly touched his face. "I think you broke my nose."

Wes paced back and forth, hands on his hips, cursing as he walked. "What were you thinking, saying something like that? Anyone could have heard you."

"Hell, it's no secret about you and your stepma going behind your pa's back. If you're gonna be such a damn fool, you'd better hide your actions better."

Wes whirled on Walt. "What do you mean?"

Taking a few steps backward, Walt braced himself. "I heard a couple of the men talking about seeing you with her the night Fergus rode to Slade."

"Other than us having supper, they couldn't have seen anything." Wes crossed his arms, thinking back.

He had gone into her room hours after eating, knowing his pa wouldn't return for two days. No one could possibly have seen him.

"You certain about that? From what I heard, they saw more than two people sharing a meal."

"They're trying to stir up trouble. Who are they?" Wes demanded. He'd make certain they never spoke of it again.

"It don't matter. I already told 'em you'd be furious hearing their lies and to keep their mouths shut. They got the message. I'm telling you, you're playing a fool's game."

Two years older than Wes, Rhoda had caught Fergus's attention, snaring him into marriage. Fergus got a young wife, while she got access to his fortune—as well as his son, a fact Wes's pa knew nothing about.

"I'll live my life the way I want with no interference from you. Fact is, she's mine whenever I want her, and there's nothing Pa can do about it."

"You sure about that?" Walt shot back. "Seems to me he can cut you off anytime he wants, leaving it all to her. He could also kill you. You better think long and hard about what you're doing." Turning his back to Wes, he pulled a cheroot from his pocket, lighting it as he walked away.

Watching Walt leave, he thought of the warning, knowing his friend was right. His father had a temper matched by few men. He'd seen him give orders for men to hang, shot his fair share, and treated people with a brutality hard to comprehend. Wes knew if Fergus ever found out about the time spent with his young wife, he wouldn't just cut him out of his will. Son or not, he'd kill him.

Taking a wife, removing the lure of his stepma, had now become a priority. Wes had just one woman in mind and he'd find a way to win her hand, no matter her feelings for another man.

"Take your seats, children." Sarah stood at the front of the class, watching as boys and girls scrambled to their seats. Within minutes, they sat silent, their hands clasped on top of each desk, staring at her with wide eyes. Touching the brooch for luck, she offered a warm smile to her students. "I'm Miss MacGregor, and I'm your new teacher."

"Good morning, Miss MacGregor," an older girl sitting near the back said, followed by a chorus of good mornings.

"It will take some time to get to know your names, so we'll start now. I'd like each of you to stand, tell me your name and the names of your parents, and how old you are."

The students were quick to do as she asked until one young boy at the back stood, his gaze focused on the desk in front of him. He didn't speak a word, his face lifting, eyes wary and frightened.

Sarah saw the boy's distress and walked up to him, crouching low, speaking in a soft voice. "And what is your name?"

"He's new. He doesn't have a name," the child next to him said. "Doesn't have parents, either."

Her heart clenched. She knew children like him existed, but her life on the ranch separated her from the realities of much of town life.

"Is it true? You have no name?"

Shaking his head, he fidgeted, and Sarah could see he fought the urge to run.

"All right. Tell me what name you want to use and it will be so."

Big, round eyes lifted to hers. "Jamie." He whispered it so low, she almost missed it.

"Good." She stood, looking at the rest of the students. "I'd like to introduce Jamie. Please say hello to him."

She kept an eye on him all day, through his time outside and while he studied. Not once did she see him around other children, nor did he try to join in their games. While outside, he'd sit alone on a stump, watching. When the others opened their sacks for lunch, he sat in stoic silence, busying himself by fiddling with a small stick.

Opening her lunch, she pulled out an apple and walked forward. Talking to the children as she made her way to the back, she casually set the fruit on Jamie's desk, making no issue of it, then returned to the front. Eating her lunch, she glanced up several times, letting out a breath when his hand moved toward the apple and grasped it.

Finishing the lessons, she excused the students by midafternoon, watching until the last student, Jamie, looked up with a small smile, then dashed out the door. Grabbing her bonnet and reticule, she hurried after him, determined to find out where he lived. Pulling the door closed behind her, she turned and gasped. Wes Bell leaned against the side of the school, arms crossed.

"Good afternoon, Miss MacGregor. I heard you had taken the teaching position." Giving her his most sincere smile, Wes straightened, offering her his hand as she took the few steps to the ground.

Nodding a greeting while ignoring his hand, she glanced around, trying to spot Jamie. He'd already disappeared.

"Are you headed to your new house?"

She winced, not wanting to engage in conversation, but having little choice.

"Yes, Mr. Bell, I am, and I have much to do. If you'll excuse me..."

"Miss MacGregor...Sarah, please. Give me a moment of your time."

Coming to a halt, she turned. It wouldn't do to be rude to one of the most prominent men in town, even if he represented a day she wanted to forget.

"All right, Mr. Bell."

"I want to apologize about what happened on your birthday. It hadn't been planned to embarrass you."

"Then what did you and my father plan it to be?" Skepticism laced her voice as she crossed her arms.

Taking a step forward, he leaned toward her. "A genuine proposal of marriage."

"You don't even know me. Why would you want to spend your life with a woman you've barely spoken with in five years, and one who doesn't love you?"

"Ah, Miss MacGregor, had I gotten to know you better, I'd have noticed much more than your beauty. Believe me, I would have spent time getting to know you before offering for your hand. However, when your father approached me, his urgency was clear. I don't know his reasons, but he'd made up his mind to find you a husband and he wouldn't be dissuaded." When she didn't comment, Wes continued. "All I ask is a chance to plead my case. Have supper with me tonight."

"I don't think that would be wise. If you recall, I've never given you the slightest indication of interest in being courted by you. In fact, just the opposite. Besides, I'm already betrothed—"

"To a boy who has never come to claim his prize."

Sarah glanced away. She'd been plagued by the same thoughts, but wouldn't allow herself to give up on Colin. In her heart, she knew he'd come.

"My promise knows no limit as to time. Rest assured, Mr. Bell, he *will* come for me."

"I appreciate your devotion to him, however misplaced. It's been five years. That's a long time to wait with no word from him. Do you truly believe he'll come after all this time?"

Lifting her chin, she glared at him, disliking him more with each comment. "Yes, Mr. Bell. Colin MacLaren will come for me. Of that, I am certain."

Wes studied her, admiring her spunk, more determined than ever to turn her dedication toward him.

"All right. I'll no longer attempt to change your mind...*today*. However, I would still like to invite you to supper. You must eat, correct?"

"Yes. However, I've already accepted an invitation from Mrs. Olford. Now, I really must be going. Good day, Mr. Bell."

As she turned to leave, he called after her. "I'll not give up. You will be seeing more of me, Miss MacGregor."

Chapter Seven

"We'll not be able to go further today. Best we find a place to camp for the night." Colin turned his collar up as the rain pounded down. The trail had already turned into thick lumps of mud, forcing them to ride through the brush where the leaves and thick undergrowth made the ground easier to traverse.

"Up ahead, in those boulders." Brodie pointed to a spot further off the trail where several large rocks came together, forming a partial shelter, providing some protection from the storm.

Thirty minutes later, they'd found a dry area to start a fire. It had been almost a week since they'd left the girls in Mindell. They'd spoken little about them, although Quinn had mentioned how quiet the ride seemed. Riding with Coral, Pearl, and Opal for several days had allowed them to form a partial bond with the sisters, none more noticeable than Coral's attachment to Colin.

"I wonder if the reverend found homes for them." Quinn sipped his coffee, cradling the tin cup between both hands.

"Hope he did. Having two younger sisters to feed, clothe, and keep safe is a big burden for anyone, even for a girl who appears to be as strong as Coral." Colin sat between his cousins as they huddled against a large boulder.

"At eighteen, she's a woman, Colin." Brodie quipped as he tossed out grounds from his cup, then poured more coffee. "All three acted older than their years."

"You grow up fast when you're on your own." Colin leaned his back against the rock, pushing his hat low over his forehead. He didn't want to think of the girls, preferring to let his mind wander to memories of Sarah.

The last time he'd seen her, she'd been running back to her wagon, clutching the brooch tight in her hand. He wondered if her golden brown hair still held wisps of yellow when catching the rays of the sun, and if her bright blue eyes still sparkled when she smiled. She had freckles sprinkled across her nose and cheeks five years ago. He tried to envision them darkening from work on their farm, spreading to form a thin blanket of color across her face.

At least he thought they'd planned to farm. It's what the MacGregors had done for generations and he doubted Dougal would change. Angus had said Dougal was a man lost in the past, and it would take a miracle to bring him into the present.

Quinn nudged Colin, pulling him from his thoughts. "Did you hear me?"

"What did you say?" Colin pushed his hat back enough to cast a glance at Quinn.

"I told you he'd been thinking of Sarah." Quinn grinned at Brodie. "The man has lost his mind over that one."

"Aye, he has," Brodie agreed, handing Colin some hardtack and jerky. "How many more days before we can have some real food?"

"If the rain stops, maybe as soon as tomorrow." Colin took a bite of the hardtack, chewing slowly, then swallowing it down with lukewarm coffee. "The reverend said the first town we'll come to is River City. The last he'd heard, the town had close to two thousand people, a few restaurants, and one hotel."

"Any saloons?" Quinn chuckled before a sharp shove from Brodie sent him sprawling. "Ach. What was that for?"

"For asking an eejit question. Of course they have saloons. Right, Colin?"

Standing, Colin rested his hands on his hips, looking down at them. "In my mind, you both are eejits. Of course there'll be saloons." At least he hoped so. He figured he'd need at least one drink if he learned the MacGregors had settled in River City. Not for courage to see Sarah, but he'd take whatever fortification he could before confronting Dougal. Even after five years, he didn't expect the man to have softened his hatred of the MacLarens.

While they ate, the rain had stopped, allowing the ground to dry enough to lay out their bedrolls. Grabbing his blanket, he spread it out near the fire before tossing more sticks into the dwindling flames and lying down. He listened for a few minutes to the good-natured bantering of his cousins before allowing his thoughts to once more turn to Sarah.

Over their weeks of riding, he hadn't allowed himself to consider the idea she might have found someone else, married, and started a family. All his plans the last five years had been made believing Sarah waited for him.

Colin knew some in his family thought he embarked on a fool's journey, going after a woman who pledged herself to him at seventeen. Others, including Quinn, Brodie, Blaine, his parents, and uncles, stood by him, encouraging him to make the journey. Most interesting, it was his aunts and female cousins who were the skeptics. His nine-year-old twin sisters, Chrissy and Alana, stood by him, no matter what. They had a vague recollection of Sarah, the girl who'd played with them and read stories of warriors and knights, but not much more. A smile teased his mouth thinking of them. In their minds, he could do no wrong.

Lowering his hat to shield himself from the light of the emerging moon, he closed his eyes. Tomorrow would be Saturday. He wondered what Sarah would be doing. An image of her appeared, eyes sparkling as she glanced over her shoulder at him, holding the brooch to her heart.

"More tea, dear?"

Settling her hand on her stomach, Sarah eyed the remaining cookies, shaking her head. "Thank you, but I believe I've had my fill, Mrs. Olford."

She'd spent Saturday morning at the house, doing laundry and helping Bessie with her mending. Now late afternoon, they had time to speak of her first week teaching, her new house, and the boy, Jamie, who hadn't missed a day.

"I can't find out where he lives or if he has parents. The other children tell me he doesn't, but how else would he live?"

"Describe him to me." Bessie picked up another cookie, then took a sip of tea. Each year, she and her husband made a trip north to Portland, a growing city of close to four thousand people. The journey gave her a chance to stock up on items in scarce supply in town, such as tea, chocolate, and nuts.

"Jamie is about this tall." She held a hand above the ground to estimate his height. "He told me he's eight. His hair is long and dark brown, he has clear, soft gray eyes, some freckles, and a wonderful smile—if I can get him to show it."

Bessie pursed her lips, trying to picture him. "I can't think of anyone in our congregation who looks like that and doesn't have parents. I wonder how he got here."

"The other children say he showed up in town over the summer. I'd never say this to anyone else, but they think he stays near the back of the buildings, waiting for trash to be tossed out so he could go through it." Sarah shivered at the thought of any child scrounging in garbage for food.

"Have you tried following him after school?"

"Aye, twice. He's quick. I think he saw me each time and took off." Her eyes glittered, remembering him looking over his shoulder, then taking off like a scared rabbit.

"Does he bring food to school?" Bessie leaned forward, curiosity consuming her.

Sarah slumped back in her chair, her heart sinking. "No. I bring a little extra each day, which I try to give him without the other children seeing. I don't want to embarrass him."

"You can't let him starve." Bessie sympathized. They had two or three almost destitute families in their congregation. People were as generous as possible. Still, parents and children went to bed hungry more than she wanted to consider. With the population booming and new businesses starting, she believed the situation had to be addressed. Perhaps Jamie's appearance would be what she needed to induce the town council to take action. She pushed the plate toward Sarah. "Pack these cookies up and take them to Jamie on Monday. I should also have some meatloaf for him. Then tell him you have somebody you want him to meet after school and bring him here."

"What a wonderful idea."

They both turned toward the sound of knocking on the front door.

"I'll get it." Sarah crossed the living room to the entry, smiling when she saw who stood outside. "Caleb. It's so good to see you. Come in." Caleb followed as she walked back to the kitchen. "Mrs. Olford, we have a guest."

"I heard. How are you, Caleb?" She set a cup of tea and a few extra cookies in front of him.

"Quite well, Mrs. Olford. I wanted to thank you again for recommending me to Fergus Bell."

"No problem at all, young man. And how is it going at the Bell Ranch?"

Caleb took a sip of tea before replying. He wouldn't say a word about his thoughts on Wes. However, he'd learned Wes had made several attempts to invite Sarah to supper over the previous year. She'd spurned him each time. The concern he felt about Bell trying to court her came from his extreme unease about the man. Although Caleb said nothing, he'd heard Walt's comments about Wes and his stepmother. He grimaced, learning of Wes's betrayal of his own father. Sarah deserved much better than a man such as him. "Lots of hard work, which is good. It keeps me busy and my mind occupied."

"Do you have plans for supper, Caleb?" Sarah asked, wanting to learn more about him.

"You know you're welcome to join us," Bessie added.

He glanced between the two women, hoping this came out right. "Actually, I came by to ask if Sarah would be available to join me for supper."

Her face flushed at his offer. "Mrs. Olford, if you don't mind…"

"Of course not, dear. You've both worked hard and deserve some time to celebrate your new jobs. Go before the reverend returns and tries to talk you into staying."

Ten minutes later, they crossed the street, Sarah's arm through Caleb's. He led her to a small restaurant at the other end of town, finding a table near the window.

"I hope this is all right." Caleb pulled out a chair for her.

"Wonderful. I've never been here."

"One of the ranch hands said they eat here most Saturday nights before going to the, well…before moving on."

Sarah laughed at his attempt to shield her from the nighttime activities of many of the cowboys. "Do you mean go to the saloon?"

Caleb's brows lifted. He should have known better than to try and bamboozle her. Chuckling, he watched her eyes glitter in amusement. Other than the woman who'd deceived him, leaving him with a shattered future, Sarah was the only woman who caught his interest. What a pity he no longer had a heart to give, and hers had been promised years before. He hoped Colin MacLaren knew what a jewel he had waiting for him.

After they finished their simple meal and were waiting for coffee and dessert to arrive, Caleb crossed his arms, relaxing back in the chair. "I've told you some of my reasons for being in River City. Why are *you* living in town when your family's home is so close?"

Sarah stroked the brooch pinned to her dress, thinking of the last time she saw her father. A chill passed over her at both his and Wes's face when she made it clear she had no intention of marrying anyone except Colin.

"I don't know how much you remember about Da, but he can be quite a stubborn man."

"Oh, I recall. His temper is something not easily forgotten."

"Yes, he does have a temper. He's also steeped in the old ways, prejudices, and hatreds. Years ago, at least two hundred, a feud began between the MacGregors and MacLarens. They held adjoining lands in the southernmost part of the Highlands. I don't know what caused it, but I know some MacGregors have never forgotten. During the trip west, when he'd learned I'd become friends with

Colin, he forbid me from speaking to or seeing him again." Sarah stopped when the server arrived with their coffee and pie. She picked up the cup, watching as Caleb took a healthy bite of pie before he nodded for her to continue.

"Going against his wishes was hard, but I refused to not see Colin again. One night, Colin approached Da about marrying me. Da refused, threatening Colin if he tried to see me again."

"I remember. My father and I weren't far away and saw most of it. If it helps, I would have had the same reaction as Colin. I would've fought for you…or any woman I loved."

His comment warmed her, even though she knew Caleb also referred to the woman who'd turned her back on him.

"We did ignore Da, seeing each other for the last time the night before we turned north for Oregon. He gave me this brooch, asked me to marry him, and said he'd come for me. I said yes."

Caleb had wondered about the beautiful jewelry she was never without. Now he knew its meaning.

"Is that why you left home?"

"In a way, yes." Taking another bite of pie, she allowed herself to show the slightest amount of pleasure at the way she'd stood up to her da. "We were celebrating my birthday at the hotel restaurant. Da invited Wes Bell to join us. With no warning, Da announced he'd made an agreement with Wes for the two of us to marry."

Caleb's brows knit together. He'd heard as much from the men who worked for the Bells, wondering if it were true. "You refused?"

"Most certainly. And I wasn't quiet about it. I announced my promise to Colin and refused to honor the agreement Da made. Then I left."

"And moved in with the Olfords."

"Even if they hadn't offered a room, I still would not have returned to the ranch. It no longer felt like my home. Does any of this make sense?" she asked, pushing away the rest of her pie.

"Believe me, it makes complete sense. You're a grown woman, Sarah. A fact your father refuses to accept. He thinks he can tie you to the hatreds and traditions of the old country. Don't misunderstand. Many of the traditions are good and should be continued. However, feuds shouldn't be a part of them. They have no place in our new lives."

"You speak as if you know a bit about it."

A grin touched the corners of his mouth. "As a Stewart, we know both hatred and strong alliances. You may not know this, but the Stewarts and MacLarens were once allies. We fought next to each other at Culloden." Finishing his coffee, he leaned forward, reaching across the table to cover her hand with his. "The same as the MacLarens, we put aside our hatred of those who fought against us and moved on. Your father should do the same."

The rain had stopped as Colin, Quinn, and Brodie turned in for the night. By morning, the sun shone bright, allowing them to make good time, stopping once before continuing to River City. If the information provided in Mindell could be trusted, they should reach their destination in time for supper.

They heard the pounding of hooves before seeing the group of men appear in the trail ahead of them. Not liking the look of them, Colin rested his hand on the butt of his gun and waited. Brodie and Quinn reined their horses to a stop on either side of him, no one speaking, even as each felt the tension in the others.

"Gentlemen," the one in front called out. Sitting tall in the saddle, he moved his horse forward.

"That's close enough." Colin signaled his cousins to spread out.

"Where you boys headed?" the leader asked, not missing the way Brodie and Quinn put distance between themselves and Colin.

"I don't believe it's any of your business." Colin kept his gaze on the leader while trying to keep track of the others.

"I'm Sheriff Joe Walker and these are my deputies." He pulled his coat aside so they could see his badge. "We're following four brothers who robbed a bank and rode south. You want to tell me what you're doing out this way?"

Colin relaxed, but didn't move his hand away from his gun as he spoke. Introducing himself, Quinn, and Brodie, he explained where they were from and a little about their trip. "We hope to be in River City tonight."

"Well, then, you won't mind if my deputies search your saddlebags." Walker nodded toward his men.

Glancing at Quinn and Brodie, he nodded. Walker seemed to be satisfied with their story when the deputies failed to find the money from the robbery.

"You looking for someone in particular when you reach town, or are you planning to pass through?" Walker asked, riding closer to get a better look at the three, deciding if he and his men were in danger.

"I'm looking for my fiancée, Sarah MacGregor. Do you know her?"

Walker glanced at the men with him, then back at Colin. "Can't say as I do. Is she related to Dougal MacGregor?" He had heard talk of Dougal and a man named Bell.

"Aye, sir. She's his daughter."

"Well, you're headed in the right direction. Before we rode out of River City, I heard talk of a prominent rancher setting his sights on Dougal's daughter."

Colin's gut clenched at the news, the first he'd heard about Sarah in five long years.

"That a fact? Well, the man will have a fight on his hands if what you heard is true. I appreciate the warning, Sheriff. If there's nothing else, we'll keep going."

"Watch your back. We don't know where the robbers went, but we do know they have no problem killing." He sent Colin a twisted smile that could best be described as disturbing, then signaled his men to follow him.

Colin watched, disquieted in a way he couldn't define. Shaking his head, he figured it was the news of Sarah and nothing more.

"All right, lads. Let's get moving."

Chapter Eight

"There's one that's open." Quinn turned Warrior toward a restaurant down the street.

Colin didn't want to waste any time eating now that he knew Sarah lived here. He wanted to speak with the locals, find out where she lived. His stomach's loud growl, however, told him finding her could wait a little longer, at least until he filled the hole in his gut.

Sliding down from Chieftain, he stretched his arms above his head in an attempt to work out the kinks after the long ride. They'd been in the saddle all day, only stopping once.

"Come on, Colin. I can't wait any longer for some real food." Brodie strode up the steps, holding the door open for the others.

Colin led the way, glancing around before spotting an empty table close to the front. One other couple sat near it and as he moved closer, he noticed the man's hand covering hers. *A couple*, Colin assumed as he continued forward. Then she looked up.

Sarah...

His breath caught and he couldn't help the tremor rolling through him at his first glimpse of her in five years. She hadn't changed—the same golden brown hair and blue eyes so radiant they sparkled. A few more freckles covered her nose and cheeks, and without question, she was still the most beautiful woman he'd ever seen. Then his gaze moved back down to the table where she gripped another man's hand, and his movements froze at the same instant he saw recognition dawn on her face.

When something hard knocked into him, he didn't budge.

"Ach, Colin, what's holding you up?" Brodie's voice came from behind him a moment before his cousin looked over his shoulder. "Ah, hell," Brodie muttered, not hesitating in his recognition of Sarah.

The knot in Colin's stomach grew to a cold, hard lump as he stared into her eyes. He'd come too late. The realization swept through him as his hands closed into fists.

"Colin?" Her voice trembled as her eyes widened in stunned disbelief.

His mind cleared at Sarah's use of his name. Although little comfort, at least she hadn't completely forgotten him. The muscles of his jaw tightened. He opened his mouth to speak, then clamped it shut, unable to say what he wanted. Instead, he turned and stomped toward the door, slamming it behind him.

"Colin, wait!" Sarah jumped from her chair, pushing past Brodie and Quinn, uncaring of the stares which followed her. "Colin MacLaren, you stop right now," she called, following him toward his horse.

Taking a deep breath, he turned and stared into a face which had consumed his thoughts for a long time. He cleared his throat, searching for calm.

"Sarah...Sarah MacGregor, right?" He shot her a look of what he hoped was total disinterest. "What a surprise after all these years."

Swallowing the sour taste in her mouth, she searched his eyes, trying to find any trace of the man she loved in them. "You...you didn't come here for me?" Her eyes teared at the same moment she sensed movement next to her.

Reaching a hand toward Colin, Caleb smiled. "Good to see you again, Colin. I'm Caleb Stewart. I doubt you'll remember me, but we traveled west in the same wagon train."

Colin's gaze moved from Sarah's face to the outstretched hand.

"I remember you, Stewart." Ignoring Caleb's attempt at friendship, he turned toward Chieftain and grabbed the reins.

"Colin, wait. Where are you going?" The desperation in Sarah's voice cut through him and he wondered what game she played.

"Good to see you again, Sarah. Perhaps we'll see each other again before I leave." Swinging into the saddle, he started to rein his horse away.

"Don't be daft, MacLaren," Caleb shouted in a cold, stern voice. "No woman could have been more devoted to a man she hasn't seen in over five years than Sarah MacGregor. At least show her some respect after all this time. Then open your eyes before you throw away a prize any man would covet."

Caleb's words shot through Colin as doubt filled his mind. Forcing himself to take another look at Sarah, he let his gaze roam from the hair he wanted to run his fingers through, to her eyes, now filled with pain. Not allowing his gaze to linger, he continued down until his eyes locked on a bright silver object pinned to her dress. His gram's brooch. Closing his eyes tight, he felt the pain in his chest recede.

"Sarah..." he breathed out a moment before dropping to the ground and crushing her to him. "When I saw you with Caleb I thought..."

Burying her face in his chest, she wrapped her arms around his neck, holding on as if she'd never let go. Feeling tears soak his shirt, she pulled back to swipe them from her face. Choking back a sob, she looked at him.

"I would've waited forever for you, Colin."

"Seems you've lost your girl, Wes. The man she talked about showed up in town tonight to claim her." Walt took a long drag from a cheroot as he leaned against the bunkhouse. Foregoing his night at the saloon, he'd ridden back to the Bell Ranch as soon as he finished eating at the restaurant where the scene unfolded. "Guess you're going to have to find another woman to get your mind off your stepma."

Wes paced a few feet away, paying little attention to Walt's last comment. He and Dougal had been certain Sarah's objections to marrying him were a way of getting away from her father rather than a rejection of Wes's desire to marry her. Neither believed her declaration of being betrothed to MacLaren, or that the man would ever come to claim her. Looks like they'd been wrong.

"You're certain it's MacLaren?"

"Yep. They both took off for a spell, but when they returned to eat, I could hear it all. He rode into town with two other MacLarens. There's something else. Our new man, Caleb Stewart, was having supper with Sarah before MacLaren arrived."

This got Wes's attention. He knew little about Caleb except he seemed to be a hard worker, kept to himself, and could handle ranch work better than most. It hadn't occurred to him that his hired hand knew Sarah. In Wes's mind, accepting a supper invitation from one of his hired men couldn't be overlooked. He'd given her time to make the right decision. With MacLaren in town, his patience had been exhausted.

"Where is MacLaren staying?" Wes needed to get MacLaren alone, explain who Sarah belonged to.

"The hotel."

"Then that is where we start."

Situated in a section of town several hundred yards from the school, Sarah's house faced the back of the lumber mill. A stream, where she often walked before supper, ran behind it. Tonight, she and Colin strolled along the edge, holding hands as they spoke. After supper, he'd asked Quinn and Brodie to get him a room while he walked her home, unable to put distance between them now that he'd found her.

"You've changed since I last saw you." Colin tightened his grip on her hand.

"Oh?"

"You're even more beautiful than I remember." Turning her toward him, he stroked his knuckles down her cheek, watching as her eyes glowed. She didn't resist when he moved his hand behind her neck to draw her close. "I want to kiss you, Sarah."

"Aye, it's been too long." She sucked in a breath, waiting, as he lowered his head, brushing his lips across hers once, then twice before taking her mouth.

Pulling back, he rested his forehead against hers.

"How many boys have you kissed while you waited for me?" He knew asking wasn't fair, yet he couldn't stop the words.

"I've kissed only one boy. You. Is it so obvious?"

He made no answer other than to place a trail of kisses down her face, stopping at the corner of her mouth.

"More, Colin. I want more."

Seconds turned to minutes as the kiss heated, their arms tightening around each other. His hands moved to her hair, threading silken strands through his fingers as he positioned her for better access. Tracing her lips with the tip of his tongue, he encouraged her to open as his hands moved to her hips.

An intense shudder heated her body, her heartbeat pounding in her ears as she squirmed to get closer. The force of the desire she felt shocked her.

Feeling his hands tighten on her hips, sending an involuntary tremor through her and a strange aching in her limbs, she moaned against his mouth.

Breaking the contact, Colin pulled back, his breath coming in deep gulps. "We need to stop, lassie. We cannot continue like this."

Her grip on him tightened, confusion replacing the passion he saw moments before.

His strong hands cupped her face as his eyes locked on hers. "If we don't stop, we may do something you'll regret."

Her flesh tingled as his warm breath fanned her face. "Do you not want me, Colin?"

He mumbled a soft curse, realizing she thought his actions were a lack of desire.

"Nae, lassie. I've never wanted anyone more."

Her tongue darted out to moisten her lips, her brows furrowing at his words. "I've waited five years for you, Colin MacLaren. I'll not wait a minute longer."

He didn't believe he could feel any more desire for Sarah than he already did. Her open, innocent admission broke through the craving he'd been trying to contain. Bending, he swept her into his arms. Capturing her mouth with his, he took long strides to the back of her house, kicking open the door.

"The bedroom, Sarah," he ground out, walking through the one door inside the house. Gently easing her onto the bed, then lying down beside her, Colin touched his lips to hers. Wrapping her in his warm embrace, he unfastened the small buttons of her dress until he reached her waist. Pushing the material aside, his breath caught at the sight of her thin chemise rising and falling as she took in deep breaths, her chest swelling with the effort.

Lowering his head, he took her mouth in a searing kiss before moving to the creamy expanse of her neck, then to the swell of her breasts. Lifting his gaze to hers, blood surged through him at the look of trust on her face.

"Are you certain, lassie? If you aren't, we'll wait."

Lifting a hand, she cupped his face. "I love you, Colin. I'll never love another."

He nodded once, his heart hammering against his ribs. "I love you, too, Sarah. Never doubt it."

Curled into the curve of Colin's body, Sarah's eyes drifted open as the morning sun sent warmth radiating onto the bed. Shifting, she felt the strong arm around her waist tighten.

"Where are you going?" His warm breath washed across her shoulder, his voice still husky from sleep.

Turning in his arms, she faced him, seeing a smile tilt the corners of his mouth upward. Touching her lips to his, she felt his body stir, her own blood surging from her fingertips to her toes. They should be exhausted, too tired to move after making love most of the night. Instead, she wanted him again. Judging by his reaction, Colin felt the same.

His hands moved down her back to caress the curve of her hip. The gentle massage sent renewed currents of desire through her.

"Once more, then you'll need to feed me." His hoarse whisper broke the silence as he shifted her beneath him, taking her mouth with his.

A loud pounding on the front door stopped him. Leveraging up on his elbows, he listened again. This time the knocking was accompanied by a brash shout.

"Colin! Are you in there?"

"Quinn," Colin muttered. "I'll kill him." Giving her one more kiss, he slid from the bed, snagging his trousers, then closing the bedroom door. Slipping his legs into them, he grasped the knob, pulling the door open to see Quinn and Brodie standing outside, smug grins on both faces. "Are you both daft, shouting so others can hear? On with you." He started to close the door, Quinn's boot stopping him.

"And where are we to go, laddie? Surely Sarah can offer us coffee." Quinn's broad smile annoyed Colin.

Cursing, he shoved Quinn away, then stepped outside, closing the door behind him. Looking around, he was grateful to see no one else on the street this early on a Sunday morning.

"Listen to me, both of you. There will be no embarrassing Sarah. No teasing or comments. She deserves better from the two of you louts." Moving to within inches of Quinn, he leaned closer. "Hear me on this, or we *will* come to blows."

Quinn's face lost all its humor. Stepping away, he held both arms out, palms up. "You know we'd never hurt Sarah. Never, Colin." His voice contrite, he glanced at Brodie, who nodded in agreement.

"Colin, is everything all right?"

He turned at Sarah's voice to see the door open a crack, her face peeking out at him.

"It's Quinn and Brodie. I'll be in shortly."

"Nonsense. Don't stand out there where the whole town can see you. Come inside. I'll make breakfast." Stepping aside, she pulled her wrapper tight.

Colin shook his head as his cousins walked past, sending him smug smiles.

Sarah scurried around the small kitchen, fixing eggs and potatoes. "I have no bacon, so you'll have to go without."

"Or go to the restaurant and order what you want," Colin prompted, hoping they'd take the hint and leave.

"Eggs and potatoes are fine, lass." Brodie winked at Colin over the rim of his coffee cup.

Placing filled plates in front of them, she took a seat, smiling at Colin as the others dug into their meal.

"Do we start back tomorrow then, Colin?" Brodie asked, pushing his plate away.

"Back?" Sarah's face lifted, her eyes locked on Colin's. "You're leaving so soon?"

Taking her hand, he squeezed. "We want to start for home before the bad weather starts. Soon would be best. Of course, you're coming with us."

Biting her bottom lip, she set down her cup, sliding her hand from his. "What of my job, Colin? I can't leave the students now. I've just started."

They'd talked of her job last night. He knew it mattered to her, yet it never occurred to him she couldn't walk away. Or wouldn't want to leave to be with him.

"Are you saying you won't come back with me?" Crossing his arms, his voice took on a hard edge, his eyes narrowing to slits.

"Of course not." Standing, she grabbed the empty plates. "I need time to speak with the men who hired me, find out if they can replace me."

"*If?*" Colin asked, uneasy at what she implied.

"All right. *When* they can replace me. I know they can find someone, but not how soon." Setting the plates on the counter, she turned to him. "Please understand. I didn't know when you'd come for me. This job is what I've always wanted and I have an obligation to the town. It doesn't mean I don't want to marry you and move to California." Walking up to him, she placed a hand on his shoulder. "You're all I've dreamed of for five years. I won't give you up."

Colin listened without comment. It hadn't occurred to him that once he found Sarah, she'd have obligations stopping her from leaving. September nights had already turned cold. They had at least a month on the trail before crossing over Boundary Mountain, Circle M Ranch stretching along its base. As best as he could figure, they had two, maybe three, weeks before they had to leave to avoid bad weather.

"Three weeks at most, Sarah. That's all the time you have before we must start back." Rising, he strode to the bedroom.

Tossing down a towel, she started after him, stopping when Quinn grabbed her arm.

"You need to understand, Sarah. You're all he's thought of since we all parted at Fort Hall. Everything Colin's done since then has had one purpose—to get back to you. Now that he's found you, there's no reason we can't leave."

"Except for my job..." Her voice trailed off as she thought of the faces of her students. It had been a short time, yet she felt as if they were hers. She'd miss them. "I'll tell them tomorrow after school, help them find someone." Offering a grim smile, she walked to the bedroom, then turned. "I won't hold you up. We'll leave within three weeks, no later."

Chapter Nine

"I'm so glad he found you and came with you to church today." Bessie's warm gaze traveled from Sarah to Colin.

It had taken some cajoling to get him to accompany her, explaining it would appear unnatural if she didn't attend. Besides, she wanted to show Colin off, introduce him to the people who'd helped her, letting everyone know he'd finally come for her.

"It's my pleasure, Mrs. Olford," Colin assured her, looking decidedly uncomfortable under the undisguised stares of the congregation.

"Sarah mentioned your cousins rode in with you. Are they here also?" She looked around for signs of anyone she didn't know.

"Uh...nae, ma'am."

"Well, they'll have to come next week." Bessie glanced over Sarah's shoulder. "Oh dear..."

"What is it, Mrs. Olford?" Sarah turned in the direction of Bessie's stare, then sucked in a breath, her face draining of color. Her reaction prompted Colin to look behind him at what had caused the stress on her face.

A buggy came to a stop under the limbs of an expansive tree, an older man jumping off to help a woman. As soon as he turned, Colin recognized the man who'd caused him and Sarah so much grief.

Dougal MacGregor stood beside his wife, his gaze wandering over the crowd. Robena slid her hand through his arm, seeing Sarah first, pointing toward her.

"There, Dougal. Sarah is next to Mrs. Olford. Now's the time to settle your differences with her."

Irritation sliced through him. He had no interest in settling their differences. He'd come for one reason...to take Sarah home, no matter her objections and despite her new job as the town school teacher. Without acknowledging Robena's comment, he strode forward, locking his gaze on Sarah. He'd gotten within several feet before the young man standing next to her turned to face him.

"MacLaren." The one word hissed from him. The hatred in Dougal's voice could be heard by all those within earshot, including Colin.

Robena tightened her hold on his arm. "Do not cause a scene, Dougal."

Shaking her off, he took several steps forward, halting two feet from Colin. As a boy, he'd been shorter than Dougal. The man who stood before him had grown to well over six feet with broad shoulders and, from what Dougal could tell, a strong back. Still, he'd not let MacLaren take Sarah from them.

"Hello, Mr. MacGregor." Colin extended his hand, hoping Dougal would take it without causing embarrassment to Sarah. For himself, he didn't care. In fact, he'd be more than happy to set Dougal straight with words or fists. It didn't matter which.

Ignoring Colin's gesture, he focused his attention on Sarah. "You'll come home with us now, Sarah."

Moving closer to Colin, feeling his arm wrap around her, she straightened.

"Nae, Da. I will go nowhere that doesn't include Colin." The strength in her voice surprised even Sarah. Her confidence building, she took a step forward, never leaving Colin's protective embrace. "As you can see, he's come for me, and I'll be leaving for California as soon as possible."

The color in Dougal's face changed from blotchy pink to red, and the arteries in his neck bulged at Sarah's announcement. Robena did her best to hold him back, but he shoved her aside. A collective gasp came from the onlookers. If another man hadn't steadied her, she'd have fallen to the ground.

"Da, stop it—"

"Stand aside, child. This is between MacLaren and me."

Colin moved her behind him, glancing at Bessie, nodding for her to take Sarah aside, away from what might happen between him and Dougal. Colin knew if her father hurt Sarah in any way, he'd kill him.

"I'll not be fighting with you today, Mr. MacGregor. Not at church, and not in front of Sarah." He held his ground, ready for whatever the man decided.

Dougal pointed a finger at him, his rage barely contained. "You're the reason Sarah turned her back on us. If you'd left her alone, we'd never have come to this. She'll never marry a MacLaren." He shifted his gaze to Sarah, who now stood between Bessie and the reverend. "If you leave, know this. You will no longer be a child of mine. You'll be cut off from your family—dead to us."

Colin didn't turn to see Sarah's response. He knew the pain he'd find on her face. It took all his strength to hold back on the immediate impulse to grab Dougal by his collar and slam a fist into his hostile face. At the same time, a wave of pity passed through him, knowing the man might be throwing away much more than his oldest daughter. Decisions such as these had a way to haunt families for generations, and he had no doubt the MacGregors would feel the pain of his actions for a long time to come.

"Nae, Da. You cannot do this." Until now, Geneen had stayed back, not wanting to interfere. She had no intention of losing her sister to her father's rage. "She's your oldest daughter. How can you even consider this?"

Rounding, Dougal focused his rising anger on Geneen. "Back in the buggy. Now. I will not have you interfering."

Stepping forward, she moved around him in measured steps until she stood near Sarah. "I will not return to the buggy and will not watch as you tear our family apart. If you disown Sarah, I will leave with her."

Although his face remained impassive, Colin groaned inwardly. The entire situation had deteriorated to where both Sarah and Geneen might be tossed out of the MacGregor clan. The MacLarens would welcome both, but nothing about it gave him peace. Staring at Dougal, he waited for the response he dreaded.

"Dougal, you cannot let this happen." Robena's shrill plea did nothing to dissuade her husband. Digging her fingers into his arm, she tried to turn him toward her. As before, he pushed her aside.

"So be it. If you leave with MacLaren and Sarah, neither of you will ever be welcome again."

"Please, don't force us to make a choice, Da. Think of what you're doing." Sarah's voice shook, her eyes pleading with her father to reconsider.

"Dougal, my friend, go home. Think through what you're asking." Reverend Olford stepped between Colin and Dougal. "I know this is hard for you, but old feuds have no place in your new home. They're best left in Scotland where they belong."

Unwilling to continue with the townsfolk standing around, Dougal stepped away. For the first time, he noticed the wide-eyed, shocked, or pitying faces of his neighbors. He didn't know with whom their sympathies lay, though.

"I'll leave, Reverend, but know that my mind is set. If Sarah and Geneen do not return with me now, they will no longer be accepted into my home." Taking one more look at his daughters, he whirled away. His shoulders slumped as he made his way through the crowd to his buggy, where his youngest daughter, Isla, waited, tears streaming down her face. Ignoring her, he called for his wife. "Robena, we are leaving."

Colin could see the indecision on her face. He couldn't imagine the pain she felt at leaving her daughters behind. Knowing Robena had little choice, he stepped closer, lowering his voice.

"You will always be welcome in our home, Mrs. MacGregor, as will your husband...if he ever forgets his hatred."

"Thank you," she choked out. Giving Sarah and Geneen long hugs, she kept the tears away until she took one last look at each. "You'll be getting your clothes and whatever else you want before you leave. Your Da cannot keep me from doing that for you." Cringing at the sound of Dougal's second order to return to the buggy, she dashed away, swiping at the dampness on her cheeks.

"Ach, that did not turn out as I'd hoped." Geneen took Sarah's hand in hers. "It appears, Mr. MacLaren, you have another person joining you on your trip."

Nodding, he took Sarah in his arms. "Are you all right, lass?"

Burying her face in his chest, she held Colin to her, hoping to absorb whatever strength she could. Waiting until her head cleared, she pulled away.

"Aye. I will be all right."

Tilting her chin up with his finger, he studied her face. "Is it still your intention to go home with me?" Colin needed to hear her agreement once more. What Dougal had said shook them all, no one more than Sarah.

"Aye. I'll not change my mind. Da will have to change his."

"Aye, Sarah. Da needs time, and Ma won't let him rest until he reconsiders. We've the unpleasant fate of having a stubborn man for a father."

Sarah smiled through her tears. Geneen always could make the worst situations seem bearable.

"Aye, Geneen. You're right. If he doesn't, we'll both start new lives in California. Right, Colin?"

"Aye, love, you will."

Bessie walked up to them. "I will not take any arguments. I've a roast cooking and two pies. You will all have supper with the reverend and myself, and that includes your cousins, Mr. MacLaren."

Colin's mouth twisted into a grin. She reminded him of their own reverend's wife at home, who had a heart of gold and a robust constitution. People seldom argued with her. He guessed the same was true of Bessie Olford.

"We'd be pleased to have supper with you. I'll round up my cousins and bring everyone back to your house. Now, I believe Sarah and Geneen might require some time alone."

Nodding, she patted each girl on the back. "We'll see you when you've rested."

Escorting Sarah and Geneen back to her house, he couldn't get his mind off Dougal. The anger he showed was beyond reason, bordering on madness. Worse, he couldn't shove away the feeling deep in his gut that this wasn't over. The man may have disowned his daughters, but he hadn't given up on his war against the MacLarens.

"When will I see you again, Wes?" Rhoda Bell sat up, pulling the covers up to below her neck.

Grabbing his trousers from the floor, he slid them on before turning to look at his stepmother.

"You'll see me when I need you."

His curt answer didn't seem to bother her. She'd become used to his rude, often biting replies to her questions.

"Tomorrow night?"

"Hell, no. Pop will be back. I may be reckless, but I'm not suicidal."

Tossing off the covers, Rhoda slid into her wrapper, letting it hang open. She knew he found her attractive, and if she'd waited, perhaps she'd have snagged him rather than his father. Although Fergus wasn't bad in bed, he would never best his son. Wes made being married to his father bearable.

Buttoning his shirt, she stilled his hands, letting hers flatten on his hard chest. "You know, I like it when he's at home and you're in my bed. It's more...exciting." She continued to play with his crisp chest hair, glancing at him with a sultry expression. "Since I won't see you for a while, why not one more time before you leave."

Wes didn't want to stay, yet his body had already started to respond. Gritting his teeth as her hand moved to his stomach, then lower, he cursed. Grabbing her by the shoulders, he pushed her onto the bed, dragging up her clothes, then loosening his own.

"This what you want?" he ground out.

"Oh, yes. Just what I want."

Not worried about her pleasure, he made it quick, then shoved away, continuing to dress. Finishing, he grabbed the doorknob, then turned around.

"We can't keep doing this, Rhoda. Tonight ends it. No more."

If it wasn't for the look on his face, she would have laughed. From the first night, it had always been up to him. Although she'd been more than willing, Wes was the one who pursued it, coming to her the first night his father left the ranch—two weeks after the wedding. He'd been coming to her ever since.

"If that's what you want, Wes." With casual grace, she rolled off the bed, letting her wrapper fall into place, knowing how this always affected him. "I'll see you at the supper table."

He cursed at her knowing smile, then slammed the door closed. Storming through the house, Wes walked out the back door on his way to the foreman's place where he lived. His father had fired the previous foreman weeks before, believing the long-time hired hand to be incompetent. Wes picked up the extra work, figuring it had been his father's plan all along. He liked hard work, enjoyed playing cards with the men, and didn't wither, as others had, at his father's harsh rule. As long as you did as he asked, Fergus would leave you alone. Defy him and the consequences would be severe.

Falling onto his bed, he settled an arm over his face and thought about tonight. He had to stop his raging desire for Rhoda. At first, their rendezvous were exciting and quite fulfilling. Now he couldn't stay away, as if she'd cast a witch's spell. He had to break her hold over him.

At twenty-five, there had only been one other woman who attracted him. One who might be able to fulfill his needs and make him forget Rhoda. That's why he'd pursued and agreed to marry Sarah. Tomorrow, he'd speak with MacGregor, figure out a way to get her to spurn MacLaren. He couldn't put it off any longer.

"I've got to send a message to Da, then I'll meet you." Colin finished buckling his gun belt, then shoved his hat down on his head. Several days had passed since meeting the Olfords. Even though it killed him, he slept alone each night, not wanting to risk anyone seeing him leave Sarah's house or let Geneen know the extent of their relationship. Instead, they'd ride out of town after school let out each day, find a quiet place, and make love.

The first time, they disappeared until early evening. Sarah guided him to a beautiful glen covered in dense, green growth and trees with wide canopies. Taking his hand, they walked along a nearby river, stopping at the edge of a ravine, the sound of water catching his attention. Pushing through thick brush, they came upon the falls. Water plummeted over the edge and into a deep pool below. Tightening his grip on her hand, he'd led her down the path, finding a wide expanse of flat ground along the pool's edge. Pulling her to him, he captured her mouth with his, heat pulsing through both of them within seconds. Taking their time, they removed each other's clothing, making love with every touch and each kiss until both were spent. They'd returned to the same spot each day since.

"We'll save you a place at the table." Quinn followed Brodie to a nearby saloon. They'd spent considerable time there since Colin found Sarah. Stuck didn't begin to explain how Quinn felt at their inability to start for home. He knew she'd asked the town leaders to find a replacement. All they could do now was wait.

Colin nodded, even though he had no desire to spend another evening drinking and playing cards. He wanted to be with Sarah, not with his two rowdy cousins, no matter how much he loved them.

Bessie had encouraged them to marry while in River City, letting Reverend Olford perform the rights. Even though it appealed to them, Colin wanted his family around when he wed Sarah. It no longer mattered to her where they married. Her father disowning her and Geneen had changed her feelings on having family present. Geneen would be there, and that's all that mattered to Sarah.

"Here you are." Colin handed the message he'd scribbled to the telegraph clerk, dropping coins on the counter.

"MacLaren, huh? I believe there's a message waiting for you." Searching a file, he pulled out the telegram. "This came a few days ago."

Reading it quickly, smiling at the brief query from his father as to their safety, Colin made a slight change to his original message. "You'll find me at the hotel if you get a response."

Stepping into the chilled evening air, he pulled out his pocket watch, knowing Sarah and Geneen would be at the Olford's for supper. If they'd accept, Bessie would have them all over every night.

The week had dragged by, with few men in the saloon most nights. Tonight, every chair was taken, except for one next to Quinn.

"Sit down, laddie. I've a run of bad luck. Maybe you'll help me turn it around." Quinn tossed back his whiskey, smiling at the barmaid who stopped next to him. "A whiskey for my friends and another for me."

After Colin arrived, Quinn's luck *did* improve, as did Brodie's mood. At twenty-two, the same age as Quinn, Brodie had always been more brooding and wary of strangers than either of his cousins. Tonight, he drank his whiskey at a slow pace, even when two untouched drinks sat before him.

"The whiskey not to your liking?" Colin asked, also sipping his drink, in no mood to let alcohol get the better of him. Throughout the evening, Colin had watched two men across from him, each taking unexpected interest in him, Quinn, and Brodie. Their continued perusal irritated him, yet he had no reason to expect trouble from the strangers.

"I'm out." Brodie set down his cards, glancing around the saloon, trying to determine what bothered him. Leaning over, he kept his voice low. "I've a gnawing in my gut."

The comment produced a quick response from Colin, who straightened. Since they'd been children, Brodie had an uncanny ability to foretell danger. Whenever his eyes looked cold and restless, his kin had learned to be watchful. Most of the family had learned to heed his warnings. The fact Colin felt unease at the same time as Brodie made him all the more on edge.

"I need some air." Colin finished his drink and started outside, Brodie close behind. Putting the noise of the saloon behind them, they crossed the street. "What is it?"

Brodie turned his head, looking for the movement he expected. "We're being watched. I don't know who, how many, or what they want. All I know is there are eyes on us, Colin."

He'd no more than finished his sentence when gunshots came from the saloon.

"Quinn," Brodie muttered before dashing across the street, his chest tightening. Shoving through the doors, his gaze landed on Quinn, prone on the floor, blood pooling around him.

Chapter Ten

"Get the doctor." Colin's shout moved people to action. Grabbing one of the men who'd been at their table, he dragged him forward. "Who did this?" The man stammered before Colin yanked him closer. "Who. Did. This?"

His voice shook as he pointed to a door behind the bar. "They ran out that way." He swallowed a lump of fear. "I didn't recognize either of them."

Colin pushed the man away, turning around. "Does anyone know who shot Quinn? I need a name."

The crowd moved away as men shook their heads or stared at the ground.

"I've seen them in here before. They were asking about work, but I don't know if they found jobs." The bartender set his unfired shotgun on the bar as the door swung open and the doctor hurried toward Quinn. Kneeling, he took a quick look, shaking his head.

"It's bad. We need to get him to my office."

"You and you," Colin pointed to a couple men. "Help us put him on this table." He turned toward Brodie. "We'll carry him to the doc's place on the table."

"Someone get the sheriff," one of the men they'd played cards with yelled.

"He and most of his deputies are gone, trailing some bank robbers. You may be able to find someone at the jail." The bartender watched as one of the men took off to find a deputy, then walked around the bar, helping them lift the table and carry it down the street.

"Careful, now," the doctor warned. Too wide to make it through the clinic door, they set the table down outside, lifted Quinn, and carried him the rest of the way. "Put him here." He indicated a bed in the back, then shooed everyone away, including Colin and Brodie, who took a few steps away and crossed their arms.

"We won't get in your way, Doc," Colin answered the look of frustration on the doctor's face.

"Either of you have any medical training?" He started removing Quinn's clothes, needing to get started before he lost any more blood.

"We've tended men who've been injured at our ranch. Nothing like this, though." Colin planted his feet shoulder width apart, having no intention of leaving Quinn with a doctor he knew nothing about. Watching every move, he winced at the sight of two bullet holes—one in his left shoulder, one a little lower.

Cursing, Brodie took a step forward. "How can we help?"

Without looking up, the doctor nodded over his shoulder. "Hot water, towels, bandages, and alcohol...in the cupboard." He looked at Colin. "Help me get his shirt off and remove his boots."

The doctor worked for over an hour removing two bullets, cleaning the wounds, and stitching, Colin and Brodie assisting with whatever he asked. His wife, who usually acted as his assistant, had fallen ill with a stomach ailment. Their help had been crucial. The blessing had come when Quinn didn't regain consciousness the entire time.

Infection loomed as the biggest threat. The doctor told them if he made it through the next few days, Quinn had a good chance of recovering.

Colin wanted to let Sarah know what happened, needing the comfort he knew she'd provide. By the time the doctor finished, it was well past midnight, so he settled for falling asleep in the small waiting area, Brodie snoring next to him.

"What happened?" Wes asked the two men he'd hired to send a warning to MacLaren. Their job had been to scare him, soften him up for the talk Wes planned. The nervous twitch on the face of one and the way the second shuffled his feet signaled their failure.

"We had a problem, but it's handled. No need to worry." The smug voice of the one with the twitch did nothing to diminish Wes's concerns.

"Did you scare him the way I asked?"

"We did more than that. Two of them walked outside, leaving the third playing cards. We called him out for cheating. When he went for his gun, we put a couple slugs in him. That'll scare MacLaren better than any words could."

Wes paced around the desk, his face devoid of expression, other than the deep red color. He didn't betray his feelings as he planted his feet in front of the man, then grabbed the front of his shirt.

"He pulled his gun on you?"

"Truth is, boss, we drew first and before he could react, I fired." The man licked his parched lips, recognizing the rage on Wes's face.

"You fool. That's *not* what I ordered you to do." Even though his voice stayed low, it hissed with anger. "He needed to fear we'd do something to one of his cousins, believe they were in danger—not kill anyone." Without warning, he let go, landing a blow to the man's jaw, watching as he clutched his face, then fell to the ground. Not finished, Wes repeatedly kicked him until Walt and the other man hauled him back.

"Enough, Wes. You'll kill him." Walt tightened his grip when he tried to shake free.

"Maybe I *want* to kill him. Did you hear what they did?"

"Yeah, I did. I'll ride into town, find out if he's still alive." Walt stared at Wes, then shifted his gaze to the other men. "You two, get back to your camp. Don't go into town or ride back here until one of us comes for you."

"What about the money you promised us?" The man held a handkerchief to his bloody face.

Never breaking his hold on Wes, Walt took a step forward. "I'll forget you said that. *If* you get paid, it'll be when you do the job right." He waited until they scrambled away, heading toward their horses. "I doubt we'll ever see them again." Glaring at his longtime friend, Walt's voice took on an urgent tone. "If they killed him, it's the end of it. Do you hear me? You find another woman. Sarah MacGregor is not the only female in River City. Hell, I don't know what's so attractive about her that you're going to all this trouble."

"Sometimes, Walt, I don't believe you have anything useful between your ears. Her father owns a ranch almost as large as ours. Combining the two would give us the biggest spread south of Salem." And there it was. The main reason he wanted her. But there was one other reason.

"And you're willing to kill a man to get to MacGregor's land? Hell, until he's dead in the ground, the man has no intention of letting you take what he's built."

Wes hesitated a moment. "I didn't order a *killing*. They were to scare MacLaren, nothing more. Sarah isn't like any woman I've ever known. Not only is she beautiful and honest, she's good and pure. She's the kind of woman I need to keep me away from Rhoda."

"Damn, Wes. Is that what this is about? You want some woman to save you, change your ways? If it is, I can tell you right now it isn't going to work." Walt held on to the disbelief he felt, not wanting to rile Wes further.

"And why the hell not?"

"'Cause you've got ways about you no woman can change. A woman like her will expect you to be faithful, and we both know you'll never be completely free of Rhoda. That woman's got her claws in you something fierce. You listen to me. If you don't find a way to stop seeing her for good, your pa's gonna learn of it, and he'll kill you."

"I've already stopped. She doesn't like it, thinks she can change my mind, but she won't. I'm finished with Rhoda. That's why it's so important I marry Sarah." Wes slammed his hat down on his head. "Let's get back to the ranch, then you can ride to town. We've got to know what happened with MacLaren. I've waited long enough to speak with Dougal about changing Sarah's mind."

A cold chill washed over Walt. He'd never seen Wes get this serious about a woman. His friend didn't know how to lose or let another man get what he figured belonged to him. By the look in his eyes, Wes had already convinced himself she'd be his and no one else's.

Pulling her hair in a rough grip, Fergus Bell pushed Rhoda onto her knees, her tears doing nothing to change his actions. He'd ridden in late, well past midnight, anxious to get back to his young wife. First, he'd met with one of his men.

The ranch hand had seen her with a man while Fergus was away. Although the cowboy hadn't gotten a good look at his face, he'd seen enough to know what they were doing. They'd been stupid enough to leave a curtain pulled back and the window ajar.

"Wife or not, you will tell me who he is or I will kill you. And believe me, no one will ever find your body." Fergus yanked her by the hair again, glaring into her frightened face. "Did you think I wouldn't learn of it, that I didn't suspect you had someone else in your bed?"

Trying to control her sobs, Rhoda swiped at her damp face, her eyes pleading with him. "You're wrong, Fergus. It's you, no one else. I don't know what your man saw, but I haven't been with anyone but you."

"You're a lying whore, Rhoda. Always knew it, but I ignored it. I can't ignore it any longer and allow you to make a fool of me. Now, who is he?"

She tried to shake her head, her scalp burning in pain as his grip held firm. "I swear, you're wrong, Fergus. I'm always at the ranch, making this a nice home for you. Who would dare come here to see me? No one, Fergus. It would be lunacy."

As if a powerful blow had been dealt to his chest, her words sparked a vision so strong, he couldn't shake it. An instant later, he shoved her away, hearing her cry out as she slammed into a wall. Her scream of pain held no power over him, but the certainty of betrayal did.

Cursing, he leaned over her. "Wes. While I've been away, you took Wes as your lover." He slapped her, drawing blood.

"No," she whimpered, unable to take a breath as pain ripped through her.

Too angry to hear her denial, he paced away, then whirled back to face her. "My own son," he roared, his fists clenching at his sides. "You turned my son against me."

She watched his fury mount, knowing he could kill her with one blow. Taking a shaky breath, Rhoda raised her head.

"He forced himself on me. Threatened me if I didn't do what he wanted. I swear, Fergus. I didn't want to, but I had no choice." Sobbing, she grabbed his leg, begging him to believe her.

His face contorted, his lips curling in disgust. "You're a beautiful woman. Anything a man wants, you give him." Pulling from her grasp, he stepped away. "You're also a terrible liar. I don't know why I didn't see it before." Pacing back and forth, he whirled on her, his angry gaze boring into hers. "I will send you away, but not yet. I need you for one more task." He shot her a wry smile. "A job for which you are eminently suited. When it's over, you'll pack your belongings—only what you brought to the marriage. You'll be taken into town, given some money, and put on the first stage. I don't care where you go or how you'll survive. I never want to see your face again."

Colin woke with a jerk. Twisting, he saw Brodie in a nearby chair, head lowered, long legs stretched out, arms crossed. Recognition as to why they weren't in the hotel came quickly, a jolt of fear ripping through him. Pushing open the adjacent door, waking Brodie, he sighed in relief when he saw Quinn asleep, his chest rising and falling with each breath.

"How is he?" Brodie's hoarse whisper snapped the doctor awake.

Rubbing his eyes and standing, the doctor leaned over Quinn. A moment later, he straightened.

"He made it through the first night. His heartbeat is strong and color is good. His breathing is shallow, but that's to be expected."

"Did he wake up at all last night?" Colin stepped forward, resting a hand on Quinn's arm.

"Moaned and muttered a few times, but I couldn't make out what he said. He's as strong as any man I've ever seen. His body isn't letting him give up, and there's no sign of infection so far. I'm optimistic he'll pull through. If you boys are going to stay here a while, I believe I'll get some breakfast."

Neither heard the door close, their attention fixed on Quinn.

"We need to find out who did this, Colin."

"Don't worry. We will."

"The sheriff is still searching for the bank robbers. From what I heard, he didn't leave much help behind." Brodie shoved his hands into his trouser pockets. "I can't stand here and wait."

Colin knew how he felt, but they couldn't leave Quinn alone. "I'll keep watch while you go to the jail. Maybe the deputy has learned something."

Nodding, Brodie took another look at Quinn, then headed for the door.

"Grab breakfast while you're out. No sense going hungry."

Pulling up a chair, Colin sat down, never taking his gaze from Quinn. His chest squeezed, watching his cousin's chest rise and fall. There was so much he wanted to say. Leaning forward, he placed his mouth close to his cousin's ear.

"You will pull through, lad. There's no way Brodie and I will ride home without you next to us." He took a shaky breath, his voice choked with emotion. "I promise, we will find out who did this and they *will* pay."

"It's no longer my fight. Sarah's made her decision and I'll not be trying to change it." Dougal continued saddling his horse, preparing to ride out to check on the stock. Glancing at Wes, he felt a stab of pain at the way the family had split, cursing his luck at having such stubborn daughters.

"You can't give up. Together, we can force MacLaren to leave without her."

"He's listened to nothing I've had to say. What makes you believe he'll change his mind?"

"Money, MacGregor. We offer enough money and he'll leave, forgetting why he came."

Dougal threw back his head and laughed. "You're a fool if you think MacLaren will be swayed by money. The man's waited years to claim Sarah, ridden hundreds of miles, and defied my demands in front of the entire town. He won't be swayed by money."

"Then we'll persuade him in other ways."

Dougal turned toward him, not liking the menacing tone in Wes's voice. Settling fisted hands on his hips, he narrowed his gaze. "What are you suggesting?"

"You may not have heard, but one of the MacLarens was shot last night. From what I hear, he's alive, but not by much. Seems to me it wouldn't be hard to convince them leaving was the best for their health, and Sarah's."

For a large man, Dougal moved fast, grabbing Wes by the front of his shirt. "Are you threatening my daughter?"

"Easy, MacGregor. I'd never hurt Sarah, but MacLaren doesn't know that."

Dougal shoved him away. "I'll not be part of a killing, not even to keep Sarah away from him."

This wasn't the answer Wes expected. He'd heard MacGregor had threatened MacLaren, implying he'd do anything to keep him away from his daughter.

"It can be done without anyone suspecting us. I have men who will rough them up, make believe we'll do whatever is needed to get them out of town without Sarah."

"I said *nae* and won't be changing my mind. The deal is off. There'll be no marriage between you and Sarah. I've accepted it. It's best you did, too." Swinging into the saddle, Dougal stared down at Wes. "I'm warning you. You'll not be putting Sarah or Geneen in danger. Let her go. I have."

Wes's jaw dropped at the way Dougal had given up, allowing his daughters to ride away, perhaps never to be seen again. "You'll regret this, MacGregor."

Reining his horse back around, Dougal glared at Wes. "Hear this, Bell. Any harm comes to Sarah, you'll be the one who regrets it."

"I couldn't find out any more. No one knows either man who shot your cousin," the deputy explained. "Descriptions vary from one witness to another. Not much more I can do until the sheriff gets back in town."

"You telling me you want to wait around while the men who tried to kill him are out there somewhere? Hell, we don't even know why they pulled a gun on Quinn." Brodie had never been good with lack of action or excuses.

"From what the bartender said, the gunmen accused him of cheating. There's mixed accounts of who pulled their gun first. The bartender swears it wasn't Quinn, but others disagree." The deputy rested his arms on the desk and leaned forward.

"You don't know him, but he'd never cheat. It's not in his blood. It was an excuse to shoot, nothing more."

Shrugging, the deputy showed no remorse at his inability to locate the shooter. "Look, you want to try to find them? Go ahead. You'll be on your own until the sheriff returns."

"When will that be?" Brodie scrubbed a hand down his face, frustrated at the lack of help. In his mind, a good lawman did whatever needed to be done to capture those responsible for breaking the law. The man before him didn't measure up to what the job required. Brodie glared at him, believing *he* could do a better job of tracking down the men who'd shot Quinn.

"Don't know. He's after a group of bank robbers. Could be days. Could be longer."

Knowing he'd learn nothing more, Brodie headed out, stopping for a quick breakfast before returning to find Colin sitting next to Quinn.

"Any change?" Brodie handed him a muffin and coffee he'd gotten from the hotel restaurant.

"Nothing. His eyes fluttered a couple times, but he never woke up." Setting the muffin aside, he took a sip of coffee. "What did the deputy say?"

"The man may not be a complete eejit, but he's close. He found out nothing. You and I could've learned more than he did." Leaning against the door, he crossed his arms. "I'll sit with him a spell. Why don't you go find Sarah, tell her what happened? I know you want to."

Finishing the muffin, Colin swallowed the last of his coffee and stood. "Aye. I do want to see her."

Brodie nodded, taking Colin's chair. "I'll find you if anything changes."

"Are you ready?" Wes waited for Walt to mount his horse.

"I still don't think this is a good idea. What if the discussion turns to threats and people overhear us? You know you've never had much patience." Walt swung up on this horse, pulling up next to Wes.

"You worry too much. Trust me. We'll talk, nothing more. I'll make him understand leaving town is in his best interest. Besides, he now has his cousin to worry about. He sure as hell isn't going to risk anyone else. By this time next week, the MacLarens will be out of the way and I'll be planning my marriage."

Wes's assurances did nothing to calm the apprehension in Walt's gut. If anything, his worry grew the closer they got to town.

Chapter Eleven

Paying little attention to the afternoon activity in town, Colin returned to Sarah's house, thinking of Quinn. He'd spent the morning talking to anyone who might know of the incident in the saloon. His first stop had been to see the bartender. As Brodie learned from the deputy, the gunmen were unknown to the locals, having come to town looking for work a few days prior. The description he pieced together could fit about any man in River City.

They already knew they'd get little help from the law. Finding the men who shot Quinn, then disappeared like ghosts would take time. Right now, that's all he and Brodie had. Between Quinn's recovery and the town council locating a replacement for Sarah, he had more time on his hands than he cared to consider. And it would be put to good use.

"Good afternoon, Geneen. Is Sarah at home?"

"She's still at school. It shouldn't be too long, but you could go wait for her, maybe encourage her to send the children home early." She sent him an encouraging smile.

"I suppose I could." Colin didn't move from his spot on the porch.

"Colin, are you all right?" Geneen studied his face, seeing lines of worry around his eyes.

"I will be. Right now, I just need to see Sarah."

"All right then. Come with me." Shutting the door, she took off at a fast pace toward the school, then dashed inside as Colin waited. Not a minute later, Sarah stepped outside, leaving Geneen to take over with the children.

"What is it, Colin?"

He held out his hand. "Walk with me, Sarah."

The silence stretched, Colin saying nothing as they approached the stream lined on both sides with thick brush and trees, the foliage hovering between green and light yellow. Even in September, some wild berries still appeared on the bushes. Reaching out, Sarah picked a few, handing half to Colin, then popping the rest in her mouth.

Seeing the pleasure on her face, he couldn't help the desire to take some of it for himself. Drawing her into his arms, he lowered his mouth, kissing her until they were both breathing heavily, aching with need. He required Sarah's touch as much as he did air to breathe, the feel of her body aligned with his, offering the comfort he craved. Letting his hands splay across her back, he tightened her to him, enjoying her soft curves. Her arms encircled his neck, pulling him down. Her soft moans ignited a fire inside him, while bringing reason back into his world. Ending the kiss, he set her aside, air coming in ragged breaths.

"It's best we stop, lass. No sense starting what we can't finish." He nodded toward the school not fifty yards away.

Using shaky hands to smooth her dress, Sarah inhaled deeply. "You're right. I don't know what came over me, behaving such as this with the children so close by."

Colin cast her a knowing smile, then tensed, remembering why he wanted to speak with her.

"Quinn's been shot."

"My God. What happened?" Gripping his hand tighter, she turned to face him, listening as he told her what he knew. "No one can identify either man?"

"They joined the game as Brodie and I walked outside. We weren't gone long before we heard the shots. They couldn't have played more than a hand before they accused Quinn of cheating and drew their guns. He didn't have a chance to get his own out of the holster. I should have taken a better look at the men in the saloon when Brodie mentioned his concerns. Instead, I walked out, needing air."

"And Brodie left with you."

"We left Quinn alone."

Moving her hands up his arms, she tightened her hold, staring into his tortured eyes. "It's not your fault. How could you know what those men planned?

If you'd stayed, you and Brodie may have been shot as well."

"Not likely, Sarah. Quinn doesn't cheat. There's no doubt in my mind or Brodie's that the gunmen ambushed him. They wouldn't have had the guts to confront all three of us."

"Why? You've done nothing to provoke an attack such as this."

Colin turned away, breaking Sarah's hold. Pacing a few steps from her, he turned, hands fisted on his hips. "There is one man with a reason to do this."

"Who?"

"Your father."

"Nae, Colin, you're wrong." Her voice hardened at his accusation. Although she and her father were estranged, she understood him well enough to know he'd never stoop to such means to get her back. "He would never hire men to gun another down. I'm certain of that."

"You're sure, Sarah? You've no doubts at all?"

"None. Although there is one other person who might be angry enough at your sudden appearance. However, he would've been recognized by everyone."

"Who?"

"Wes Bell."

"The man who wanted to court you, the one who made the agreement with your father to wed you?" Colin couldn't keep the edge from his voice at the thought of another man with Sarah, wanting her the way he did. Although she'd waited a long time for him, Colin couldn't help but wonder how much longer she would have held out with a wealthy rancher interested in her affections.

"He meant nothing to me, and I told him so. More than once." Rubbing a hand across her forehead, she pushed strands of hair from her face, wishing she'd never mentioned Wes. "I shouldn't have said anything. Wes might be angry I turned him down and that you came for me, but he wouldn't kill an innocent man."

"Why do you say that?"

"Because he'd confront you straight on. Try to talk you out of it. Maybe even try to, um…negotiate with you."

"Are you trying to say Bell might try to pay me off, bribe me?" Colin stalked toward her, his face a mask. "Do you think for one minute I'd wait this long, ride hundreds of miles to claim you, then turn around and leave with my pockets full of money? Do you think so little of me?"

She took a step away, casting her gaze to the ground to still the anger at his words, then glared up at him. "That's a ridiculous thing to say, Colin MacLaren, and you know it. I never should've mentioned Wes. Forget that I did." Leaving him behind, she stormed toward the school, then stopped as a strong hand gripped her arm, turning her around.

"Come here." Colin's gentle tug drew her to him. Enfolding her in his arms, he rested his chin on top of her head. "Quinn's been shot, is fighting for his life, and I have no idea as to who shot him or why. I need answers and I'll listen to whatever you have to say."

Wrapping her arms around his waist, she relaxed, letting her face nestle against his chest. "Well, there is one other possibility."

"And what is that?"

"The war. We see many men coming west, trying to forget the carnage back east. Some are good and build new lives. Others have made killing a way of life. Perhaps the shooting was as the people said. Two men accusing Quinn of cheating and looking for an excuse to kill. If the sheriff were here, you'd get more help. Walker is a good man, as are most of his deputies."

"We met him on our way here. He and his men were searching for bank robbers." Colin thought back to the men they'd met not long before reaching River City. "Regardless, we'll get no help from him. We'll have to figure it out on our own."

Looking up, she gripped the front of his shirt. "Let's leave, Colin, and forget about finding the men who shot him. As soon as Quinn can travel, we'll go home—to our home."

"It sounds good, but that still leaves two men out there who kill at will. They can't go unpunished."

"But—"

He touched a finger to her lips. "While Quinn recovers, Brodie and I will try to learn who did this. If we have no success, we'll make a decision. All right?" He didn't want to leave without bringing the men to justice. At the same time, Sarah's idea made sense. They had no idea who did it and little hope of finding out. They turned at the sound of laughter and yelling from the direction of the schoolhouse.

"Appears Geneen has let the children go home. We should start back." Sarah reached for his hand. "We'll figure this all out, Colin. Now, take me to see Quinn, then Geneen and I will bring supper to you and Brodie."

"Afternoon, Wes, Walt. What can I get you?" The bartender stood with his hands braced on the bar.

"Two whiskeys. I'm also looking for information. Do you know where I can find Colin MacLaren?"

Setting the drinks in front of them, the bartender cocked his head. "What do you want with him?"

"I'd say that's my business." Wes sipped his whiskey, waiting.

"And I'd say it's mine since people seem to be trying to kill the MacLarens in my saloon."

"I heard about the shooting, but I had nothing to do with it. It's a civil discussion I want with MacLaren, nothing more."

"In that case, you'll find him at the clinic or the hotel."

Finishing their drinks, Wes and Walt set their glasses down and started for the door.

"One more spot you might look. Miss MacGregor's place."

Sarah sat with Quinn for over an hour while Colin and Brodie took another turn around town, hoping to uncover any lead that would help them find the men responsible for the shooting.

While they were gone, Sarah talked with Quinn, telling stories as she would a child, trying to get him to open his eyes. Gripping a pitcher to pour a glass of water, she heard a groan. When she looked back, his eyes were open to slits, staring at her.

"Quinn. We've been so worried about you."

His lips moved, but nothing came out. Shutting his eyes tight, he groaned and tried to push up.

"You need to stay still. You've been shot."

Ignoring her, he tried once more to sit up, then fell back with a deep moan.

"You are a stubborn man, Quinn MacLaren. This time, however, you'll do as I say and stay down. I'm going for the doctor."

Returning a few minutes later with the doctor in tow, they found Quinn asleep.

"Did he speak to you, Sarah?"

She shook her head. "He moaned some and tried to sit up, then fell back."

"How about I sit with him a while and give you time to go home and fix supper?"

"Geneen's been cooking most of the day, but she'll need help bringing it all over here. If you're certain, I'll go help her."

It took no time at all for the two women to pack plates, the stew, and biscuits into baskets. By the time they returned, Colin and Brodie sat with Quinn as the doctor watched, leaning against a nearby wall.

"We'll take those, Sarah." Colin stood, taking a basket, placing a kiss on her cheek.

"Has he stirred again?"

"Nae," Colin sighed.

"He will. You weren't here before, but he tried to sit up. He's going to make it, Colin. I'm certain of it."

"This all smells real good, lassies." Brodie took a peek into the stew pot, breathing in the rich aroma.

"Now, Geneen and I don't want to haul any of this back to the house, so I expect you to eat it all." Sarah filled plates with chicken stew and biscuits. "Doc, there's broth here for Quinn, if he's up to it."

"I don't know how much he'll get down, but I'll eat whatever you have, Miss MacGregor." The doctor took the plate Geneen held out to him.

They ate in silence, the only sound was the clicking of utensils on plates and occasional labored breathing from Quinn. Each moan or movement had them all watching, hoping he'd wake again.

"Looks like you men finished every bit." Sarah set the lid back on the pot as Geneen collected the empty plates. Packing their belongings, her movements stilled at the sound of a groan.

"Quinn? Quinn, lad, can you hear me?" Colin stood over him, hands resting lightly on his shoulders, watching as Quinn's eyes fluttered, then opened.

"Colin..." Even hoarse, Quinn's voice was still the best sound any of them had ever heard.

"I'm here, as is Brodie, Sarah, Geneen, and the doctor."

"We almost lost you, young man." The doctor looked him over, checking his heart rate and breathing.

Clearing his throat, Quinn tried to speak. "Water?" he rasped out before being overcome by a wheezing cough.

Waiting for the convulsions to pass, Sarah handed the doctor a glass of water. Supporting Quinn's head, he lifted it, holding the glass to his lips.

"A small amount," Doc warned, pulling it away when he tried to take too much.

"How..." He swallowed. "How long have I been here?"

"Almost a full day. Do you remember getting shot last night?" Colin asked.

"Shot?" Quinn closed his eyes, trying to think. "At the saloon..."

Colin nodded. "Aye. A man accused you of cheating. Called you out."

Quinn pursed his lips, his eyes glazing before they closed. The others thought he'd lost consciousness until he let out a slow hiss. "I remember..." His eyes drifted shut.

The doctor glanced around the room. "He needs his rest. I'll send word when he wakes again."

"I'm not leaving, Doc." Colin pulled up a chair and began to sit when Brodie spoke up.

"Why don't you walk Sarah and Geneen home? I'll stay with him." Turning the chair around, Brodie straddled it, resting his arms on the back. "Go on with you. Come back when you're ready."

"Send word if he wakes or there's a change."

Brodie nodded, never taking his gaze off Quinn.

"We've been to the hotel and Sarah's place. If he isn't at the clinic, I say we head back, try to find him again another day." Walt crushed the cheroot he'd been smoking under the heel of his boot.

"If he's not at the clinic, we'll go back to the saloon, then start over. I'm not riding back until I've spoken with him."

"Well, I'll be damned. Look who's walking our way with two of the MacGregor women. Appears you'll get your chance after all."

Paying little attention to their surroundings, Sarah carried on a conversation with Colin and Geneen, oblivious to the men coming toward them. Seeing the two men, Colin turned to Sarah.

"Do you know them?"

Sarah had no time to respond before Wes and Walt were upon them.

"Good evening." Wes tipped his hat at Sarah and Geneen, paying particular attention to the man with them. "I don't believe we've met. I'm Wes Bell." Holding out his hand, he noted the holster with what appeared to be a .45 slung low on Colin's hip.

"Colin MacLaren."

"Ah, the mysterious fiancé Sarah mentioned to me. I see you are real after all."

"Very."

"I wonder, Mr. MacLaren, if you and I might have a word."

"As you can see, I'm escorting the women home."

"I have no issue waiting. I'll be at the saloon when you're finished." Not waiting for Colin to answer, he looked at Sarah. "Good evening, ladies."

Leaning into Colin, Sarah let out the breath she'd been holding.

"What do you think he wants?" Colin draped one arm over her shoulders, offering his other arm to Geneen.

"Honestly, I don't know, unless it's what you and I discussed before."

"I wouldn't trust anything Wes says. He's been after Sarah far too long to give up because you've come for her." Geneen glanced over her shoulder, seeing the men retreat toward the saloon. "He's a devil, that one." The disgust in her voice emphasized her deep dislike for the man.

"You should take Brodie when you talk with Wes. Geneen's right about not trusting him. I don't believe he'd kill anyone, but he's not above using other methods to get what he wants." Sarah shivered, even though the night held no chill.

"I don't want to leave Quinn alone. I'll meet with Bell alone, hear him out so I know what the man's about. It may be about you. It may not. We won't know until I talk with him." He tightened his hold on Sarah, placing a kiss on her temple. "He won't do anything to me at the saloon. There would be too many witnesses."

"That didn't stop the men from shooting Quinn." Sarah paused outside her house, crossing her arms, worry etched on her face.

"No one knew those men. I'm certain most everyone in town knows Bell."

"I can sit with Quinn if you want to take Brodie," Geneen offered.

"And I can go with her."

Exasperated with both women, Colin walked up the steps and opened the front door. "Wait inside while I speak with Bell."

"You'll come back when you're done, let me know what he said?" Sarah realized there'd be no changing his mind.

Circling her waist, he took her in his arms, lowering his mouth to hers. They could've stayed like that for hours, tasting each other, letting the passion build, but now was not the time. Loosening his hold, he touched his forehead to hers.

"I'll come back. Now, in with you. Let me find out what the man wants."

Chapter Twelve

Enjoying the cool night air, Colin took long strides toward the saloon. He felt no danger at meeting Wes alone. Stepping inside, he spotted both men at a table near the end of the bar. Nodding a greeting to the bartender, he pulled out a chair, sitting so he had a good view of the other patrons.

"Glad you could join us, MacLaren. Whiskey?"

Colin nodded. Taking the glass from Wes, he held it up. "To Sarah's happiness." The toast had Wes's eyes narrowing into slits, although he recovered within seconds, holding up his glass.

Taking a long swallow, he set the glass down with a thump. "Her happiness is why I want to speak with you." He glanced at Walt. "Why don't you find a card game while MacLaren and I talk?" Filling his and Colin's glasses as Walt walked away, Wes leaned forward, resting his arms on the table. "Has she mentioned my interest in her?"

"You don't mince words, do you, Bell?"

"I've never seen any reason to and certainly not when it comes to Sarah. My interest in her is no secret, extending to offering marriage."

"She turned you down and for good reason. Sarah and I promised ourselves to each other years ago. Now I've come to claim her and she's willingly agreed. We'll be leaving for my ranch as soon as my cousin heals." Never taking his gaze off Wes, Colin rolled the glass between his fingers, wondering where the conversation would go next.

"Yes, I heard about the shooting. A real tragedy." His voice was more mocking than sincere, his eyes showing none of the compassion the words implied.

"He'll pull through, then we'll be on our way. Now, what is it you want to say to me?" Colin had grown impatient. He wanted to check on Quinn, see if he'd awakened.

"I believe it's the remains of a young girl's infatuation that has Sarah agreeing to your suit. She's left her family, gave up a teaching job she loves, and has agreed to move hundreds of miles away. For what? A dream that doesn't exist. Sarah deserves better."

"And you believe you can provide her with what she deserves?" Colin sat back, crossing his arms.

"I do. She'd want for nothing and stay near her family. Most importantly, she'd fulfill her father's wishes that she and I marry."

"Do you love her?"

Wes chuckled at the question. "Love? Let's say I have a strong fondness for her, which is more than many marriages are based on. I do have considerable wealth, a strong standing in the community, and the ability to provide for her in ways I'm certain are beyond your means. Love means nothing when you cannot offer what's important."

Colin sipped at his whiskey, pondering Bell's words. Some were nonsense, although others were true. The MacLarens had land, cattle, horses, and a strong family. All assets in building a lasting legacy. Their ranch encompassed close to two thousand acres. His da and uncles had plans to add more, and if successful, they'd have three thousand acres within another year. That's where their wealth lay, not in money in the bank or precious gems. They were a simple people, valuing family and honor above all else. His doubts began on those last few thoughts.

Did Wes know Sarah better than Colin thought? Had she become used to a finer lifestyle he had no way of providing? The fact she'd walked away from her family to honor her promise to him, found a job in town, and lived a frugal life told him what mattered to Wes held no meaning for her.

"If you've ever had a long, serious conversation with Sarah, I believe you'd find what's important to her isn't wealth or position. She's a passionate woman, expecting love and commitment from the man she marries. A good part of me believes those are unknown concepts to you, Bell."

"What the hell does that mean?"

Colin leaned forward, one hand moving to the butt of his gun, the other gripping the glass of whiskey. "I doubt you plan to provide her with either love or fidelity."

The air thickened between them as tension grew. Both men held the other's gaze, neither wavering. Without warning, Wes leaned back, opened his mouth, and let out a belly churning laugh, garnering the attention of many in the packed saloon.

"You know me, yet you don't, MacLaren. I don't know a whit about love. And being faithful? In truth, it *would* come hard for me. What I can offer is what, over time, strengthens a marriage, regardless of archaic traditions. Money and power. Those are what will make a marriage successful."

Colin heard his chair scrape against the rough wooden floor as he pushed away. "It's been a fascinating discussion, Bell. Thanks for the whiskey."

"Sit down, MacLaren. We're not finished."

"I believe we are." Standing, Colin picked up his hat.

"Five minutes more. I think you'll find it quite worth your time." Wes's smug expression riled Colin, although his curiosity had him reclaiming his seat.

"Five minutes. No more."

Refilling their glasses, Wes set the bottle down.

"As I mentioned, I'm a man of considerable means. My father and Sarah's are quite set on this union." Reaching into his pocket, Wes pulled out a pouch, setting it in the middle of the table. "You'll find there is perhaps more money in that than you've ever seen in your life. And that's just one. There are nine more waiting for you when you ride out of town."

Sarah told Colin how Wes thought, warned him not to be surprised if he tried to bribe him to leave. Even her caution hadn't prepared him for the anger raging through him at the insult. Fisting his hands on his thighs, he counseled himself to stay calm, even though every instinct in him vibrated to reach across the table, grab Wes by the collar, and beat the breath right out of him.

"Think of it. You'll return to your ranch unencumbered by marriage, with wealth beyond what you could accumulate through years of toil. Your family will welcome you for bringing back true riches and not another mouth to feed." Placing a hand against the pouch, he pushed it forward. "Take it, MacLaren. The rest will be ready when you ride out."

Colin's jaw tightened and his nostrils flared, his eyes sparking in contempt. Forcing calm, he grabbed the bag and flung it back at Wes.

"I fear you have misjudged me, Bell. My love for Sarah has no monetary value. It's based on what I hold dear and which you hold in little esteem. Take your money. Use it to buy the affections of another woman. Sarah is mine." Tipping his chair backward in his haste to stand, Colin cast one more menacing look at Wes. "A word of caution. Do not go anywhere near Sarah, Geneen, or my family. I don't want them breathing the same air as you."

Pushing his hat down, he slammed the doors open, and stepped into the fresh air. Taking a deep breath, Colin began the process of ridding himself of Wes's words and disgusting proposal. Walking toward the clinic, he sent a silent prayer for Quinn's quick recovery. They needed to leave as soon as possible. The more distance between them and Bell, the safer Sarah would be, and the better he'd sleep.

"How is he?" Colin put a hand on Brodie's shoulder as he peered at Quinn.

"He's woken twice. Each time, the eejit tries to get up, then falls back. Doc says he'll tear the stitches and get an infection if he doesn't stay down. If he rests, Doc says we could move him to the hotel in a few days, but he'll need at least two more weeks before he can ride. Longer, if at all possible." Brodie noticed the grim expression on Colin's face. "What's going on?"

Colin grabbed a chair, lowering his weary body onto it before dragging a hand down his face. "Wes Bell tried to bribe me into leaving Sarah behind."

"Sonofabitch," Brodie murmured, shaking his head at the man's bold stupidity. "Can't imagine what you might have told him." He chuckled, figuring he knew exactly how Colin would have responded.

"He got the message."

"How much?" Brodie asked, brow raised.

"Did he offer me? Hell, I don't know for certain. He tossed out a bag full of coin and told me nine more would be waiting when we left without Sarah." A grim smile passed over Colin's face.

"Some men aren't cut out to be human. It takes someone special to act that low." Standing, Brodie stretched his arms above his head. "I could use a drink. You?"

"You go ahead, but keep watch for Bell. He's got a man with him and I doubt he's in a mood to be sociable right now."

"I won't be gone long." Pulling the door open, he turned back toward Colin. "I suppose we could get a wagon for Quinn. Might be better than a horse."

"The hell it would."

Brodie shut the door and walked back toward the bed at the sound of Quinn's raspy voice.

"I'm ready to go now if someone will help me on my horse."

Colin chuckled at the absurdity. "He's talking crazy," he said to Brodie. "Has the doc been giving him laudanum?"

"Matter of fact, he has. Still doesn't excuse him for not using his brain, though." Brodie's words were harsh, although full of relief. "You still with us, Quinn?"

Eyes flickering open, he nodded. "Aye, I'm here. Any whiskey in this place?"

"You'll get water and nothing else." Colin supported his head as Brodie held the glass to his lips. "No alcohol, cards, or women for you until you heal, lad."

Sucking in a labored breath, he winced in pain. "Then I'd better get to it…"

"Damn fool. He should've taken the money. It's more than any man could refuse." Wes had finished the bottle of whiskey, then stormed out of the saloon, climbing on his horse, and taking off without a word to Walt. It had taken his friend a good amount of time to catch up with him.

"Well, he didn't, and I can't say as I'm surprised. The man came here for one purpose—to claim Sarah after years of waiting. He won't be swayed by money." Walt lit a cheroot, taking a long pull on the thin cigar. "You can have any woman you want, Wes. Put her behind you."

Wes rode in silence. The fact MacLaren couldn't be bought weighed on him. No man had ever refused him. Yet, as he came to terms with not winning the prize he coveted, he now felt a sense of freedom to move on. He'd tethered himself to Sarah after agreeing with Dougal to marry her.

His father and Sarah's pushed for the union. He wanted to please both men, gaining access to MacGregor's land. Pride had also been a factor, especially when she'd turned him down in such a public way, then continued to refuse his requests to court her. He didn't often give up on something he wanted, but nothing could be gained by continuing his pursuit.

He'd done all he could. Walt was right. It was time to move on. Besides, Dougal had no sons who'd inherit his ranch. Sarah and Geneen would both leave with the MacLarens, and from what Wes knew, the youngest daughter, Isla, had no interest in the ranch. There would be other ways to get the land without entering into a marriage of convenience.

"Short of killing the man, I've done all I can. I won't win this battle. Let them go and to hell with them both. I've got choices and Rhoda waiting at home."

Walt threw out a disgusted curse. "You listen to me. Don't you go seeing that woman again. Rhoda offers nothing good and all kinds of trouble. You've stayed away since your pa got home and there's no sense going back now."

Arguing would do nothing at this point. He'd do what he wanted, no matter his friend's concern. "Sure, Walt. Time to forget both Sarah and Rhoda."

Taking a detour they used many times, they arrived at the Bell Ranch to learn Fergus had plans to leave in a few days.

"I'll be gone at least a week, maybe longer. I know you'll take good care of the ranch while I'm gone and keep a careful watch on Rhoda. All right, Wes?" Fergus looked up from his desk as he said the last.

"Sure, Pa. Don't I always?"

"That's what I hear." Fergus fought the gnawing ache in his gut. He'd been betrayed by both his wife and the son he counted on to continue the Bell legacy. The death of his first wife years before had almost killed him. He'd become older, yet no wiser in trusting those close to him. "You're welcome to come with me, meet some of the ranchers up north." Reaching out in this last effort, he hoped Wes would agree.

"Another time, Pa. There's a lot to be done before the weather turns, and I don't want to leave it all to the men."

"Whatever you think best." Fergus walked around his desk to the table holding a decanter of whiskey. He poured two glasses, handing one to Wes. Holding his in the air, he tilted it in salute. "To continued growth and new beginnings."

If Wes thought it an odd toast, he said nothing, returning his father's salute, then swallowing the drink in one gulp.

"I'm beat. Guess I'll head to bed. Night, Pa."

Fergus watched him leave, closing the door behind him, and felt a heaviness in his heart he knew would never fade and time would never heal. "Goodnight, son."

Chapter Thirteen

"What the hell are you doing?" Hands on hips, Colin stared at Quinn as he struggled to fasten his trousers. It had been almost two weeks since the shooting, a little over one since the doctor released him to stay at the hotel, and each day had been a test of wills to keep Quinn from pulling the stitches loose.

"Getting out of here, and don't you be trying to stop me," he growled. After another minute of fighting the buttons, he turned a frustrated expression toward Colin. "Help me with these."

"Where do you think you're going?" Colin finished closing the shirt, then stepped back, his head tilting.

"The saloon for a drink. After that, I don't know, but I'm not coming back here until I'm ready."

Crossing his arms, Colin considered another option. "I have a better idea. I'll get Brodie and the three of us will take a ride. We need to know how you'll do on Warrior so we can decide how soon we can leave."

Slamming his hat on his head, Quinn nodded. "Let's go."

Brodie took over saddling Warrior when Quinn couldn't get the leverage needed to swing it over the horse's back.

"I'll do that." He pushed Brodie's hands away to finish cinching, then grabbed the bridle. Using his good right arm to mount from the other side, he slumped before forcing his spine to straighten.

"You ready, Quinn?" Colin studied him for any signs it may be too soon.

"More than ready." Nudging his horse forward, he reined it around and headed out of town.

They followed the stream to a spot where it joined the river. Taking their time, an hour passed, then another before Quinn showed signs of fatigue.

Brodie spoke first, knowing Quinn would never admit to being tired. "It's been a while, lads. I need a rest." He reined Hunter to a stop under a wide maple and slid from the saddle. Stretching, he glanced up at Quinn, his mouth twisting into a grin. "Need some help?"

Quinn shot him a venomous look. "Not from you." Dismounting in slow, somewhat jerky motions, he swiped the sweat from his brow and took a few unsteady steps. "Now, if you were a beautiful woman…"

"Don't be rushing it. I'm guessing it'll take longer to continue some activities than others." Colin's smirk had Brodie laughing.

Stepping up to Quinn, Brodie rested a hand on his good shoulder. "You shouldn't fret about it. You've got plenty of time to get back to your old self by the time we get home."

"Off with you," Quinn growled, shrugging off Brodie's arm. Drinking from his water pouch, he slid it back in his saddlebag. "How soon can we leave?"

"Sarah's last day at school is Friday. Any time after that." Colin studied him, knowing Quinn would push it. "She and Geneen will need time to pack. Middle of next week is soon enough, but the doctor has to agree to the trip first." That would give Quinn almost another week.

"I don't need him to tell me when I'm good to ride. It's my decision, not his."

Colin stepped up to within inches of him. "We all agree or we don't go. We'll have two women with us and several hundred miles to cover. You need to have all your strength back, not just enough to start the trip. Brodie and I don't have time to nursemaid you along the way."

His eyes narrowing, Quinn stared at Colin as heat rose in his face. They needed to leave before the weather turned and he wouldn't be the one to hold them up.

"Fine. You get the girls ready to leave by next week. I'll see the doc and get his blessing. Then we'll not talk of it again."

"How about we ride into town with the men? It's been a long week and I'm ready to relax." Walt pulled on a clean shirt, then his boots. "Wouldn't hurt you to get away."

Wes had stopped by the bunkhouse before walking up to his own place. Most Saturday nights, he'd go into town with the others. Tonight, though, he needed something else. "You boys go ahead. I think I'll grab supper and get to bed early."

Walt's gut clenched at the announcement, knowing Rhoda was alone in the house. Since Fergus left the week before, he'd kept a close watch on Wes. As far as Walt knew, Wes had kept his distance, sleeping in the bunkhouse most nights without making the journey to his own place.

Looking around at the others, Walt lowered his voice. "Don't be thinking you'll get one more chance at Rhoda while Fergus is away. You've kept out of her room for several weeks now and there's no reason to take the chance. Put her behind you for good and come with us."

"You worry too much. I have no plans to see her again." Wes stood, grabbing his hat. "I'm heading to bed." Stepping outside, he considered stopping at the big house, then thought better of it. He'd stuck with his decision to stay away from her while his father had been out of town, yet it hadn't been easy.

Within minutes of entering his house, he sat in a large chair, a glass of whiskey in his hand, the half-full bottle on a table a few inches away. He'd come to terms with MacLaren showing up for Sarah, deciding her leaving didn't bother him as much as his damaged pride. Being rebuffed in such a public way had stung, but he'd soothed the embarrassment by bedding Rhoda. Her warm body and experienced ways never failed to provide the comfort he sought. The fact it didn't last long didn't bother him. She had nowhere to go, and despite his decision to the contrary, he knew she'd still make herself available whenever his pa left the ranch.

This time, however, something kept him away...at least until he swallowed the third glass of whiskey. Becoming restless, he paced around the small room, fighting the urge to forget his earlier resolution. He drank one more shot of whiskey, then stalked outside. Seeing the light on in Rhoda's bedroom, Wes took slow paces toward the ranch house, cursing himself with each step. Fueled by alcohol, his raging desire replaced common sense. *One last time*, he told himself, *then I'll be done with her*.

Climbing the stairs, he glanced around, satisfied his father hadn't returned home without his knowledge. Stopping outside her door, he took a deep breath, then pushed it open, his mouth tilting up in an appreciative smile.

Rhoda lay on top of the bed, wearing his favorite lace dressing gown with the wide, pink sash closed at the waist. His eyes darkened, knowing she wore nothing under it.

"You're ready for me, I see." Closing the door behind him, he wasted no time stripping off his shirt.

"You shouldn't be here, Wes. Remember your words the last time?" Rhoda's heart beat faster as he continued to undress, showing off his hard, lean muscles. "You were right. It isn't right for us to continue. What of your father?"

"He's gone. No one is in the house except you and me." He moved to the edge of the bed.

"And the housekeeper."

"Even if she found out about us, she'd say nothing." He leaned across the bed toward her. "Come here, Rhoda. We both know he can't give you what you need."

Jumping out on the other side of the bed, she held up a hand when he walked toward her.

"No, Wes, we can't. We never should've started this. Your father is my husband."

Chuckling, he stalked forward until he had her trapped in a corner of the bedroom. Gripping her behind the neck, he hauled her to him, lowering his mouth to within inches of hers. "That's not what you said when you kept offering yourself to me, encouraging me to take what I wanted. Are you saying you never wanted it?" He didn't wait for an answer before crushing his mouth to hers, letting his hands wander up and down her back, feeling the heat rising off her almost naked body.

So lost in the feel of her, Wes didn't hear the footsteps behind him. His only warning was a feral growl before a strong hand gripped his shoulder, spinning him around, a fist connecting with his jaw. Spiraling backward, Wes slammed against the wall. He hadn't recovered when another blow crushed his nose, the sound of breaking bones and cartilage loud enough for Rhoda to react with a shrill scream.

Lifting his arms to defend against the punishing blows, Wes gazed up to see his father, rage and hate on his face, standing over him. Grabbing Wes by his shirt, Fergus pulled him up, sending another smashing blow to his face. Letting him drop to the ground, Fergus kicked him in the stomach and ribs, not letting up when Wes begged him to stop.

"Fergus! Stop. You'll kill him." Rhoda tried to insert herself between the two men, only to be shoved aside.

After a few more savage kicks, Fergus stepped away, letting out a savage roar at the sight of his son, broken and unable to move. His shoulders slumping, he lowered himself to the bed, scrubbing a hand down his anguished face.

Rhoda lowered herself to the floor, kneeling beside Wes. "Can you move?" she whispered, ignoring the tension streaming off Fergus. At any moment, she expected him to grab her by the collar and toss her aside. Instead, she heard the sound of sobs behind her. The sight of Wes's broken body and the tortured cries of Fergus were more than she could handle. Standing, she dashed from the room and ran down the stairs, calling to their cook for help.

"Why, Wes? You could have any woman you want. Why Rhoda?"

Even through the haze of pain, Wes heard the torment in his father's voice. His attraction to Rhoda had never been about hurting his father. In fact, he didn't even consider the impact the illicit affair would have on the older man. Each time Rhoda used her body and considerable charms to tempt him to her room, selfish desire consumed him. Fergus's name almost never followed them to the bed.

Leveraging himself enough to lean his back against the wall, Wes tried to open his rapidly swelling eyes. Pain racked his body as if he'd been run over by a stampeding herd. Never had he thought his father capable of such a brutal attack on his own son. Walt's warning that Fergus would kill him had never registered until now.

Shaking his head, he opened his mouth, then clamped it shut. He had no idea what to say. Realizing it didn't matter—he was already a dead man, at least in his father's eyes—he cleared his throat, trying to straighten his spine.

"Every time you left the ranch, Rhoda offered herself to me. I knew it was wrong, but that didn't stop me." Choking, he swallowed the bile in his throat. "After the first time, I couldn't stay away." Slumping back against the wall, Wes shook with pain and regret. He knew Fergus would either kill him or send him away. His place alongside his father had vanished when he took Rhoda to bed.

Fergus sucked in a deep breath. He couldn't summon any compassion for the man before him. Wes had betrayed him in the worst possible way.

"Get your stuff together. I want you off the ranch by sunrise. If you ever have the notion to come back, don't. You'll be shot on sight." Turning his back, Fergus walked to the door, ignoring Wes's plea to stop. Reaching into a pocket, he took out an envelope and tossed it on the bed. "Take that with you," he said before slamming the door behind him. His mind fogged, barely registering Rhoda and their cook coming up the steps with warm water and towels.

Shoving the bedroom door open, Rhoda dropped beside Wes as the cook set the pan of water on the floor. Soaking the towels, then wringing out the excess water, she wiped his face and neck.

"Get him clean clothes," she murmured to the cook without taking her gaze off Wes. "Can you stand?"

His eyes slits, he looked up at her. "I don't know."

"Well, you're going to try." Putting her arm around his waist, he leveraged himself with one hand, propelling his body toward the bed. Cursing, he crashed onto it before Rhoda could break the fall. "We need to get these soiled clothes off you."

Carrying fresh clothes as she entered, the woman who cooked, cleaned, and helped raise Wes since his mother died did her best to hide the tears as she assisted Rhoda. She could guess what transpired to prompt such a violent act by Fergus. Seeing it first-hand was almost more than the older woman could bear.

An hour later, the cook left, leaving Rhoda to watch over Wes.

"He ordered me to leave by dawn. I don't know that I can even get on my horse..." His voice drifted off as his eyes closed. He needed sleep if he were to leave in a few hours.

She'd never seen the smug, arrogant man who'd shared her bed so defeated. Rhoda had grown up with nothing. Starting over would be hard, but she knew it could be done. Not so with Wes. He'd grown up as the egotistical heir to a ranching empire, certain of his fate. Now everything had been stripped from him.

Spotting an envelope on the floor next to the bed, she opened it, her eyes widening. Tucking it into the almost full satchel at the side of the bed, she stretched out beside Wes, a plan forming in her mind.

"No sense keeping him in River City any longer. As far as I'm concerned, he's fit enough to start back to your ranch." It had been almost three weeks since the shooting and Quinn had shown considerable improvement. "Wish I'd say it's been a pleasure, but..." Doc offered them a tired smile.

"We understand. Quinn isn't the easiest man to be around, even in the best times." Colin shook the doc's hand.

"Colin's right. We'd have nothing to do with the lad if we weren't blood kin." Brodie clasped a hand on Quinn's shoulder.

"Enough," Quinn grumbled. "I've been injured and all you eejits can do is give me grief." He took the doc's hand in a firm grip. "Thanks, Doc. I'd have died without your help."

"I don't know as I'd go that far, but you were in pretty bad shape. And don't think the trip south will be easy because it won't." He looked at each of the men. "I'm certain you'll ignore what I have to say, but at least let me get it out. You'll need to stop more often and earlier each day. Don't push him if he's tired. And make sure he eats something more than just hardtack and jerky.”

“We can do that, Doc.”

The men turned to see Sarah walk in, Geneen a few steps behind.

“We’ll be taking an extra pack horse with food and other supplies.” Looking at Colin’s surprised expression, Sarah smiled. “Geneen and I have it all arranged. At least we can get a few days out before we have to resort to trail food.”

They’d discussed taking a wagon, but there weren’t enough funds to buy one, plus the animals to pull it. Using their well-bred horses would be a risk—one the men weren’t willing to take.

“Anything else you and Geneen have planned?” Colin slipped an arm around her waist, drawing her close.

“Oh, I might have a few surprises left for you.” Sarah winked, her eyes sparkling.

“We’ll say goodbye, Doc. We hope to get on the trail by dawn two days from now and I have no idea when we’ll be back.” Opening the door, Colin stayed behind while everyone walked outside. “I’ll send you the money as soon as I return to Conviction. Thanks for not letting our lack of funds hold up your work on Quinn.”

The doctor’s eyes narrowed, although his expression stayed friendly. “I never considered *not* helping him. It’s what I do, son. Now, you have a safe ride home. If you're ever up this way again, I'd be honored if you stopped by to see me."

"Have you seen these, Wes?" Holding the documents in her hand, she waved them in front of his face.

She'd helped him up not long before. At least he'd had a few hours of fitful sleep. The sun would be up in an hour and he'd need to be well on his way by then. While he slept, she'd packed the rest of her clothes and loaded them in a wagon. She'd then made her way to Wes's house, stuffing what she could into saddlebags and the rest into satchels, which now sat behind the seat of the wagon. Harnessing a draft horse, then tying her own to the back of the wagon were the last tasks before she returned to the bedroom.

"No," he rasped out. "What is it?"

"The deed to some property and a stack of cash. I'm guessing it's Fergus's way of not letting you leave a complete pauper."

Grabbing the document from her, Wes read it twice. He didn't know why his father had done it, but he'd accept whatever help he could. Slipping the deed and money in a pocket, he took hesitant steps toward the door.

"Wes?"

Leaning a hand against the door, he turned toward her. "What?"

"Take me with you. Fergus is tossing me out, too. We can leave together, maybe, um…maybe help each other." She gripped her hands tight in front of her. Even if he said no, she'd follow as best she could. After all, she had nowhere else to go.

He'd never seen Rhoda with hope in her eyes. Desire, pleasure, and fear, yes, but never hope, as if his response meant a great deal to her.

"I'll make no promises to you. If you want to ride along, it's your choice. Just don't go thinking it makes us a couple because it doesn't."

Her body visibly relaxed. Even if it wasn't all she hoped he'd offer, at least neither of them would be alone on the trail.

"Thank you. You won't regret it."

"I may not, but you might."

Making his way downstairs and out the back door, he saw the wagon and his horse saddled, all ready to go. With help from Rhoda, he swung into the saddle, then took one more glance around. He'd never see this place or his father again. Somehow, the sharp pang of regret he expected didn't come. Instead, he focused on a future far away from River City. "Are you ready?"

Nodding, she climbed onto the wagon and took the reins. "Ready."

Fergus stood at his upstairs window, watching the two disappear around a bend in the road, the pain in his chest so intense, he thought he might collapse. He'd lost his wife and son, leaving him to run a ranch no one would remember once he died. All the hard work, years of toil, meant nothing to him anymore.

He'd expected Rhoda to leave with Wes and hadn't tried to stop her when he heard her harness the horse to the wagon. The wagon and horses were a small price to pay to get her out of his life. Tomorrow, he'd ride to town, file the necessary papers to end the marriage, and change his will. He didn't know who he'd leave all his land and wealth to, but it didn't matter right now. Today, he'd drink his breakfast, dinner, and supper, then he'd drink some more. Maybe if he lost himself in a few bottles, he'd be able to forget the sting of betrayal and get on with his life.

Chapter Fourteen

"Are you certain we can't talk you into staying a few more days so I can marry you?" Reverend Olford leaned back in his chair as Bessie placed the last platter of food on the table. His wife insisted they all have one final supper together before the three men and two women left on their journey south. "I know it would relieve Bessie to see you hitched before you left."

Sarah and Colin shared guilty glances, not wanting to disappoint the Olfords. The older couple had been their staunchest supporters, but that still didn't sway their decision to marry at the MacLaren ranch. Taking Sarah's hand, Colin repeated what they'd told them several times in the past few weeks.

"We appreciate all you've done, but it's important to us and my family that Sarah and I marry at home. I've already sent word to Ma to start the wedding plans. There'd be no living with her if I put a stop to them now."

"Understood, Colin. Thought I'd ask once more." They all turned to the pounding on the front door.

"I wonder who that could be." They were used to having neighbors and church members stop by at any time. However, Bessie had hoped they'd get through one meal without interruption. She hurried to the door, ready to shoo whomever it was away. Pulling it open, her smile widened. "Caleb Stewart. We're just sitting down to supper and there's plenty. Please, come in and join us."

Clutching his hat in his hands, Caleb hesitated. "I don't want to intrude on your supper."

She reached out and grabbed his arm. "Nonsense. You get in here this minute before the food gets cold." Closing the door behind him, Caleb followed her toward the sound of laughter. "Guess who's come to join us?"

"Ah, Mr. Stewart. Come in." The reverend stood, extending his hand as the other men did the same. Bessie went in search for another chair.

"I'll get that, Mrs. Olford." Brodie slid a chair to the table between Geneen and Quinn.

"Well, now, shall we say grace?" The reverend bowed his head.

Between talk of the trip, Quinn's recovery, and plans once they reached the ranch, the conversation never stopped, lasting into late evening. The biggest news concerned Jamie, Sarah's young student. With the help of Colin and Brodie, she and Bessie had been able to locate an abandoned shack a mile from town where he stayed each night. The four visited him late one evening, waking him from a deep sleep. He struggled, not able to break the hold of Colin's strong arm around his chest.

It took time for him to calm down and talk. When he did, the details came spilling out in quiet sobs. He'd been abandoned by his family on their way to Portland. The youngest of ten children, his father had taken him aside late one night, giving him a sack of food and a few coins. Jamie didn't understand until he woke the next morning. His family had disappeared, leaving him behind.

Living on scavenged food from the restaurant garbage and what he could steal from the general store, Jamie had been on his own for several months. Within a week, Bessie and Sarah had found a home for him, with a childless couple. Although it would take time for Jamie to adjust and trust them, the new arrangement seemed to be working well for everyone. Sarah knew she'd miss him as much as anyone when they left.

"And what brings you to town, Caleb?" Bessie asked as the last bits of food had been piled onto plates.

"I heard these folks were leaving tomorrow. Thought I'd come and say my goodbyes." During Quinn's recovery, he'd spent several nights in the saloon with Colin and Brodie, even joining them for supper at Sarah's one night. They'd become friends and he'd miss them.

"No need to say goodbye. Why don't you come with us?" Colin asked as if it were a natural suggestion.

"Excuse me?" Caleb's eyes widened in surprise. He'd thought of traveling south at some point, just not this soon.

"You've got nothing keeping you here. We've a good deal of acres and can always use more men." Colin set down his fork, resting his arms in his lap.

"And it would get you that much closer to San Francisco," Brodie added, remembering Caleb mentioning his desire to see the rowdy bay town.

"It's a wonderful idea. Caleb, please say you'll come with us." Sarah flashed a brilliant smile at him. For some reason, she hated the thought of leaving him, knowing of his desire to see more of the country. "It's the perfect opportunity for you."

Chuckling, Caleb tried to hide his eagerness at their offer. Joining them would make the journey easier and much more pleasurable. Lone riders were always at a higher risk of danger than those traveling within a group. "I hadn't thought of leaving so soon, but your offer does sound good."

"Excellent. Then you'll meet us tomorrow morning at dawn in front of my house." Sarah scooped up another bite of potatoes, a self-satisfied smile on her face.

"All right, if you're certain. I'll ride back to the Bell place tonight, let the new foreman know of my plans, and meet you tomorrow." He dug into the rest of his meal, eager to start another phase of his journey.

"New foreman? Isn't Wes the foreman?" Sarah's brows drew together.

"Not any longer. Guess he and Fergus had a falling out. Wes took off before dawn this morning. Could be he'll be back, but his father didn't waste any time giving Walt the job." Caleb didn't add that Rhoda Bell had left with Wes. He figured it was no one's business except the Bells.

"Oh, he'll come back. That's probably why Mr. Bell gave the job to Walt. He knows Walt will give it up when Wes returns." Sarah finished her last bite, then set down her fork. "His father would be lost without him."

Caleb said no more. He knew Fergus Bell was in for a tough future. One he'd have to face alone.

"Is everyone ready?" Colin checked the pack horses once more. The men planned for one to carry Sarah's and Geneen's belongings, while the women loaded the second with extra food and supplies. Satisfied everything looked secure, he gave Sarah one more kiss before joining Quinn at the front. "Let's go."

Caleb and Brodie rode at the back, each leading one of the pack horses, leaving Sarah and Geneen to take places in the middle. The men would change positions each day while the women would stay between them. If the weather held, Colin figured they could travel about twenty-five miles a day, arriving at the ranch in twenty days, well before winter weather slowed them down. A significant unknown factor remained—Coral, Opal, and Pearl.

"What will we do if the reverend hasn't been able to find homes for the girls?" Quinn rode alongside Colin on day five, keeping watch on the trail ahead. No one had mentioned the runaways until now, as if discussing them might curse their luck.

"We promised to take them with us. I don't see how we can back out if they are still at the church." Colin rode in silence a few more minutes, his gaze trained on the trail, his mind focused on the girls. "And I don't feel comfortable leaving them in Crocker."

"Even if they have kin there?" Quinn asked.

"I doubt they'll stay if they were running away from someone, even if it's their own family. That town isn't a place for young girls—or anyone else who upholds the law. We all know it. Taking them home isn't something I want to consider, but if they have no other place to go, I don't see any way this works out with our consciences in one piece."

Quinn nodded, wondering what his father and uncles would say to three more mouths to feed.

Colin glanced over his shoulder, sending a warm smile to Sarah riding a few paces behind him. "Another issue is our lasses. Sarah and Geneen have a real fondness for children. If they become attached..."

Quinn understood Colin's concern. "Aye. We may have little choice but to take them to the ranch. Have you told Sarah about them?"

"Nae. It's not something I wish to think on." He *did* want to figure out a way to sleep with Sarah while on the trail—and not just beside her in separate bedrolls. He wanted to wrap his arms around her, hold her tight against him all night, feel her warmth. They'd had little time together since the unexpected arrival of Geneen, and Quinn's injury. Not for the first time, he regretted the decision to refuse Reverend Olford's offer to marry them. The best they'd been able to do was a few private minutes at night after supper, taking walks or finding some other excuse to leave camp. Tonight, he hoped to disappear with her for more than a few minutes.

By evening, they'd made good time, traveling significantly further than Colin's projection and, assuming they could continue at this pace, saving themselves at least two days on the trail. It also put them a day's ride from Mindell and the girls.

Glancing around at the clearing near a stream, Colin turned to Quinn. "Let's stop here for the night. We'll get settled, eat, then I'll talk with Sarah about the girls." Sliding off Chieftain, he helped Sarah down, pulling her to him for a long kiss, unmindful of those around them. "We'll take a walk after supper." He gave her a meaningful look, seeing the understanding on her face before her lips tilted into a playful smile.

"Well then, I'd better start supper."

The men started a fire, then laid out the bedrolls while Geneen and Sarah unpacked the remaining food. Tonight would be the last night they'd have a regular meal before resorting to hardtack, jerky, and dried fruit.

"Smells wonderful, ladies." Caleb lowered himself onto a log near the fire, brushing his hands down his trousers. Removing the lid on the large pot, he moaned at the aroma.

"Enjoy it as it's the end of what Geneen and I prepared." She glanced up as Colin, Quinn, and Brodie joined them, plates already in their hands. Each of them packed their own, cleaned up after themselves, then stored them for the next meal. "Eat all of it. There won't be enough for another meal."

Colin finished first, settling a hand on Sarah's back as she took her last few bites.

"Come. Walk with me." Standing, he held out his hand. "We're heading toward the creek," he called over his shoulder, grabbing his rifle before they disappeared into the trees. When out of sight, he turned her to him, letting his hands drift up and down her arms, his gaze raking over her body before he lowered his mouth. Seconds passed as the kiss deepened. He could already feel his heart hammering against his ribs, the result of the acute anticipation he'd fought all day. Breaking the kiss, he rested his forehead against hers. "We need to get further away."

Walking at a brisk pace, he led her toward the creek. Looking up and down the bank, he found what he wanted—a row of rocks creating an easy path across the water. Stepping behind Sarah, steadying her so she wouldn't slip, Colin followed her to the other side, then continued on a deer trail toward a small opening in the trees. He set the rifle aside, slipped off his coat, laying it on the ground, then turned a heated gaze toward her.

"Come here." Colin reached for her hands. "We have little time..." His voice drifted away as he dropped her hands, cupping her face. Reclaiming her lips, then moving his hands to her back, he crushed her to him.

The kiss was hungry, demanding, not at all slow and savoring as she'd come to expect. She gave herself over to the heated passion as an acute craving spiraled through her. Gripping his shoulders, she matched his urgent need. Her lips parted, allowing him the access he sought, their tongues tangling in a savage intensity. Her knees trembled as wave after wave of his fiery possession overtook her.

Without breaking the kiss, Colin's hands moved lower, resting on her hips, gently easing her down onto his coat. Moving a hand between them, he unbuttoned her dress, interrupting the kiss to push the material aside. Gazing down at her, his breath hitched at the sight of her chest heaving, straining against the thin fabric of her chemise.

His tongue caressed the soft column of her neck, taking his time placing feathery kisses along the swell of her breasts. One hand slid down to rest on her stomach, moving lower to the swell of her hips, then to her stockinged legs. Bunching her skirt, his hand moved under her dress to skim her hips and rest on the heated skin of her thigh.

A moan escaped her lips as his gentle massage created a surge of desire. Wrapping her arms around him, she drew him down, caressing the hard planes of his back. Feeling heat radiate off him, she squirmed to get closer, pulling him against her warm, pulsing body.

On a ragged gasp, she pulled back. "Colin, please..."

He chuckled, knowing what she wanted and having every intention of providing it. "I know, lass..." he breathed out, unable to hold back any longer. Hovering above her, his eyes searched hers, chest tightening from the love he saw on her face. "I love you, Sarah."

"There are three men and one woman. They won't be expecting trouble." Ralph, a short, round man with thick black stubble crouched low, glancing over the shoulders of his two companions. "Pretty even match, Clem." He looked at the tallest and oldest of the three Baldwin brothers. They'd parted ways with the gang they'd been riding with after relations went sour. Although they'd pulled a couple good jobs, they'd ridden out with little.

"Did you see any guns?" Clem asked. They wouldn't have stopped when they saw the light from the fire, except they needed food, water, and money.

"Each is wearing a gun, and I spotted rifles near their gear."

"What do you think, Emory?" Ralph asked the middle brother. Quiet and thoughtful, Emory was also the most ruthless of the three.

"We need food and money to make it up to Portland. Don't know what other chances we'll get before we reach River City. I say we take what we can get."

"Then it's decided." Clem stood, checking his gun, motioning for his brothers to fan out.

Moving at a slow pace, the three surrounded the camp, Ralph and Emory nodding to Clem when they were in place.

"Don't anyone move." Clem's voice boomed in the quiet night. "If I see you go for your guns, the first bullets will hit the woman."

Everyone froze, except Quinn, whose hand slowly moved toward his gun.

"Don't be stupid, mister." Clem swung his gun toward Quinn. "If you give us what we want, no one will get hurt. Take your guns out of the holsters and drop them on the ground."

Doing as he asked, the three men glanced at each other, knowing the other's thoughts. All carried knives strapped to their belts, hidden underneath their coats.

"What is it you want?" Brodie shifted, looking around him. He could see the outlines of three men, but not their faces.

"Food and money. Give us what you have and we'll ride out."

"We don't have much other than hardtack and jerky. Same with money, but we'll give you what we have." Caleb glanced at Quinn, seeing him nod.

Clem looked at Caleb, signaling with his gun. "You, collect the money and get the food. The rest of you stay where you are."

Caleb moved from Brodie to Quinn, taking the money each pulled from their pockets.

"Now get what you have in the saddlebags." Clem nodded toward the gear on the ground near the horses.

Mumbling a curse, Caleb checked each saddlebag, taking out as little as possible without raising suspicion.

"What about the food, Clem?" Ralph asked, feeling the pangs of an empty stomach.

He looked at Geneen. "You, pack up your food. All you have."

Standing, she crossed her arms, face red with anger. "No. You're taking our money, but I won't give you what little food we have."

"Watch them," Clem instructed Ralph and Emory as he stalked toward Geneen. Reaching for her, he grabbed the back of her hair, drawing her close. "You'll do as I say, little lady, or you'll wish you had." He shoved her away. When she still hesitated, he took a menacing step toward her. "Now!"

Chapter Fifteen

"Sarah, wake up." Colin tightened his hold around her waist, brushing a kiss on her shoulder.

They'd fallen asleep under the stars, talking of their wedding and future. Colin didn't think they'd been napping long when the sound of male voices woke him. Sitting up, he'd listened, unable to understand what was said, but certain the discussion wasn't friendly.

"Sarah, lass, we need to get back to camp."

Her eyes opened on a low hum of satisfaction. "Can we not stay here longer?"

The sounds came again. This time Colin stood, extending his hand to her. "Something isn't right at camp. We need to return. Now."

Picking up his coat, grabbing her hand, he moved through the brush. The voices grew louder as they approached the camp. Glancing over his shoulder, he put a finger to his lips, then crouched low when he saw three strangers, their guns trained on his family. Containing the fear ripping through him, Colin turned to Sarah.

"Do not move from this spot unless they come after you. If that happens, run."

Grabbing his arm, Sarah's fingers dug in, forcing Colin to look at her. "I know you have two guns. Give me one. I'll help."

Cocking his head, he cupped her face in his hands. "Nae, Sarah. You stay here."

"But—"

"I'll waste no more time on this," he hissed. Pulling from her grasp, he moved closer, watching as Caleb stood, then walked to Quinn and Brodie, taking money they pulled from their pockets. Colin saw their guns on the ground and knew each had a knife. He didn't know about Caleb, but Quinn and Brodie were quite skilled. Moving quietly, he stopped behind a thick bush several yards behind the tallest of the outlaws. If he could distract them, disable or kill one of the robbers, Quinn, Brodie, and Caleb might have time to draw and throw their knives, surprising the other two men.

He held his gun steady as the oldest man ordered Geneen to pack their food. Colin held his breath, hoping she'd do as the man asked, getting her out of danger when the fight started. He cringed when she stood, hands on hips, and defied the man. However, the outlaw's threats had her changing her mind and moving toward the pack animal carrying their supplies.

Moving to get a better shot, Colin's gaze shifted when Caleb crouched by the saddlebags, taking out the money each had stored inside. Before he stood,

Caleb's head turned to the side, then nodded. Looking past Caleb to the bushes on the other side of the camp, Colin cursed as a patch of white fabric disappeared into the darkness. Sarah. They'd have a stern discussion when this was over.

Standing, Caleb looked at the tallest outlaw, then behind him, sending Colin a slight nod when their eyes locked. Opening his hand, Caleb held out the money.

"This is all we have."

Clem sneered at the pittance, turning his attention to his brothers. "Ralph and Emory, why don't you two go through those bags and see what else you can find?"

His gun moving away from Caleb was all the break Colin needed. He aimed and fired at Clem's back, sending him sprawling seconds before Caleb drew his knife and sent it flying toward Ralph. The outlaw grabbed the protruding handle, then collapsed to the ground, the blade buried in his throat. The distraction gave Quinn and Brodie the time needed to draw their own knives and hurl them toward Emory. Both lodged in his chest.

Colin moved to kneel next to Clem, checking his pulse. Finding none, he watched as his cousins shook their heads, indicating neither of the other two had survived. He started to dash toward the last spot he saw Sarah, then let out a breath when he saw her arms wrapped around Geneen, both of their faces blank, as if in shock.

"Are you two all right?" Colin rested a hand on Sarah's shoulder.

Swallowing the fear she'd felt moments before, she turned toward him, shifting her embrace from Geneen to Colin. Stroking her back, he placed a kiss on her forehead, then stepped back.

"I'd better help them with the bodies."

"Do you know who they are?" Geneen asked Colin, her voice surprisingly calm.

"Nae. Do you recognize them?"

"I've never seen them. The oldest is named Clem. He called the other two Ralph and Emory."

Colin nodded. He needed to speak with the others, decide what to do with the bodies, then find where they'd left their horses.

"What do you want to do with them, Colin?" Quinn checked his knife again, then slid it into the sheath.

"Search them for anything that may identify who they are. We'll bury them here and let the sheriff in Mindell know what happened. He can decide what to do next."

"Cursed outlaws," Brodie muttered. "I hate wasting good time burying such scum, but guess it has to be done."

Colin slapped him on the back. "That it does, lad."

It took several hours for them to dig shallow graves, then toss rock, branches, leaves—whatever they could find—on top. They'd done what they could. If animals got to them, so be it.

Collapsing on their bedrolls, they slept a few hours, then ate before riding south. From what Colin could tell, Sarah and Geneen seemed fine given all they'd been through. Neither had slept while the men worked, using their time to provide coffee, then helping gather rocks and branches to mark the graves.

Today, he rode alongside Sarah in the front, while Brodie rode by Geneen in the middle. Caleb and Quinn stayed at the back with the pack horses and the three mounts the outlaws used, their usual banter giving way to stoic silence. Although proficient with their knives, none of the three had ever used them to kill a man. It wasn't a sight they'd soon forget.

Reining Chieftain to a stop at the top of a hill, Colin took a breath, his gaze settling on the town of Mindell a couple miles below.

"Is that it?" Sarah stared into the distance, seeing nothing more than a few buildings in a clearing not more than a quarter mile in diameter.

"That's Mindell." He had yet to tell her about the girls. Their time together away from camp the night before had been short and he didn't want to waste it talking about the runaways. During the ride, he had little desire to talk, his thoughts still focused on what happened at camp. Like the others, Colin had never killed a man, hoping he'd never be forced to. Even though the outlaws had given them no choice, the burden of ending a life would still weigh heavy on him for some time.

"Will we be stopping there?"

"Aye. There are some people we need to see about."

Sarah cocked her head, waiting for him to finish. Instead, he started down the hill, giving no further explanation.

Deciding to stop at the jail first, he and Brodie reported the shootings, giving the sheriff the names of the outlaws from wanted posters they found in their saddlebags.

"Wondered about those Baldwin brothers. They were a mean bunch. I think they were part of a gang that robbed our bank a few weeks ago. It's a miracle you and your family got away without them killing anyone. They'd usually shoot first, not worrying about the consequences." The sheriff wrote down the approximate location of the graves, even though he doubted anyone would care. "There's a small reward for each. Where do you want it sent?"

"Send it to Reverend Olford, River City, Oregon, with a message to give it to Jamie's new family," Colin said before walking out with Brodie.

They headed straight for the church. He'd no more than slid off Chieftain when the door burst open and Coral ran outside, launching herself at him.

"I knew you'd come back, Colin." Her arms gripped him tight.

"Ah, lassie. I told you we would." He stroked Coral's hair, glancing up to see the astonishment on Sarah's face. He hadn't anticipated the reception, believing if they hadn't found homes, the girls would have already run.

"That's what I told Opal and Pearl, but I don't think they believed me. But I knew..." Her voice trailed off as she settled her head against his chest.

Squeals from the church, then the sound of running feet signaled the arrival of her sisters. Opal ran up to Quinn, while Pearl threw herself into Brodie's arms before he swung her in a circle.

"What do we have here?" Geneen walked to Colin, glancing up at Sarah sitting atop her horse, a look of complete confusion on her face.

Gently pulling Coral's arms from around his waist, he turned her toward Sarah and Geneen. "This is Coral and her sisters, Opal and Pearl. Girls, this is Miss Geneen MacGregor and her sister, Sarah

MacGregor. Sarah and I are getting married. That's the reason Quinn, Brodie, and I rode to Oregon."

Sarah almost felt bad at the look of total dejection on Coral's face. The girl had an obvious affection for Colin, perhaps even believed herself in love with him. Sarah could understand. She'd been in love with Colin from the first day they'd met.

Sliding off her horse, Sarah walked up to Coral. "It's a pleasure to meet you and your sisters. Do you live here in Mindell?"

Straightening and showing the attitude Colin had seen when they first met the runaways, Coral stared at Sarah. "We're going to live with the MacLarens at Circle M Ranch."

Colin settled his hands on his waist, tilting his head up, looking at the sky. Quinn choked on the news, while Brodie crossed his arms and shook his head.

Coral spun around, casting a defiant gaze at Colin. "That's what you told us. You said if the reverend and his wife didn't find a home for us, you'd take us to yours."

"Coral, what I said was—"

"The MacLarens." The reverend's booming voice came from the front steps of the church, his arms spread wide. "You are as good as your word." Walking up to them, he held out a hand to each of the men. "I don't recall meeting you," he said to Caleb.

"Caleb Stewart, sir. I met up with the MacLarens in River City and decided to ride south with them. We all traveled west together in the same wagon train a few years ago."

"Ah, then you know them to be the same fine men I met when they left the girls with us." Turning to Colin, he looked at Coral. "We did try, but there wasn't a family able to take all three girls, and they refused to be separated. It's good you came as I don't know how my wife and I would have been able to feed them over the winter."

"I understand. You've done more than we expected and we thank you. I wish I had more money, but…"

"No need, young man. You provided enough, and the girls weren't shy about helping my wife. I know she'll miss the extra hands."

Colin introduced Sarah and Geneen, then huddled with his cousins and Caleb. "We do have the three extra horses. We'll need to buy extra supplies, enough to get us to Crocker."

"Quinn said the girls are from there. You know the town's reputation isn't the best." Caleb shot a look at the girls. They didn't appear to be as rough as Quinn led him to believe when he'd explained the situation during the ride.

"Hell, the place is fit for outlaws and no one else," Brodie growled. In his mind, any town not fit for decent citizens shouldn't exist.

"I don't see as we have much choice except to take them home with us. We can ask around about a family to take them in once we're at the ranch." Colin didn't like it any better than the others. "Agreed?"

They nodded without enthusiasm, resigned to three extra females until they could find a home for them.

"All right, girls. Pack whatever you have. We'd best get going."

As the others helped them load their belongings onto the horses, the reverend took Colin aside. "You need to know about a group of bank robbers who were here a few weeks ago. We heard they rode south, but no one knows for certain. Not sure if they headed for Nevada or not, but you should keep watch. They killed a farmer making a deposit when they robbed the bank here."

"The sheriff told us about the bank robbery. Outlaws hit the bank in River City not long before we arrived. Their sheriff took off after them, riding south. I wonder if it was the same gang."

Rubbing his face, the reverend thought a moment, then shook his head. "Could be. There's more than one gang roaming the country around here."

Colin sure hoped they didn't run into them on the trail home.

"Thanks again, Reverend. Look us up if you're ever around Settlers Valley."

Taking Colin's outstretched hand, the reverend nodded. "I'll do that, son. You be safe."

"Are you planning to take the girls into Crocker with us?" Caleb rode up front with Colin, each taking turns scouting ahead as they got closer to the wild frontier town. They'd rotated positions every few hours, keeping watch on their surroundings. No one trusted what they'd find ahead of them.

"Nae. They'll stay with Sarah, Geneen, and Brodie while you, Quinn, and I go into Crocker. We'll get supplies and get out, then take the trail heading west to avoid all of us riding through town."

"And ask about the bank robbers?"

Colin shook his head. "All they have are outlaws in that town. Bank robbers, murderers, men running from the law. I doubt they even have a sheriff. The last I heard, theirs was killed in a shootout months ago and they never found anyone fool enough to take the job." Taking off his hat, Colin ran a hand through his hair, then shifted in the saddle toward Caleb. "We may ask about the girls' kin, though. Find out if anyone's heard of them. That is, if they'll tell us their last name."

"Coffman."

"One of them tell you that?" Colin had tried several times to get Coral to tell him.

"Coral. She told me last night over supper."

"Did she tell you her parents' names?"

"No. Said their parents are dead and they're orphans, the same as they told you." Caleb glanced over his shoulder, hearing Coral laugh at something Quinn said. "Truth is, I don't believe it. I think they have kin somewhere in that town."

"Why is that?"

"I've caught Coral scolding her sisters a couple times, saying something about us not finding out or we might leave them in Crocker. Of course, if they're that afraid, taking them to your ranch may be for the best. I'm heading to the back with Brodie. I'll send your lady up here." Caleb smiled before reining around.

It surprised Colin the way the younger girls kept up with the pace he set. They'd ridden harder and longer than anyone expected, allowing them to make up more time. And they'd yet to encounter any foul weather. If nothing changed, they'd be home by the end of the week.

"Brodie doesn't need to stay with us. Why don't you take him with you into Crocker?" Sarah felt no unease staying with Geneen and the girls while the men rode into town. They didn't plan to be gone long, and they hadn't encountered another soul since leaving Mindell. "Who'd bother us way out here when there's food and alcohol to be found a couple miles away?"

Wrapping his arms around her, he lowered his mouth for a searing kiss. Resting his chin on the top of her head, he let out a deep breath. "We didn't count on the Baldwin brothers riding by our camp, but they did. We were all lucky to come through it alive. I won't leave you without protection. Brodie has no issue staying and that's what's going to happen." Colin stepped back, checking his guns once more, then fixed her with a hard stare. "You'll do as I say this time. Don't follow us or try to send Brodie into town. While we're gone, I want to know you and the others are safe, protected, and far away from the blackguards in Crocker. Do you understand?" A ball of ice formed in his gut at the thought of what could've happened with the Baldwin brothers. He had to keep reminding himself how much life at their ranch differed from the lawlessness of much of the land. The Baldwins were a harsh reminder.

"Sarah?" he asked again when she didn't respond.

After life with her da, Sarah hated being ordered around. No matter how much it stung, she had to remind herself Colin had to do what he felt necessary to keep her and everyone else safe. Still, she crossed her arms and glared at him. "I'll stay and won't try to send Brodie after you. Does that satisfy you now, Colin MacLaren?"

He'd already learned when Sarah used his last name, he'd crossed some imaginary line. So be it. She'd cross one of his if she defied him on this.

Grasping her shoulders, his lips turned up into a smile. "Aye, Sarah MacGregor. It does." Looking around, he saw everyone else occupied with their own preparations. "Come with me." He took her hand, pulling her behind a stand of thick-trunked cedars, quickly drawing her into his arms before capturing her mouth. Resting his hands on the curve of her hips, he drew her close, hearing her moan at the intense contact.

"Colin? Are you ready?" Quinn's voice had them pulling apart.

Dropping his arms, Colin took her hand, placing one more kiss on her lips before returning to the camp. "I'm ready."

"All right then. We should be off." Quinn chuckled at Sarah's flushed appearance.

Watching them ride out, Sarah couldn't shake the feeling of dread that washed over her. Lifting her hand in farewell, she shook her head. Although her instincts had always been good, she felt too much happiness to take the latest warning seriously. The men would purchase supplies, ride back, then they'd leave for the last part of their journey...and her new life with Colin.

Chapter Sixteen

"What can I get you, fellas?" The bartender rested his hands on the bar, leaning forward.

"Three whiskeys." Colin turned, leaning his back against the bar, getting his first good look at the customers. As expected, the faces were ruthless, cruel in their intensity. The kind of bitter, unforgiving presence he expected from those who lived in Crocker.

"How do you want to deal with this?" Quinn took a sip of his whiskey, enjoying his first taste of the amber liquid since leaving River City.

Colin focused on one group of men at a table in the corner, men who'd been keeping watch on them since they took their places at the bar. Their looks weren't subtle. More of a warning to finish their drinks and leave. He turned, nodding to the bartender.

"You know a Coffman family in Crocker?"

The man's hands stilled, one holding a glass, the other a bottle. He shot a look at the table of men Colin had been watching, not outwardly acknowledging the question. Setting the glass down, he turned his gaze to Colin, holding out the bottle.

"More whiskey?" His voice, edgy and tense, had lowered to a whisper.

Tossing back what he had, Colin held out his now empty glass. "Sure."

As the bartender filled it, then Quinn's and Caleb's, his eyes shifted to the table again. "Why do you want to know?"

Colin's eyes narrowed, brows furrowed. "We heard his name in Mindell. It sounded familiar. Nothing important."

The man straightened, setting the bottle on the shelf below the bar. "Since it's not important, I'll give you some advice. Coffman is a name you best forget. He and his men aren't the kind who take kindly to strangers, especially those asking about them." He started to move down the bar.

"One other question."

Stopping, he turned back to Colin. "What's that?"

"Is he in here now?"

Shaking his head, he let out a breath and leaned forward. "It's your life. No, he's not here, but those are some of his men at the table. The same men who haven't taken their eyes off you fellas since you walked in."

They didn't turn to look. If the bartender's warning was accurate, there'd be no point confronting them about the girls. At least they now knew Coral had lied to them about being orphans. Their father was alive.

Assuming Coffman was like the group at the table, he wouldn't be the type they'd leave them with anyway. According to Coral, the three would run again. They'd probably try to make it to Circle M Ranch alone.

"Let's get out of here. We still have supplies to buy."

"Hard bunch of men." Caleb spoke first as they walked toward the general store. "Wouldn't be too anxious to start anything with them or Coffman, if we ever figure out who he is."

"I agree with Caleb. Let's get what we need and get back to camp." Quinn glanced over his shoulder, unable to ignore the dread burning in his gut.

It didn't take long to gather the supplies they needed.

"You boys ain't from around here, are you?" The clerk totaled the purchase, giving Colin an amount. Short and lean, with weathered skin and a scrawny beard, the man looked close to seventy.

"Nae."

"Where you headed?" Picking up the cash Colin set on the counter, he placed it in a tin box.

"Conviction. We have a ranch near there."

"That a fact? You hear about the shooting in Conviction? Group of outlaws robbed the bank, killed two or three people from what we heard." The old-timer scratched his beard, eyeing them. "Heard the dead owned a ranch nearby."

Quinn reached across the counter, grabbing the man by his shirt, almost pulling him across the low divider.

"The murdered ranchers...do you have names?" he asked, his eyes burning into the man.

His face reddening as he tried to swallow, the man's eyes grew wide. "No...no name. Just heard about it. That's all."

"Let him go, Quinn. The man's done nothing." Colin placed a hand on his cousin's shoulder, his heart pounding as his chest squeezed in pain. "We need to get out of here. Now."

Not reining Chieftain to a stop before he jumped off, Colin dashed toward Brodie. "Pack up. We have to get to the ranch."

"What is it?" Brodie saw the same apprehensive look on both his cousins' faces.

"We heard of a bank robbery in Conviction. Some ranchers were killed." Turning in a circle, Colin searched for the others. "Where is Sarah?"

"She and Geneen are at the creek with the girls— a few yards that way. I'll get them."

Colin grabbed Brodie's arm. "I'll go. You help Quinn and Caleb pack."

Dashing in the direction Brodie pointed, he heard their laughter before seeing them in a clearing not far from the camp.

"Colin!" Sarah stood, running toward him, then stopped. "What is it?"

Wrapping an arm around her shoulders, he turned her away from the others. "There's been a bank robbery and killings in Conviction. We need to get there as soon as possible."

"Do you know who was killed?" She could feel heat radiate from his body, see the dread in his eyes.

"Just that it was local ranchers."

"My God, Colin. Do you think...?" Her shaky voice signaled her own fear.

"I won't think the worst, Sarah." He dropped his arms, turning toward the others. "Hurry and pack. We're leaving."

On their way north, it had taken them several days to travel from their ranch to Crocker. Riding each day until they felt compelled to stop, the trip back took almost three days. Three agonizing days of not knowing if one of their family members had been murdered.

"Is that it?" Sarah pointed toward the valley ahead dotted with several houses, barns, and corrals. Her breath hitched at the beautiful sight before her.

Colin had told her of Circle M Ranch, the large spread owned by his father and three uncles, but nothing could have prepared her for the impact of the first view.

"Aye. That's home."

"It's...magnificent..." Her voice trailed off as Colin gave her one more glance, then pushed Chieftain faster, not waiting for the others to catch up as he rode straight for the main house.

"I'll stay with the women. You two go on," Caleb offered when he saw the anxious looks on Quinn's and Brodie's faces.

Not answering, they moved their horses into full gallops, following Colin to the house. Reining to a stop in front of the big wraparound porch, they sat frozen at the way Colin wrapped his arms around his mother, Kyla, muffling her sobs as her body shook. Pulling back, her tear-streaked face searched Colin's, misery edging her features.

"They didn't have time to draw their weapons. They were murdered in cold blood." Her voice broke, the cries of agony slicing through each of them.

Sliding from their horses, Quinn and Brodie approached in slow, tentative steps, not wanting to know the truth, but needing to hear it.

"What happened, Colin?" Quinn's hands fisted at his sides, anticipating the worst.

Colin's shocked face, eyes red and swollen, turned toward him. "They're dead. My da and yours...dead."

Quinn stumbled backwards, pain like he'd never felt before wrapping itself around him, drowning him in unspeakable agony.

"Ma? Where's Ma?" Quinn asked, breath labored, his chest tight.

"Heather and Bram are with her at your house. From what I know, she hasn't eaten or slept since Gillis was murdered." Kyla stepped away from Colin to wrap her arms around Quinn. "Doc said they died right away, without pain..."

Quinn swallowed the growing lump in his throat, swiping at the hot tears streaming down his face. He didn't notice Caleb and the others ride up, and wouldn't have cared even if he had.

Brodie stood to the side, disbelief, anger, and hatred warring within him. "Do they have the men who did this?"

Kyla looked at him. "Nae."

"What is the sheriff doing about it?" Brodie demanded. "He must have a posse out looking for them."

"For one day, then they stopped, giving up without any explanation. Ewan and Ian may know more about what's going on, but they've been wrapped up in their own grief." Kyla referred to the two remaining brothers. Ewan was Brodie's father and the third oldest.

"Then I'll speak with Da. We need to find the men who did this and make sure they hang." Brodie stormed from the porch, swinging up on Hunter, riding at a gallop toward his family's home.

Sarah walked up the steps, stopping next to Kyla, placing a hand on her shoulder while the girls stood, listening. Coral fidgeted, wrapping her arms around her waist, staring at the ground. Beside her, Opal and Pearl did the same, not looking at the adults.

"Come on, girls. Let's put away the horses." Caleb had heard enough to learn the two eldest MacLarens had been murdered with little being done to find their killers. He'd help get the girls settled, introduce himself to Colin's mother, then find out what he could do to help track down the men responsible.

The family had waited to have the funeral until the boys returned. *Boys*, Kyla thought, shaking her head as she stood near the open graves next to Quinn's mother, Audrey. They'd left young men, full of enthusiasm for their journey and finding the lass Colin intended to marry. Not one of them anticipated any of the trials marking their trip or the tragedy awaiting them at home.

Colin and Quinn had returned to find themselves the head of their families, forced to take over for fathers who'd died well before their time. As for Brodie, his father, Ewan, was now the eldest. Therefore, as with Angus, he held the deciding vote, a role he didn't want or embrace. Kyla believed he'd look to Ian, Colin, and Quinn for guidance, leaning heavily on them before making decisions.

"Da and Uncle Ian won't speak of the sheriff's decision and won't ride out on their own. With winter approaching, they've too many burdens here at the ranch to hunt the men who murdered Uncle Angus and Uncle Gillis." Brodie slammed a hand against a wall in the study of the big ranch house where Kyla, Colin, and his brothers and sisters lived. He and his cousins shared Angus's favorite whiskey, each wrestling with their own hate and bewilderment at the senseless killings.

Slamming his glass down, Colin crossed his arms, turning toward the others. "I'm tired of excuses. We need to speak with the sheriff ourselves, find out what the man is doing to find the murderers." Colin had been filled with a burning rage since coming home to learn of the deaths. The depth of the hate scared him, fueling his need for revenge. Someone had to pay for what happened, and he wouldn't rest until they did. The one person who gave him solace was Sarah. Taking long rides after supper each night, she'd let him rage, burning through his anger until exhausted, then wrap her arms around him, telling him over and over that all would be well.

He felt the same. Everything *would* be all right, but not until the killers had been put in their own graves.

A week after the funeral and one week before Colin and Sarah's wedding, nothing had been solved. The murderers were still free to continue their robbing and killing, no one answering for the deaths. The frustration Colin and Quinn felt at the sheriff's lack of action ate at them until they could wait no longer.

"Tomorrow morning, I'll ride to town and meet with the sheriff. I'm tired of waiting. I want answers." Colin picked up his glass and downed the remaining whiskey, letting it burn a path down his throat.

"I'll ride with you," Quinn growled.

"Hell, Colin. We'll all go. The sheriff has to know we're in this together." Although Brodie's father still lived, he felt the pain of losing his uncles. He wanted the guilty caught and made to pay for their crimes.

Colin glanced around the room at the determined faces. "Then it's settled. We leave at dawn tomorrow."

"It was Coffman, pure and simple." Quinn slammed a fist on the sheriff's desk, tired of listening to the man trying to appease them.

"Listen here, Quinn. No one got a good look at any of them. They wore bandannas and never spoke. I took a posse out, searched for the men who killed Angus and Gillis, but lost them." Sheriff Yost stood at least six inches shorter than any other man in the room, having a slight build, inconspicuous features, and a soft voice more suited to a librarian than a lawman.

"One damn day," Quinn growled, his voice hard and threatening as he took a menacing step toward Yost. "You searched from morning until night, then gave up. You. Gave. Up." Quinn wanted nothing more than to pull the man across the desk by his collar and toss him against a wall. As far as he was the concerned, Yost was a worthless piece of humanity. The man hadn't made it as a rancher, store owner, or telegraph clerk in San Francisco, so he'd ridden east, landing in Conviction at a time when the sheriff's job sat vacant. A year later, all he did was take up space.

Face reddening at Quinn's accusation, Yost held his arms out, palms up. "There were no tracks. They rode east out of town, then disappeared." He glanced from Quinn to Colin, then the others.

Jaw tight, Colin's narrowed gaze ripped into the man. "Who'd you use as a tracker?"

"What?" Yost looked bewildered at the question.

"A tracker, Yost. Who did you use?" Colin growled, barely containing his disgust.

"Me and the boys…" Yost's voice trailed off. He'd taken his one deputy, the deputy's brother, and a local ranch kid who happened to be in town the day of the shooting.

"You didn't take anyone with you who had knowledge of tracking or following trails, did you?" Colin stepped closer, stopping at Blaine's hand on his shoulder.

Straightening, trying to preserve his reputation, Yost glared at him. "We did our best. Don't know what else to tell you."

"Admitting you're incompetent and finding someone who can do the job would help," Brodie spat out, unable to remain silent any longer. "I understand. You're afraid of Coffman. Hell, everyone is. It's your job to find the men who robbed the bank and killed our kin. If you can't, or *won't,* do it, the town needs someone who will." He slammed his fist down, then turned and stormed outside, afraid of what he might do if he stayed.

Colin watched him leave, feeling the same anger, yet needing to get what he could out of Yost before leaving. "I want to know who else was in the bank when it happened, plus the names of anyone who saw the shootings or the outlaws ride out."

"But—"

"*Now*, Sheriff. I want to know everything you learned, then we'll leave."

Quinn tossed a branch on the open fire. He, Colin, Brodie, Blaine, and Caleb had begun gathering at this spot almost every night since their return. After the meeting with Yost, they had to decide what to do next. Tonight, however, Heather, Quinn's sister, had learned of their meeting and refused to be left out of further conversations about avenging their father.

At first, Quinn had argued with her, saying she'd not be included in whatever their decision concerning punishment for their father's killer. But she wouldn't let it go, arguing that allowing someone who wasn't family, such as Caleb, and not her was wrong. She could ride and shoot as well as any of her kin and had a right to be a part of any decision the men made. Besides, she didn't trust Caleb, wondering at his motives for leaving his family in Oregon to venture hundreds of miles south to work for a family he'd not seen in years.

The bigger truth was the unease she felt around him. She'd felt the same sense of discomfort during their journey west years ago. It seemed no matter where she rode or what she did, Caleb wouldn't be far away. He never spoke or intruded, which irritated her even more.

Now he'd shown up again—older, taller, well-muscled, a man in every sense. Unlike her female cousins, she didn't see the reason for wanting a man as a permanent part of her life. Every suitor who'd spoken to her da, trying to court her, had been soundly rebuffed until few came around any longer. She'd felt nothing for any of them—until Caleb. Never had she felt such odd feelings for a man—nervous, unable to form a coherent thought, as if she were a daft lassie. She had no idea what bothered her so about him, but Heather was determined to push the nonsense from her mind.

"Yost says we can't be sure it's Coffman. They wore bandannas, and never spoke, only gestured at each other." Blaine scrubbed a hand down his face.

"The man's a coward," Quinn spat out. "More worried about his own hide than seeking justice. The way I see it, we're the ones who'll have to do what's right."

"Are you thinking we ride out, leaving your families here to take care of themselves?" Caleb asked. "I'm not sure that's a wise idea. And remember, Coffman is Coral, Opal, and Pearl's father." Most every MacLaren, except Heather, had accepted Caleb right off, put him to work, and treated him as if he'd been a part of their family forever. He glanced at Heather now, her arms crossed, staring at him as if he were an unwanted insect. His lips tilted into a grim smile, remembering her from the wagon trip west. Beautiful and wild with a free spirit, she defied the ordinary definition of a female. She also had a natural distrust of those outside of the family.

"Hell, I don't know what's best. All I know is we need to find who did this. There won't be peace for any of us until we do." Quinn stood, pacing toward Colin, who'd taken a spot near the horses.

Crossing his arms, resting a hip against a post, Colin listened without comment. His sentiments mirrored Quinn's. If it weren't for Sarah and his impending marriage, he'd already be on the trail, searching for the killers.

"What do you say, Colin? Are you with me on going after them?"

"Aye, Quinn. Just not yet."

"And why not? The longer we wait, the harder it will be to find them."

"For one, I'm getting married in a few days—"

"And he won't be getting out of his bed for days afterwards," Blaine added, seeing Colin's mouth quirk up in a slow grin. It was the first smile he'd seen since his brother returned.

"Aye, Blaine, you're right. And I'll not be leaving the others until we know where we're headed."

"After Coffman." Quinn paced back to the fire, dropping onto one of the logs.

"Aye, but there are questions I'd like answered before we rush off to kill the man. As Caleb said, he's the girls' father. Even if they ran, killing someone's kin is never easy. Also, we need to be certain he's in Crocker before all of us ride out, leaving the ranch with a partial crew."

"But you agree Coffman and his gang are responsible for the murders?" Heather asked. She'd believed the same, yet she'd never been able to convince her uncles of it.

"I do. It's moving into winter. They'll hit what banks they can before the snows force them to stay in Crocker. That's when we go after them. They'll settle in, not expecting anyone to be brave or foolish enough to take them on in their own town. We do what we need to do, then ride out without anyone knowing."

"That will also give us time to learn more about him from the girls." Caleb understood they couldn't let the killers go unpunished. At the same time, he didn't want to cause the girls more pain.

"So you aren't planning to tell Yost?" Blaine asked, unsure of the wisdom of keeping the man out of it.

"I'm not planning to tell *anyone.*"

Blaine's jaw dropped open. "Not even our uncles?"

"No one." Colin glanced at the men around the fire. He'd trust his life to each one. "We're the only ones who'll know what we plan."

"When?" Quinn relaxed for the first time since their return.

"We ride to Crocker as soon after the wedding as possible. Brodie and Blaine will ride into Crocker, leaving the rest of us a few miles outside of town. No one will recognize either of them. We'll wait until they return, confirming Coffman is there, then we all ride in. We were able to get here in three days, and that was with the women."

"We'll make it in two each way. Won't be gone more than a week." Quinn liked the idea. He'd ride out tonight if they could.

"And if we learn it wasn't Coffman?" Blaine asked Colin.

"It was. I'd bet my life on it."

Chapter Seventeen

"It's so good to have you and Geneen here." Kyla continued stitching the wedding gown Sarah would be wearing on Saturday. The work kept her mind off Angus and the life she faced without him. The days weren't so bad, but the nights were complete agony, crying herself to sleep, then reaching over in the early morning to find the space next to her cold and empty. How she wished he'd lived long enough to see what a beautiful woman Sarah had become. "Now, tell me more about the girls."

Geneen and Sarah stayed close to Coral, Opal, and Pearl each day, helping with chores, trying to get them to talk about their parents and where they'd been raised. So far, she'd had little success.

"They're still somewhat of a mystery to us. You already know Coral is the oldest at eighteen, more a woman than a girl. Seems she's been responsible for Opal and Pearl for a while." Sarah looked up from stitching lace on her veil. Several MacLaren women had ridden into town a few days before to pick up the rest of the supplies for the wedding. Kyla had insisted they purchase additional lace and clear beads. Sarah would be lucky if she didn't go blind trying to apply them.

"Colin told me you think their father is the same man who killed Angus and Gillis?"

"Coral told Caleb their last name is Coffman, and neither Opal nor Pearl have said otherwise. According to what Colin has learned, Lonnie Coffman is the head of a group of notorious outlaws who live around Crocker. That's where the girls said they were living before they ran away." She opened the veil, inspecting her work.

"I wonder what made them run away."

"None of them will talk about it. Whenever it seems like Opal or Pearl might say something, Coral is quick to stop them. Whatever the reason, they don't want to go back there." Sarah stood, holding up the veil. "There. How does it look?"

"Oh, Sarah. It's beautiful. By tomorrow afternoon, I'll have the dress ready for you to try on again. Then we need to start cooking. Saturday will be here before you know it." Setting down the dress, Kyla glanced out the window, watching the girls play while Geneen watched. "Your sister is only a year younger than you?"

"Yes, she's twenty-one. Isla, the youngest, is sixteen and not at all like either Geneen or me. She loves being in the house, reading, helping Ma." At the mention of her mother, Sarah's chest tightened. If only her da wasn't so stubborn, her family might have been here to celebrate the marriage, instead of not knowing if she'd ever see them again.

Kyla sat back, folding her hands in her lap, watching Geneen lean against the barn, talking to Coral, keeping a vigilant watch on the younger girls. Her nine-year-old twin daughters, Chrissy and Alana, had taken to Pearl right away, following her everywhere.

"Does she want to teach, like you?"

Sarah laughed at the thought. "Heavens no...unless it involved being outside. Geneen isn't as accomplished as Heather around a ranch, but she can hold her own with most chores."

"I've seen them talking. Geneen mentioned Heather doesn't say much, which is true. That girl always has been a loner. Maybe in time..."

"Geneen told me the same." Sarah walked to the window, standing behind Kyla. "Of course, my sister can be quite chatty. It may take Heather a while to warm up to her." She looked at the horizon, seeing a group of riders approach. "Looks like the men are heading back."

"Guess it's time to finish supper and feed them." Kyla smiled as Sarah took off, dashing outside onto the front porch to wait for Colin. It had been the same each day since their return. Any free moment they had, the two spent it together.

Except for Caleb, she'd known the young men all their lives. Kyla's instincts warned her they had something planned, fearing it had to do with chasing the outlaws. A part of her sought justice as much as they did, wanting to put Angus's killers in the ground. Another part caused a cold lump to lodge deep in her stomach when she thought of the possible outcome. She couldn't handle losing anyone else she loved. She had to make time to get Colin alone, find out what they intended, and put a stop to it.

"What will we do if they won't let us stay, Coral? I don't want to go back to Crocker." Pearl sat on her bed in the room the three sisters shared, worry etched on her young face. At ten, she'd already witnessed too much violence, had too many sleepless nights wondering if she'd be torn from her sisters, forced to live in a house not of her choosing.

"If they wanted us to be in Crocker, they would've left us there weeks ago." Coral wrapped an arm around Pearl's trembling shoulders, pulling her close. "We can't waste our time worrying. Instead, we need to show them how much help we can be— convince them to let us stay. Now, let's help Mrs. MacLaren with supper." She let her arm drop as Pearl slid off the bed, racing down the steps.

"No running, Pearl," Coral called after her.

"Do you truly believe they won't send us back?" Opal stood at the bedroom door, glancing over her shoulder. At fourteen, she was four years younger than Coral, but already a young woman in many ways.

"Yes, I do," she sighed, walking up to place a hand on Opal's arm. "Maybe they'll let us stay here or look for a family in town, but they won't return us to Crocker." She prayed her thoughts were true. It had been years since they had a real home, people they could depend on. Living with the MacLarens had given her the first sense of peace she'd known in a long time. "I promise, no matter what they decide, I won't let them pull us apart."

"Where are you taking me, Colin?" Sarah gripped his hand tight as he led her down a path through what she knew to be a thick forest. Over her weak protests, he'd insisted on using a bandanna to blindfold her. She could hear water in the distance, feeling leafy limbs brush against her skirt as they got closer to the sound. Their rides and walks after supper had become a tradition, even in the short time they'd been together.

"Show some patience, lass. It's a surprise." Colin looked around, keeping her close as the trail narrowed. He hadn't been out here in at least two years. It used to be his special spot to be alone and think about Sarah, wondering if they had a future.

"Are you sure you can see where we're headed?"

Chuckling, he shook his head. "Aye. There's a full moon, the same one you saw rising on our ride out here." Several more minutes passed. To his surprise, Sarah didn't utter another word. Drawing her ahead of him, he stopped, gripping her shoulders in his hands. "Do you hear that?"

"Aye. Sounds like a waterfall."

"It is, but there's more." Untying the bandanna, he stepped to her side, watching her face.

"Oh my..."

He watched her eyes widen as her voice trailed off, turning to flash him one of her bright smiles, the kind that always made his breath hitch.

"It's stunning." She peered down into a lagoon, the surface sparkling from the light of the moon. "Can we get closer?"

Taking her hand, they took an overgrown path to the water's edge. "I found it not long after we settled here. I used to come here often to get away." He cast her a cautious look. "To think of us, wonder if I'd ever find you, if you'd follow me here."

Wrapping her arms around his waist, she nestled her head on his chest. "And here we are. It seems some prayers are answered. Have you ever swam in the lagoon?"

"Many times." Dropping his arms, he unbuttoned his shirt, shrugging out of it before starting on his trousers, not stopping until he stood before her, naked as the day he'd been born.

"Colin MacLaren." She crossed her arms. "What are you doing?"

"Going swimming. Join me, Sarah." Turning toward the water, he dashed in, ignoring the cold, swimming several feet from the shore. "Come on. No one will see us."

Even knowing how isolated they were, she still hesitated to remove her dress. Instead, she removed her shoes and stockings, stepping into the water.

"It's cold!"

"I'll keep you warm," he grinned, opening his arms wide.

Laughing, she loosened her dress, letting it slide to the ground, leaving her in nothing but a thin chemise. Looking around once more, she bit her bottom lip, closed her eyes, then dashed into the water before she changed her mind.

Colin swam toward her, stopping a few feet away when she stood, tilting her head back, allowing the water to run down her back. His breath caught at the sight before him. The shapeless chemise clung to her body, accentuating every glorious curve, tightening around her tiny waist, leaving little to his imagination.

"What is it, Colin?"

Shaking his head, he moved toward her, catching Sarah in his arms. "Nothing, lass," he whispered against her ear.

"It is s-so cold," she stuttered.

"Ach, it's not so bad. My body will warm you in a moment. And I know a way to help it along." Cupping her cheek with one hand, he molded his mouth to hers, letting it deepen until she clung to him. He pulled back on her soft moan, his dark gaze traveling over her, his breathing ragged. The chemise clung to her skin, a translucent covering which did nothing to hide her from his view. Crushing her to him, he held nothing back, fierce in the way he took possession of her mouth, plunging his tongue inside as her fingers dug into his shoulders.

Lifting Sarah into his arms, Colin carried her to the shore, lowering her feet to the ground, then spreading their clothes near the water. Taking her in his arms, they sank to their knees, clinging to each other as he continued to ravage her mouth, his hands molding her to him.

Sarah's heart hammered in her chest, the sensations created by Colin's soft caresses, his knowing hands moving over her body, caused a raging fire to flash through her. As his hands continued to explore, her body grew heavy and warm, a heated shudder pulsing low in her stomach.

Reaching between them, she splayed her hands across his chest, then lower, feeling the taut muscles of his stomach. On a gasp, he pulled back, slowly laying her down, stretching out beside her.

"I need you, Colin," she breathed out, unable to control her thundering heart.

"Ah, lass. No more than I need you."

Colin couldn't stop Sarah's body from violently shivering on the ride back to the ranch. He'd used blankets to dry her off, then bundled her in his coat. Placing her in front of him on Chieftain, he wrapped an arm around her in an effort to keep her warm. Nothing seemed to help as he raced toward home.

"We'll be there in a few minutes, love," he whispered, spotting the lights ahead. "It won't be long before you'll be in front of a fire." He could feel her head bob in acknowledgment as he tightened his hold. Reining to a stop, he swung off, sliding her into his arms. Kicking the front door open, he ignored the stares of his family, taking her straight to the fire.

"I'll get dry clothes." Kyla rushed upstairs while Geneen grabbed a quilt from a nearby chest.

"Here. Wrap her in this." She opened it, settling it around Sarah's shoulders.

Hurrying down the stairs, clothes draped over her arm, Kyla came to a stop beside Colin, looking around at the others.

"All of you, out. And that includes you, Colin. We'll keep her by the fire while Geneen and I get her into dry clothes. Coral, make her a cup of cocoa, please."

"Yes, ma'am." Coral immediately dashed past Colin, who stayed rooted in place.

"Colin, go!" Kyla swept an arm toward the stairs. "Put on some dry clothes, then come back down."

"Ma...I—"

Kyla stood, cutting him off and taking him by the arm. Turning him toward the stairs, she leaned up to whisper in his ear. "Ach, I don't know what was in your head, taking her for a swim on such a cold night, but you have to let me take care of this. I am not a stupid woman, lad. I know you've been together and you want to stay. For now, give Sarah the privacy she needs. Do you understand me?"

He started to protest, then snapped his mouth shut. Nodding, he glanced over his shoulder once more, then took the stairs two at a time. Slamming his bedroom door closed, he snatched dry clothes from his wardrobe, his hands trembling as he slid into them. His ma's words roared through him, the stupidity of his mistake slapping him in the face. Hurrying, he dashed down the steps.

By the time he returned, Sarah sat in his father's old chair, quilts wrapped around her, a cup of cocoa cradled in her still shaking hands. Geneen stood behind her, brushing her drying hair, then securing it in a bun. Taking a few steps, Colin knelt in front of her.

"How are you feeling?" His eyes searched hers, which had grown distant, glassy.

"All right," she croaked out, her voice barely above a whisper, her eyes closing.

Raising a hand, he stroked her face, feeling the heated skin. "Ma, she's burning up." His voice rose in panic, his eyes flaring in concern.

Kyla dropped her stitching, placing the palm of her hand on Sarah's forehead. "It's gone up some. Get her upstairs, Colin. Geneen, I need towels and a pan of cool water."

Lifting her into his arms, Colin climbed the stairs, holding her to him, feeling the heat of her body even through the heavy quilt. Kyla rushed past him, pulling back the covers before Colin laid her down.

"Colin, I need willow bark tea."

He didn't move, his gaze locked on Sarah.

"Colin, lad, did you hear me?" Kyla touched his arm. "Willow bark tea?"

Shifting his gaze to his mother, he nodded, walking through the doorway as Geneen carried a bowl of cool water up the stairs. Stopping, she looked up at him.

"She'll be all right, Colin. All her life, Sarah has taken to fever quicker than most. It's her body's way. They disappear just as quickly." She offered him a thin smile, then continued into the bedroom.

"What can I do to help?" Coral asked as he entered the kitchen.

"I need to make tea." He walked to a cupboard, pulling down a tin.

"I'll heat the water." Coral grabbed the kettle, filled it with water, then placed it on the wood burning stove.

"How is she?" Blaine walked in, reaching for a cup when he saw what Colin and Coral were preparing.

Colin shook his head. "I don't know what I was thinking, taking her to the lagoon."

"Don't blame yourself. You took her to a place that's always been special to you." Blaine placed a comforting hand on his brother's shoulder.

Shaking off the hand, Colin turned to him. "I encouraged her to get in the water. She didn't want to, but I insisted. This shouldn't have happened."

Reaching between them, Coral took the cup from Blaine's hand and the tin from Colin's. Placing several pieces of bark inside the kettle, setting the lid on top, she stood back, listening.

"Ma knows what to do. If the cool water doesn't work, we'll be preparing a bath." He pointed to the kettle. "And we've been drinking that *disgusting* tea our entire lives to reduce fever." Blaine took a breath, leaning a hip against the kitchen table. "If nothing works, I'll ride for the doctor tonight. You know he'll come without question."

"And if nothing works?"

"You're creating a problem where there may be none. She has a fever. Don't fret so much until we know how bad it will be."

Neither noticed Coral pouring the tea into a cup. "Do you want me to take this upstairs?" She held it out to them, her head cocked.

"No, I'll do it." Colin took it from her hand, ending the discussion with Blaine. Guilt plagued him. No matter what his brother said, he knew going to the lagoon was the reason for Sarah's fever. Entering the bedroom, he stopped. Her eyes were still closed, her face deathly pale, her deep coughs echoing in the small room. Setting the tea aside, he took the cloth from his mother, dipping it in the cool water and placing it on Sarah's forehead as tremors still racked her body.

"I'll ask Blaine to bring the tub into this room. We need to get her in a cool bath." Kyla took one more look at Sarah before walking out.

"Sarah, lass, I'm so sorry," Colin whispered as the coughing receded and her face calmed. Starting at her forehead, he swiped the cloth down her face, neck, and across her shoulders. Looking over his shoulder, he set the cloth in the basin, then walked to the door, shutting it before returning to unbutton her chemise. Pushing the gown from her shoulders, he pulled her arms free. Picking up the cloth, he ran the cool water over her chest and arms, then repeated the process over and over.

"We'll put it near the door—" Kyla stopped at the sight of Sarah's clothes pushed away, Colin bent over her.

"It's all right, Ma. Have him bring it in." Colin covered her, continuing to apply the cloth to her face and neck.

It took little time to place Sarah in the tub after they'd filled it. Blaine continued to haul additional buckets of cool water upstairs, replacing the water which warmed from her fever.

"I believe it's coming down, Colin." Kyla kneeled on the other side of the tub, mimicking his actions of dripping cooling water over her body.

Touching her forehead with his own, Colin let out a breath. "Aye, I think you're right."

They continued until her eyes fluttered open, her glassy stare fixed on Colin. "What happened?" Her voice weak, she closed her eyes, then forced them to open again.

"Thank God..." Colin breathed out, picking up one of her hands in his. "You had a fever, lass. It's down now. Here." He reached behind him, grabbing the cup of now cold tea. "Drink this. It will help keep it down."

She took a sip, grimacing at the taste. "Ach...willow bark tea."

He chuckled at the look on her face. "I didn't think to add sugar." Tipping the cup again, he encouraged her to drink until she'd finished it.

"All right, Sarah. Let's get you dried and back in your nightdress," Kyla said, her lines of worry beginning to ease.

Sarah blushed, noticing Colin's mother for the first time. For some reason, the knowledge of Colin seeing her naked didn't bother her nearly as much as knowing Kyla had been working alongside him to reduce her fever.

Once they had her dressed and back under the covers, Colin called for Blaine to help him empty the tub and put it away in the closet their ma insisted her husband build. One tub upstairs and another near the kitchen had been her instructions. Colin stilled at the memory of how she'd insisted on the closets, and how his da had gone along with her instructions without comment. His jaw tightened. Revenge would be theirs, and if he had his way, it wouldn't be much longer.

Chapter Eighteen

"We'll put it off a week, Ma. There's no reason to rush. I want to be sure Sarah is fully recovered." Colin still berated himself for what happened to her. He'd not put her through the stress of a wedding until he knew she had her strength back.

"Did you talk to Sarah about it?" Kyla asked, her brows knitting in concern.

"Why should I? I can see she still doesn't have her strength back. It happened just two days ago, Ma."

"I know, lad, but that girl does have a mind of her own. She helped bake pies today while you were with the herd. Her strength seemed fine to me."

Kyla had met him in the barn when she'd seen the men ride in. The wedding was two days away and he'd already told her he wanted to postpone it. From what she could tell, Sarah had no desire to wait.

Stepping back, she crossed her arms, staring at her oldest son. He reminded her so much of his father in looks, as well as the stubborn streak that defined them both. She felt a sharp stab of pain at the reminder of her loss. All of her children gave her comfort, but there'd always be a special place in her heart for Colin.

"You and Sarah need to talk. Decide together whether to go ahead with the wedding on Saturday or wait a week." She touched his arm. "You'll not be ordering her around like some women, Colin. She's the kind who'll expect to talk through decisions, and this is an important one." Without another word, Kyla left the barn and Colin to his thoughts.

"She's right."

Colin glanced at Blaine standing a few feet away, a humorless grin on his face.

A frustrated Colin turned toward him. "And you would know this how?"

"It's not hard. She's much like Ma. You know she and Da talked over everything, made decisions together. If it were me, I'd listen to Ma. Of course, it's your marriage, big brother." Blaine chuckled as he walked out.

Scrubbing a hand down his face, Colin finished grooming Chieftain before letting him out into the pasture behind the barn. Leaning against the gate, he crossed his arms, thinking of what his ma said. She almost never gave her opinion unless asked, which had him carefully considering her words. The first question he asked himself was why he felt the marriage should be postponed. He'd told himself Sarah needed time to regain her strength, but the real reason had to do with the fear that tore him apart when she lapsed into a fever. He'd never seen a fever spike so high in such a short period of time, then disappear. And he was to blame.

"Blaine told me you were out here."

He turned at Sarah's voice, opening his arms. She walked right into them, showing none of the hesitancy he expected after putting her in such danger. Fevers were serious, often resulting in death. His arms trembled around her as he thought of what might have happened. Tightening his hold, resting his chin on the top of her head, he closed his eyes, not wanting to imagine losing her.

"I'm so sorry, Sarah."

Pulling back to look up at him, she touched a finger to his lips. "You've already apologized. It's over. I'm fine. There's no need for you to fret about it any longer."

"I could have—"

"No, Colin. I don't want to hear of what might have happened or how you still think it was your fault. I made the decision to go into the lagoon, and I'd make the same decision again." She dropped her hand, nestling her face into his chest. "Do you remember what Geneen told you the night I took the fever?"

His brows furrowed as he tried to remember what was said. "Nae. I can't say as I do."

"Then I'm glad she thought to tell me," Sarah laughed. "Geneen told you I've been prone to fevers ever since I was a young girl. They come fast, spike high, then disappear. Some people get stomach pains or earaches. I get fevers. This one was no different than the others I've had."

He narrowed his eyes, trying to recall the conversation, but couldn't remember Geneen ever mentioning Sarah's tendency toward high fevers. "She's certain we talked of it?"

"Oh, aye." She dropped her arms and stepped back. "You were worried. I doubt you remember much of anything, except trying to help your ma. Now, no more of this worry. I don't want misplaced guilt to mar our wedding on Saturday." Holding out her hand to catch his, she turned toward the house.

"About the wedding..."

She shot him an evil glare, her lips thinning into a slim line. "Colin MacLaren, unless you are telling me you no longer want me, we *will* marry Saturday." Dropping his hand, she stormed toward the house.

Ach, what a fool I've become, he thought as he heard the door slam behind her. His mother had warned him. Even Blaine had seen what he didn't. Pinching the bridge of his nose, he accepted Sarah was no longer the compliant, accepting girl he'd first met. A strong, determined, and loyal woman had taken her place, and she loved him. Climbing the stairs to the front door, he whispered a prayer that he could be the kind of husband she deserved.

"Deal me in." The tall, hulk of a man with thinning dark hair streaked with gray pulled out a chair, glaring at those around the table.

"Sure thing, Lon. We'd given up on you."

Lonnie Coffman scowled, picking up the cards in his large, beefy hands. He played one hand, then sat back, not feeling the urge to continue.

"You hear any more about where the girls might have gone?" Deft tossed down his cards, leaning back in his chair. Lon trusted no one more than Deft, his friend since their time as orphans on the streets of St. Louis.

"Let's move over to the bar," Lon said, not wanting anyone else to hear their conversation. He'd learned the girls were gone as soon as they rode back to town after one of their raids. It had been over two months with no sign of them. Everyone knew the man Lon had left to guard them would never have let them leave. In his early sixties, he'd ridden with them until his gun hand gave out to the pain of gout. His job had been to guard the girls at their place in the mountains, keeping watch on them as they cooked the meals and cleaned. He was the man Lon left in charge when the men rode out. Lon held no great love for any of the three, but they were kin and belonged to him.

"Nothing. Some say they were spotted heading north weeks ago."

"Coral is resourceful and probably had it planned for months, waiting for the right time. Don't know why you're so set on finding them. They were nothing but trouble." Deft took a sip of his drink, rolling the glass between his fingers. "If you're that set on getting them back, I say we ride to either Pine Top or Mindell. Unless they were lucky enough to find passage with a group of travelers, there are only three towns they could go—Mindell, Conviction, and Pine Top." Deft leaned forward, resting his arms on the bar. "We can't show our faces in Conviction. Weather's going to be getting rough north of here in a few weeks, and the trail to Pine Top will be treacherous when the snow starts. It's your decision, Lon, but you should make it soon or accept they're gone for good."

"They ain't gone for good," Lon growled, keeping his voice low. "Coral will never leave the other two, and who'd take in three girls? They're hiding. Maybe not too far from here. Besides, you know I can't let them wander around knowing what they know."

"Suppose so. It's too bad their mama taught them right from wrong. If you'd found them sooner, schooled them in the real way of life, we might not be in this fix." Signaling the barmaid, Deft watched as she filled their glasses, then walked away.

"We both know I was looking for their ma, not them. If they hadn't seen and heard so much, I'd let them go and not waste any sleep over it." Tossing back his drink, he considered Deft's words. "It's too late to track them now. We'll wait for spring. But we *will* find them, and when we do, I won't waste time keeping them around for sentimental reasons." Glancing around once more, he leaned closer to Deft. "I've another job I want to do while we've got the chance. If we can drive a herd to Sacramento, I've got a contact who will pay a good price for however many head we bring him."

"What are you getting at?" Deft asked.

"We already heard about the rancher near Conviction who's getting married, and all his men are invited."

"I remember one of the men having drinks with a drifter who'd ridden through Conviction and overheard some people talking about it. He said no one would be guarding the herds during the ceremony and celebration. Don't know how reliable the information is, though."

"That's right." Lon glanced around, lowering his voice. "No one will be looking for us, and few would think our gang interested in moving from robbing banks to rustling. We get in and out, move the cattle south to my contact, sell them, then ride back to Crocker. The money will be easy and quick."

Deft nodded, his mouth twisting into a wry grin.

Lon looked at his men, still playing cards at a nearby table, and walked over, taking a seat. "Listen up. Tomorrow, we ride to a ranch near Conviction. We're moving into rustling for a spell."

"If anyone tries to stop us?" one of the men asked.

"Same as always. Kill them."

Circle M Ranch

"What can *I* do, Mrs. MacLaren?" Pearl clasped her hands in front of her, a hopeful look on her face. Everyone else had a job, even Chrissy and Alana.

"Well, now, let me think." Kyla wiped her hands on a towel and set it aside, her mouth curving into a smile. "How about you help me slice the meats and put them on platters?"

"Oh, yes." Nodding her head, Pearl hurried to a cupboard, grabbed a platter, and set it on a nearby table as Kyla placed a roasting pan next to it.

"Have you ever used a carving knife before? One to cut large pieces of meat?" Kyla laid a knife on the table next to the pan.

"Many times. Me, Coral, and Opal cooked all the time for the men at the hideout—" Pearl clamped a hand over her mouth, her eyes going wide as she took a step away from Kyla.

Her face blank, Kyla glanced at Pearl as if she hadn't heard the slip. "Sounds to me as if you have lots of experience, lassie."

"Um...yes, ma'am."

They worked in silence until Quinn's mother, Audrey, walked in with her oldest daughter, Heather, and her middle son, Bram, all carrying breads, pies, and plates of cookies.

"Put them on the table," Kyla instructed, clearing a large space.

Audrey looked at her sister-in-law, seeing she hadn't dressed for the wedding. "The men have the tables and benches in place, a platform for the band, and the trellis you asked them to build for the ceremony. Now, you need to let the girls and me finish so you can get ready. The reverend will be here within the hour."

Kyla glanced around, swiping a sleeve across her brow. "There's still so much to do."

"Not as much as you think." Placing an arm around her shoulders, Audrey guided her to the stairs. "Now, upstairs with you. Do you need my help?"

"Nae, I can manage. You might look in on Sarah, though. She's in the downstairs bedroom with Geneen, Coral, and Opal. I haven't heard a sound from them in a long time."

Knocking on the door, Audrey pushed it open, her jaw dropping open at the beautiful sight before her.

"Oh, my. Aren't you a vision, Sarah."

Glancing over her shoulder, Sarah's face lit up. "Do you think he'll like it?"

"Ach, lassie, Colin may well be struck speechless when he sees you." Audrey stepped closer, careful not to get too close to Geneen and Coral, who were sitting cross-legged on the floor, finishing the hem. Opal stepped around them, applying the last of the ruffles.

Compared to what they'd find in a large city, the fabric choices in Conviction were limited. Viewing the selections at the general store, Sarah had become mesmerized by a beautiful blue satin patterned with cream-colored flowers.

Kyla designed a beautiful dress, using her wedding gown as a guide. The same color of tulle comprised the veil, finished with a wide ruffle of the blue satin fabric and tiny pearls.

"How much time do we have before the reverend arrives?" Geneen asked as she stood, making certain the hem fell evenly.

"Not long. Kyla is getting ready."

"And Colin?" Sarah moved to the edge of the bed, letting Geneen spread out the dress so she could sit.

"The men are at my house. I suspect they're well on their way to helping Colin build his courage," Audrey laughed.

"You mean with whiskey? Surely he wouldn't get drunk before our wedding." Sarah's voice betrayed her anxiety at walking down the aisle toward a man dizzy on liquor.

"Don't worry," Audrey said. "I've never seen Colin drunk. Besides, he has a good head on his shoulders. I'm certain the lad will restrain himself."

"Ma, the reverend is here. He's waiting in the study with a cup of coffee. I'll let Aunt Kyla know." Heather's gaze lingered on Sarah for a brief moment, her expression unreadable, before she turned.

"Heather, aren't you going to say anything about how beautiful Sarah looks?" Audrey crossed her arms, raising one brow.

"Um...sure, Ma." She took one step closer, looking Sarah up and down. "Real nice. I like the color." She cast a quick look at her mother, then hurried out.

"I've never known a woman who reacts the way Heather does." Geneen put the supplies in the mending basket.

"To what?" Sarah asked her sister, cocking her head to one side.

"Well, anything having to do with clothes, hair, chores, boys..."

"Ach. Heather has no use for boys or much of what she considers frivolities that interest most women. Sometimes, I think she wishes she'd been born a man. I'd better check on Kyla and make sure the reverend is comfortable. Coral and Opal, come with me. I could use your help downstairs." Taking one last look at Sarah, Audrey closed the door behind them.

Geneen pulled a chair close to the bed and sat down, shooting a look at the door. "Don't say a word to anyone, but I believe Heather is sweet on Caleb."

Sarah's eyes widened. "Why would you say that? I've seen nothing to show she has an interest in *any* man." At one time, she'd thought Geneen might have feelings for Caleb. Her sister had laughed, saying he was like a brother to her.

"The way Heather looks at him when she doesn't know anyone is watching." Touching Sarah's arm, Geneen stood. "I'm going to see how long before you're to come outside. I hope it's soon."

"No more than me."

"Are you ready, lad?" Uncle Ewan clasped Colin on the shoulder. "It's time to claim your bride."

Colin finished the last of the whiskey he'd been nursing for over an hour. Quinn and Blaine had done their best to push his drinking along, holding out the bottle whenever he took the slightest sip. In contrast, Brodie and Caleb had been the voices of reason. His concern for Sarah since the fever had kept his enthusiasm under control. After their conversation, he'd allowed himself to again look forward to finally taking her as his wife. He'd let nothing ruin the day, such as too much whiskey.

"I'm ready." A broad smile spread across his face as he slammed the empty glass on the table, looking at his family. "Lads, I'm ready."

Approaching the ranch house, Colin spotted all the people mulling around, turning to look at the group of men as they reined their horses to a stop near the barn.

"Looks like Ma invited the whole town," Blaine chuckled. He knew Colin had little use for large crowds. "You'll have to endure it this once."

"I'll be focused on Sarah. Nothing else concerns me today." He scanned the crowd, looking for his bride.

"She won't be out here," Blaine reminded him. "You're not allowed to see her before the ceremony."

Colin didn't have to wait long. Within minutes of arriving, his uncles ushered him to his spot near the reverend, the music started, and all eyes turned to the front porch. Geneen came out first, taking her place at the front, across from where Colin stood next to Quinn. Chrissy and Alana, who couldn't control their giggles, came out next, almost skipping toward Geneen.

Smiling at his young sisters, Colin let his gaze return to the porch just as Sarah came through the front door. As the next oldest brother after Colin, she'd asked Blaine to escort her, thrilled when he accepted.

Keeping her eyes locked on Colin's, she took his hand. From that moment on, the ceremony became a complete blur.

When the reverend finished, announcing them to their guests, Colin turned toward her, his heart hammering in his chest. Cupping her face in his hands, he placed a firm, sweet kiss on her lips, then put an arm around her shoulders as a cheer erupted. The last five years had been long and lonely, but she was now his.

Chapter Nineteen

Lon looked down at the scene below. From his vantage point, not only could he see his men rounding up well over a hundred head, but also the party at the ranch house less than a mile away. Music, loud and raucous, wafted through the still night air, a huge advantage when rustling a herd of bawling cattle.

The best news had come when they saw where the cattle were pastured. Two small sets of hills shielded the area, silencing the noise of the herd from the ears of the revelers.

"We're ready, Lon." Deft reined up next to him. "Appears no one will discover they're missing until late into the night or tomorrow. You're right. Easiest money we'll ever make."

"Don't be too hasty. We still need to drive the cattle south, get our money, and return to Crocker. A lot can happen during that time." Lon chewed on a piece of jerky as he watched the celebration. He'd heard from a man who'd recently passed through this area that the MacLaren family owned Circle M Ranch. The name sounded familiar, but he couldn't place where he'd heard it. It didn't matter. Whether he'd met any of them or not, the cattle were now theirs and would fatten their pockets for the winter. "Let's get out of here."

Lon split the herd into two groups, lessening the chance that if the MacLarens became aware of their actions sooner than anticipated, they'd have a chance of getting at least one group to the buyer. They were to meet the buyer and his men north of Sacramento. From there, he'd take the cattle to San Francisco, where a steady demand for beef gave them the best price. Texas ranchers accounted for some of the meat, but cattle from California could be provided more profitably than those from other states, especially when Lon hadn't put a penny into raising them.

Although they kept a steady pace, pushing the cattle harder than a normal drive, the night passed without incident. Lon kept lookouts riding well behind each herd, looking for any sign they were being followed.

"I believe your bride has danced with every man here," Quinn joked, sipping the whiskey-laced punch. "Uncle Ewan and Uncle Ian both took turns. Seems those two are enjoying themselves."

"As is most everyone from what I can see." Colin watched Sarah laugh at something Caleb said as he swung her around to a fast tune.

Two fiddlers, one banjo player, and the piano man from Buckie's Castle saloon hadn't slowed down since they started an hour before. Colin and Sarah had begun the celebration with the traditional first dance. Afterwards, his uncles, brothers, cousins, and friends hadn't let her take a rest. Instead of being exhausted, she looked exhilarated, as if she could go on for hours.

"Will you be taking Sarah into town tonight?"

"Didn't you hear?" Colin shot Quinn a surprised look.

"What?"

"Your ma invited my family to stay at your house tonight. Sarah and I will have this place to ourselves."

"Ach," Quinn groaned. "You mean I'll be sharing the place with five more?"

"At least they're kin. Besides, sharing a bed with Blaine won't be so bad." Colin's eyes crinkled at the corners as his lips tilted into a grin.

Narrowing his gaze at Colin, Quinn turned to the table behind him, refilling his glass with punch, then reaching into his pocket for the flask of whiskey, adding a decent pour to his drink. Taking a large swallow, he used his glass to point to the hills behind them. "It may be a good night to stay at the hunting cabin. I'm sure we could use more game."

Colin chuckled. "Aye. Might as well tell Blaine. He said that's where he planned to go after the party."

"Your brother is a smart man." Setting his glass on the table, he rubbed his hands together. "Time to get my legs moving. I believe I'll ask Geneen to dance."

No sooner had Quinn left than Kyla walked up, slipping her arm through Colin's.

"She is a beautiful bride. You are a lucky man."

Colin glanced down at his mother to see her gaze still focused on Sarah, who now danced with Blaine. "Aye, Ma. There were times I never thought this day would come, thinking I was a fool for believing she'd wait for me." He swallowed the lump in his throat, remembering the hours he sat at the lagoon, wondering if he should forget her and move on. He thanked God he hadn't.

"From the first day you saw her, you set yourself on a path to claim that girl. Your da and I knew you'd never be happy until you saw this through. You are a stubborn man, Colin MacLaren, much like your da." She smiled up at him. "But you're a good man. Faithful, smart, with a steadfast heart. I never doubted you'd go for her." She tightened her grip on his arm, then stepped away. "I do believe you owe me a dance. And if you time it right, you might even be able to steal your bride away from all those eager men who've claimed her attention."

Knowing his mother had given her blessing for them to disappear into the house, Colin couldn't hide his enthusiasm.

"I like your idea, Ma. May I have this dance?"

"Why, I'd be charmed, lad."

Sarah needed no additional encouragement when Colin whispered in her ear they'd be leaving the party. He'd danced with his mother, taking Sarah in his arms as soon as the song ended, giving her one more dance before they retreated inside.

"We'll need to say our goodbyes." Sarah glanced up at him as the music ended.

Taking her by the arm, Colin guided her near the band and turned her toward their guests.

"Thank you all for coming to celebrate our marriage. Stay as long as you like, enjoy the food, drink, and dancing." He smiled down at Sarah. "My bride and I will say goodnight to you now."

Before Sarah realized his intentions, he swung her up into his arms. Blushing a deep red, she buried her face in his neck at the boisterous laughter and cheering that followed. Within seconds, he'd covered the distance to the porch, kicked the door open, then shut it as the guests continued to hoot and holler their approval.

Laughing, she tightened her hold around his neck, placing kisses on his jaw.

"You keep doing that and we won't make it to the bedroom," Colin warned, his body already heating.

Sarah didn't stop. Instead, she unbuttoned his shirt, reaching inside to spread her hand across his hardened chest. On a deep growl, he took the stairs to their bedroom, backing inside, sitting on the bed, with her secured in his lap.

"So you plan to tease me, lass?" He didn't wait for her to answer before capturing her mouth in a searing kiss, unbuttoning her dress as he increased the pressure of his mouth on hers.

Sarah whimpered as his tongue stroked and teased, creating an intense ache that pooled at the juncture of her thighs. As she arched toward him, he growled, seizing her hips, crushing her against him.

Pulling back, Colin stared into her face. When she opened her eyes, they were glazed with passion, while his own were dark with desire. Lowering his head, he brushed a trail of kisses down her neck, lingering at the sensitive hollow of her throat.

Sarah moaned, squirming closer to him, craving more. "Colin..." she breathed out on a ragged sigh.

"I know, love." He turned, placing her on the bed. Removing his boots and shrugging out of his coat and shirt, he stretched out beside her. Spreading the dress and the chemise open, he drew in a deep breath, marveling at her beauty. He'd never get tired of looking at her, touching her.

Tracing a line down her jaw and creamy column of her neck with his lips, he whispered words of love, exciting her with his deep, husky voice. His hands moved under the hem of her dress, searching for pleasure points as she curled into him, writhing as if trying to bury herself within him.

"Colin, please." Her whimpered plea sent a wave of urgency through his body.

He undressed her in unhurried, slow movements, then removed his own clothes, lowering his body over hers. Gathering her warm, pulsing body to his, he took her mouth in another passionate kiss.

"You're mine, Mrs. MacLaren," he whispered before he could no longer wait to claim his bride.

"You've worn me out," Colin growled into her ear as he felt her hand move slowly up his chest.

"You don't feel worn out." Her throaty chuckle sent a new wave of passion through him.

Grabbing her hands, holding them captive between their bodies, he traced the outline of her lips with his tongue, then sealed his mouth on hers. His kiss was slow, gentle, savoring, until he heard the low rumble of her stomach. Chuckling, he raised up, gazing into her eyes.

"Come on. We both need food."

As much as she wanted to continue, she also knew they needed to eat. Looking around, her gaze landed on her wedding dress, then darted back to Colin.

"My clothes are in my room." She tossed off the covers and stood.

"You could always—"

"No, I couldn't." Folding her arms, she started for the door.

Laughing, he grabbed her arm. "Stay here. I'll get them." Pulling on trousers, he headed for her room downstairs. He hadn't hit the last step when the front door burst open, Blaine and Quinn rushing inside.

"Sorry to bother you the day after your wedding, but we have bad news. We thought you'd want to know right away." Blaine glanced around.

"She's still upstairs. Wait in the study. I'll be right there." Grabbing her clothes, he dashed back up the stairs and into their room, handing them to her. "Blaine and Quinn are downstairs. Something has happened."

Slipping into her clothes, she nodded. "I'll be down in a bit."

Kissing her check, he grabbed a shirt and left, closing the door behind him.

Walking into the study, buttoning the last button of his shirt, he sighed. "All right. What is so urgent you couldn't wait a few more hours?" He slumped into a chair, crossing his ankles.

"Over a hundred head of cattle are missing," Quinn hissed. "We think it happened during the party."

Cursing, Colin stood. "Do Ewan and Ian know? Have you sent out any men?"

"Yes, and not yet. We thought we should decide how best to organize the men. Some will need to stay, but it will take quite a few to locate the herd and bring them back," Blaine answered.

"Any tracks?"

Quinn nodded. "Yes, but we stopped the men from riding out. We can't afford to send them on some wild goose chase."

"Let me tell Sarah what's going on and I'll meet you outside."

"I'll get Chieftain ready," Blaine volunteered, heading straight to the barn, Quinn not far behind.

Colin met Sarah standing outside the study. "You heard?"

"Yes. I know you must go." She clasped her hands in front of her.

He took her hands in his, a look of regret on his face. "I'm sorry."

"Don't say that. I'm a grown woman and can handle the problems of running a ranch." She leaned up, placing a kiss on his cheek, then moved her lips to his mouth.

Taking her in his arms, he deepened the kiss, then pulled back, his large hands cupping her face. "I'll be home as soon as I can." Turning, he didn't look back as he joined Blaine, Quinn, and the other men outside, vaulting up on Chieftain. "Show me the tracks."

Lon and his men were well away by mid-morning the next day, closing in on their destination. It had been much easier than he imagined. Perhaps he'd been wrong in his decision to stay clear of rustling all these years.

"They should be waiting for us over the next rise, Lon. We may want to send a couple men ahead to make sure." Deft tossed the cheroot he'd been smoking on the ground and looked toward the horizon. "It's almost been too easy."

"I was thinking the same." Lon glanced over his shoulder as if he expected the ranchers to descend upon them at any moment, guns firing. "Let's get the herd to the new owners before our luck changes."

In less than an hour, Lon and Deft reined to a stop next to a group of five well-armed men. In addition to a pair of pistols in holsters around their waists, each had a rifle at the ready.

"You Coffman?" the oldest of the group asked.

Lon guessed him to be of average height, was as round as an oak barrel, with a sallow complexion and a large, bulbous nose.

Lon nodded. "You Smith?"

"That's right. How many head you got for me?"

"Last we checked, a hundred thirty, but you should count them."

"Oh, we will." Smith turned to the man next to him. "Take the men and get started. Signal when you're done so we can finish up and send these men on their way."

"Sure thing, boss."

"Deft, you go with them," Lon ordered, not trusting any of his other men to keep a close watch on Smith's people.

"You have any trouble getting them here?" Smith watched as the men rode toward the front of the herd.

"None. Didn't expect any. 'Cept it almost seemed too easy."

Smith cocked his head at Lon, his brows knitting together. "No men were posted, keeping watch on the herd?"

Lon shook his head. "One of the ranchers was getting married. Didn't leave a single person with the herd while they celebrated. Like I said, the job went almost too well. A man could get drawn into believing it would always be this simple."

"Easier than robbing banks?" Smith asked, his hand moving to the butt of his gun.

Lon's gaze narrowed on the man. "What do you mean?" he ground out, his face a mask as a hand inched toward the revolver on his hip.

"Don't get me wrong. I don't care how a man makes his living, as long as he deals fairly with me." He leaned over and spat on the ground. "But don't get to thinking I don't check on who I'm doing business with. No one's business stays private for long."

Lon's jaw tightened, but he held his tongue. Reining his horse to get a better look at the herd, he saw Deft raise a hand at the same time as Smith's man.

"Appears we're good on a number."

"A hundred thirty head." Smith reached into his pocket, pulling bills from a pouch. Counting out the agreed upon amount so Lon could watch, he handed the money over. "Pleasure doing business with you."

Taking the money, Lon slid it in a pocket. "I'll contact you if another opportunity comes along."

"Make sure you do."

Lon rode straight toward Deft and his other men. "Let's get out of here." He had no reason to suspect Smith would try to come after them, but he didn't want to take the chance. The sooner they put distance between them, the better he'd feel.

"You mean we ain't goin' into Sacramento to celebrate, boss?" One of the older members of his gang rode up beside him, looking tired and haggard.

"Not this time. We need to get away while we've got plenty of daylight ahead of us. Besides, there's still a chance those ranchers will try to track us and I don't want to run into them." Lon didn't explain his actions to too many. Deft and this man were two of them.

"Guess I'll just save my celebrating for Crocker." Reining around, he rejoined the rest of the men, passing along the news.

"It's a lot longer, but I'm thinking we ought to take the northeastern trail, Lon. If the ranchers come after us, they'll probably be west of here."

He sent Deft a wry grin. "You still got those badges we used after killing the sheriff and deputies from River City?"

"In my saddlebag."

"Pass them out to the same men who rode with us to Oregon. We'll take the western trail to Crocker and send the others on the eastern trail. No reason all of us should waste a couple extra days on the trail. Tell them I'm being careful by splitting into two groups. As always, we'll split the take when we get to the cabin."

Deft twisted in the saddle and reached into his saddlebag, pulling out a leather pouch.

"Here you are, Sheriff Walker."

Pinning it to his shirt, Lon laughed at how easy it was to be a lawman of convenience.

Chapter Twenty

Colin, Blaine, Quinn, Brodie, Caleb, and a few cowhands rode out within an hour of learning about the missing cattle. Following the tracks from the herd, they traveled several hours before Caleb noticed someone following them and moved off the trail. Holding up, he waited until the rider got closer.

Muttering a curse, he moved back onto the trail.

"What the hell are you doing out here, Heather?" The set of his jaw and hard voice made it clear how he felt about her disobeying her Uncle Ewan's orders not to ride out with the men.

Jutting her chin toward him, she started to ride past until he blocked her path. Letting out a disgusted breath, her face turning the deep pink hue Caleb had come to expect when she was angry, Heather glared at him.

"I have every right to be here. In fact, I have more right than you. I'm a MacLaren and they're my cattle, too."

"Is that what this is about? Your pride got hurt because I'm part of the search and you aren't?" The thought she'd endangered herself by riding out alone angered him. That she'd done it out of spite caused his blood to boil.

"Of course not," she spat out. "And I don't have to explain myself to you."

"But you *do* have to explain yourself to us."

Heather winced at the hard tone of Quinn's voice. So engrossed in their argument, neither she nor Caleb had seen Quinn and Colin ride up.

"You were told not to follow us for a good reason. They needed you to help at the ranch. What were you thinking?" A muscle in Quinn's jaw quivered, betraying his deep frustration. "Well?"

She glanced at Caleb and Colin, then moved her gaze to her brother, her eyes sparking in indignation. "I'm old enough to make my own decisions. All three of you know I can ride, shoot, and handle myself as well as any man. I—"

"Stop right now," Quinn roared. "Your abilities had nothing to do with the decision our uncles made and you know it. They needed you at the ranch. What if the rustlers return, threaten the family? Or worse, Coffman and his gang ride back to Conviction?" He took a breath, trying to control his rage. "Do you ever think of anyone but yourself, Heather?" Quinn turned toward Colin. "What do you want to do?"

Colin sent her a brutal stare, not shifting his gaze as he spoke "We can't send her back now. Those clouds are threatening and it'll be dark soon."

"Fine. She'll ride with Caleb."

"*What*? No. You're not going to saddle me with your family's problem. Someone else can keep watch on her. I want nothing to do with a woman with a lousy attitude and overblown belief in herself." Caleb didn't wait for a response, reining his horse around to catch up with the rest of the men.

"I wouldn't ride anywhere near you, Caleb Stewart—even if you were the last man on earth," Heather shouted after him, her face turning the shade of a ripe tomato.

Quinn covered his mouth to control his laughter as Colin looked away so she wouldn't see his grin.

"You'll ride with Blaine, and don't even consider arguing with me," Colin added when she started to open her mouth. "There are reasons we pair up, but I don't have time to explain it to you. Do you understand me?" As the oldest male MacLaren cousin, Colin's orders were followed without question when their uncles weren't around.

She nodded, irritation crossing her face at his condescending tone.

"We better join the others so we can cover as much ground as we can before the storm hits." Quinn moved up beside Heather. "Do what you're told without hesitation or I'll treat you as I would any other brat."

Colin hunkered down in the saddle, his duster doing little to protect him from the pounding storm. It had started without warning minutes before, giving them scant time to pull on their trail coats and look for shelter.

"Up ahead." Blaine pointed to a rock outcropping. It would be a tight fit for everyone, but better than no shelter at all. He looked at Heather, who hadn't left his side since joining them. At least she had the good sense to bring her own duster.

They'd always gotten along well. He respected how much she wanted to be her own person, although he didn't condone her habit of ignoring direct orders from the uncles or Colin. She let her fierce independence and quick temper get the better of her most of the time. If she didn't learn to control it, she'd eventually put herself, or others, in danger.

"You two go ahead and check it out. I'll let the others know." Colin reined Chieftain around, motioning the men toward the shelter. "Quinn, make sure we aren't missing anyone, then have some of the men gather as much dry wood as they can."

Somehow, they found enough to keep a fire going. They'd stripped the gear from their horses, placing the animals within sight outside the shelter. Bigger than what they'd thought, it held all of them and their gear. If the wind didn't shift too much, they'd stay protected until the storm passed.

Slouching near the back wall next to Blaine, Heather dug into her saddlebag, pulling out some jerky and offering him a piece.

"Thanks."

The others barely acknowledged her, feeling the tension between Colin, Quinn, and her. No one ignored her more than Caleb, which bothered her more than a little. Heather didn't understand what about him set her off, but she refused to let herself dwell on it.

"It's a shame these rustlers had to interrupt Colin and Sarah's honeymoon." Blaine washed down his jerky and hardtack, handing the canteen to Heather.

"Guess so." She took a few sips before handing it back.

"She's a good match for him, don't you think?"

"Seems to be."

"You want to tell me what, besides Quinn and Colin being angry with you, has you so riled lately?"

She didn't answer at first, pursing her lips, furrowing her brows. Setting the rest of her jerky aside, she lowered her voice. "Do you think I'm disagreeable?"

Blaine couldn't hold back his chuckle. "Aye, lass. I do think you can be contrary."

Crossing her arms, Heather bit her lower lip, considering his words. "I don't know why I'm not like the other women. All I want to do is work on the ranch. My skills are as good as any man—even you.”

“You see, that’s where you create problems. Listen to the men talk. Do you hear them talking about how good they are at their jobs? How they can shoot or ride better than anyone? Nae. Only braggarts do that.” Standing, Blaine smiled down on her. “We all know how good you are, Heather. You don’t need to keep reminding us.”

“We have riders coming toward us.” Quinn had been taking a turn as lookout. The storm had let up, giving him an expansive view from his perch atop a large boulder. The early evening sun had yet to disappear, providing good visibility.

“How many?” Colin asked, pushing up from where he’d been resting.

“Looks to be five, but there could be more.”

“All right. Let everyone know. Brodie, spread the men out so the strangers don’t get a full count of our numbers. Try to keep out of sight so they don’t see your faces.”

“What is it?” Blaine came to stand beside Colin, followed a few minutes later by Brodie and Caleb.

“Riders. Blaine, get Heather in a protected spot and stay with her. *Warn her to keep her mouth shut.* The rest of you take your weapons and find good places to keep watch as they approach. I’ll try to get them to move on." Colin checked his gun, then slid it back into the holster.

A few minutes later, five riders came into view.

"Stop right there," Quinn called from his position.

Colin watched as the men got closer, noting something familiar about the man in the lead.

"Gentleman, I'm Sheriff Walker and these are my deputies." He took a good look at Colin. "Have we met?"

"I believe we have. We were on our way north to River City. You and your men were headed south, searching for bank robbers." Colin moved closer, extending his hand. "I'm surprised you're still out here and so far south."

Coffman shook his hand before sliding from his horse. "I do remember you. Mind if we take a rest before moving on?"

Colin turned, extending his hand toward the fire. "Feel free to share the fire. We have some coffee left, but not much else."

"Just a rest is all we need." Coffman looked around, noting the number of horses didn't match the number of people standing around the fire. He recognized one other man, but not the others. "Where you headed?"

"Back to our ranch. Been chasing rustlers."

"Any luck?" Coffman asked, warming his hands by the fire.

"None. The rain washed out the trail. We're heading back in the morning. You?"

"On our way home to River City. Never found a trace of those outlaws." Coffman glanced at his men, nodding toward their horses. "Thank you for the use of your fire. We'll be riding on."

Colin kept his arms loose by his sides until the sheriff and his men were out of sight. Crossing his arms, he continued to watch, feeling a keen sense of unease. Something wasn't right. He'd yet to meet a sheriff who traveled this far from their town chasing outlaws. They usually left that to the Rangers or federal marshals.

"What do you think?" Brodie's eyes narrowed as the last rider disappeared, his hand resting on the butt of his gun.

"I don't like it." Colin's expression clouded as doubt took hold. "We'll keep two people on watch in three hour shifts. Plan to get out of here at first light."

Those not on watch snuggled in their bedrolls, but few slept. Colin sat on the ground, his back resting against the wall of the rock shelter. He'd take the second shift on watch. Closing his eyes, it took seconds for his thoughts to turn to Sarah, wondering if she were in bed, or perhaps waiting by a window, watching for him to appear.

His chest tightened as images of her on their wedding night controlled his thoughts. Her beauty was so much more than he remembered. Gracing him with one of her brilliant smiles could stop his heart, making breathing almost painful. He still had a hard time believing they'd found each other and married. The odds had never been in their favor, yet they'd beaten them.

Leaving so soon after getting married had been one of the most difficult decisions he ever had to make. Thankfully, she'd understood, not pouting or putting pressure on him to stay as some women might. He'd chosen well, thanking God she'd also chosen him. Giving into sleep, he drifted off, a picture of Sarah in his thoughts.

"Sarah, come quick!" Geneen stood on the front porch, watching a group of riders approach.

"What is it?" Sarah dashed outside, still holding the damp kitchen towel in her hands. Looking in the direction Geneen stared, she let out a squeal, dropped the towel, and ran down the steps toward the riders.

Seeing her, Colin pushed Chieftain into a gallop. Coming to a stop, he swung to the ground, taking her in his arms and swinging her in a circle. "Ah, lass, I've missed you."

"No more than I've missed you."

Crushing his mouth to hers, he set her on the ground, tightening his grip.

"Colin...everyone is watching," she whispered against his lips, pushing away.

"So? Let them." But he dropped his arms, already missing the feel of her.

"I'll take Chieftain for you, Colin." Blaine held out his hand for the reins, nodding at Sarah.

"Welcome home." Sarah could feel her face heat, knowing they'd all seen.

"Glad to be back." He walked toward the barn, leaving them alone.

"Did you find the cattle?" Sarah asked Colin.

"No. We lost the tracks in the storm. I sent men ahead several miles, but they saw nothing. I don't understand how they could have gotten so far without us catching them." Taking off his hat, Colin swiped an arm across his forehead.

"Uncle Ewan said they had at least a twelve hour start. He and Uncle Ian rode into Conviction to let Sheriff Yost know about the rustlers." She watched as a look of disgust appeared on Colin's face.

"Ach. The man will do nothing." The mention of Yost reminded him of seeing Sheriff Walker. "We crossed paths with Sheriff Walker last night."

"Sheriff Walker of River City?" Slipping her arm through his, they walked up the porch steps.

"He and his deputies rode into our camp last night. I already told you we first saw him on our way to find you. That means he's been away for almost four months. I've never known a sheriff to travel that far tracking outlaws. And four months? It's a long time to be gone."

"True, especially given his health."

"Health?" Colin turned toward her, his brows creasing.

"Well, you met him. He's older, overweight, and Ma used to say he had a little drinking problem." Sarah started toward the kitchen, stopping when Colin reached out and grabbed her arm.

"Are you certain you're talking about Sheriff Joe Walker?"

"Of course. I've met him often enough at church and when he'd come out to the house. Why?" Sarah cocked her head, her eyes flashing confusion.

"The man we met is younger, tall, slender, and appears to be as healthy as a horse."

Sarah watched as he took a few steps away, as if trying to reconcile the man he met to the one she described. Cursing, he turned back toward her.

"I'm sorry, Sarah, but I've got to ride into town and send telegrams to the deputy in River City and Reverend Olford."

"There's not a chance I'm letting you out of my sight. I'm going with you." Untying her apron, she hurried into the kitchen, letting Geneen know where she'd be. "When Kyla returns, please let her know where I've gone." Voices from the entry indicated her mother-in-law had just gotten home. "Sounds as if she's already here."

"You're riding out so soon?"

"I have to, Ma. It's important I get confirmation about the man we met on the trail. It won't take long, but don't hold supper for us. We'll eat in town."

"Who's going with you?" Kyla asked.

"I am." Sarah slipped her arm around Colin's waist. "You don't think I'd let him go without me, do you?"

"I suppose not." Kyla chuckled, watching Colin lean down to place a kiss on Sarah's neck. "Well, you'd best get going if you want to get the message off today."

"Do you want to wait for a response?" The clerk read over the messages, collecting the money Colin set on the counter.

"You can find us at the hotel restaurant."

"Fair enough. I'll get these right off."

Taking Sarah's hand, he walked down the boardwalk toward the sheriff's office. Stepping inside, he didn't wait for Yost to look up.

"I need to see your wanted posters."

Yost set aside his pen, looking up at Colin, then standing when he saw Sarah. "I understand congratulations are due, Mrs. MacLaren."

"Thank you, Sheriff."

"Now, why do you want to see the posters?" Yost asked.

Colin explained their two encounters with the man claiming to be Walker. "I believe they're outlaws and may have been part of the group who stole our cattle."

"Well, guess it wouldn't hurt to let you look through them." Opening a drawer, he pulled out a stack of papers, tossing them on the desk. "Here you go."

Colin quickly went through them, shaking his head as he reviewed each one. He'd almost given up when one of the last posters presented a perfect image of Sheriff Walker. The name underneath was Lonnie Coffman. Holding it up, he handed it to Yost.

"This is who we saw."

Yost's eyes widened. "You're certain?"

"I am. We saw him twice. When they rode out, they headed in the direction of Crocker."

"You're not thinking of going after them, are you?"

"I'm here to let you know what we saw. It means they're still around and could be a continued threat to Conviction. What you decide to do is up to you." He took Sarah's hand. "Come on. I owe you supper."

Chapter Twenty-One

It took them several minutes to sit down at their table as several townsfolk stepped forward to congratulate them. Many had been at the wedding and chided him for disappearing with his bride so early. He laughed, taking Sarah by the elbow and escorting her to their table.

Ordering the night's special, he held her hand, settling it on his thigh as they waited for their food. He could feel tremors passing through them.

"You're shaking." Lifting her hand, he placed a kiss on her knuckles.

"What will you do if you learn Coffman killed Sheriff Walker?" Her hand tightened in his, her brow creasing with worry. She saw his jaw clench and eyes narrow.

"Not much we *can* do. It's up to the law to go after him." He hadn't told her of their plans to find Coffman and bring him to justice for the killing of his pa and Uncle Gillis. No one knew, except those who'd sat around the fire, deciding the fate of the outlaws. He didn't intend to lie to her, telling himself this wasn't a real lie. She simply didn't know what the men had discussed.

"Here you are." The server placed their plates in front of them, then walked away.

"So you don't plan to go after him in Crocker?" Raising an eyebrow, she picked up her fork, taking a small bite of roast.

He chewed his meat, taking his time, figuring out how best to answer. Thankfully, he didn't have to when he saw the clerk from the telegraph office come rushing toward them.

"These came for you, Mr. MacLaren." Holding out the messages, he nodded at Sarah. "Sorry for the interruption, ma'am."

"Here you are." Colin reached into his pocket, handing the man a coin.

"Thanks. I'll be in the office a little while longer if you want to send any other messages."

Colin nodded as the clerk walked out.

"What do they say?" Sarah leaned toward him, noting his bleak expression.

Handing them to her, he sat back in his chair, his face a mask.

"Oh no." She looked up at Colin. "Coffman killed the sheriff and his men?"

"Looks that way." He pushed his plate away, taking out a few bills and setting them on the table. "I want to send another telegram to River City, then we'd better head back home. I need to speak with Quinn and the others about this."

"Do you think Coffman and his men are the ones who stole the cattle?"

"Aye, I do."

A light snow began to fall when Colin and Sarah were within a mile of the ranch. They'd taken their horses as he'd wanted to get to the telegraph office as fast as possible. Now he wished they'd taken the wagon.

Riding into the barn, he helped Sarah down. "I'll take care of your horse. You go inside and get warm, and ask Blaine and Caleb to meet me in Quinn's barn. I need to ride over there." The houses were far enough apart for privacy yet close enough to ride between each in a few minutes.

"Can't it wait until tomorrow?"

"The information is too important to put off. We've run into Coffman and his gang twice, and I *know* they're the ones who robbed the bank and killed Da. I'm certain they're also the ones who stole our cattle. I'm not willing to take the chance they might ride back here to see what else they can take." Placing his hands on Sarah's shoulders, he turned her to him. "The man is dangerous and Crocker isn't that far away. We need to figure out what we'll do if they swoop back down on us. Now go ahead into the house. I'll be back as soon as I can."

Watching her leave, he felt a pang of guilt. What they planned had little to do with fortifying the ranch and everything to do with revenge. But no one could know that, except for those riding to Crocker to dispense justice.

Swinging by Brodie's house, they rode to Quinn's, meeting Blaine and Caleb as they entered the barn.

"I'll let Quinn know we're here," Blaine offered, dashing toward the house, pulling his collar up to ward off the increasingly heavy snow.

"You know Heather will want to be involved." Brodie moved further into the barn where the heat from the animals warmed the air.

"Aunt Audrey will never let her go," Colin said as he and Caleb followed.

"That didn't stop her from following us before," Caleb grumbled, crossing his arms and leaning against a stall. His mouth drew into a thin line as Blaine returned, followed by Quinn and Heather. Someone would have to set Heather straight, but it sure wouldn't be him.

"What have you learned?" Quinn asked, stopping next to Colin.

"Sheriff Walker isn't who he says he is. My belief is he's Lon Coffman." Colin pulled out the telegrams and passed them around.

"Sonofabitch..." Quinn's voice trailed off as he read each message, then passed them along. "We were within feet of being able to take care of the men who killed my da and yours, Colin."

"They were right in front of us, twice," Brodie grumbled, his face set.

"We know now, and there's no reason we can't go after them." Caleb handed one of the telegrams back to Colin. "What do you want to do?"

"I'm repeating what we decided before, but no one outside of here can know what we plan—not our families, ranch hands, or the sheriff." Colin looked at each person, his gaze stopping on Heather a second longer than the others. He or Quinn would have to speak with her, tell her she wouldn't be going with them. If she argued, they'd have to tie her up and leave her in the barn loft for one of her younger brothers to find. He prayed it wouldn't come to that. "We have a good idea Coffman is back in Crocker. He and his men rode that way when they left our camp. If we're going to do this, I think it should be soon."

"Agreed. It will take a few days to make sure we have all the work sorted out here. Truthfully, Colin, I think we're going to have to tell our families *something*. They accepted our decision when we left to find the herd. They'll be suspicious if we all ride out again now." Brodie dragged fingers through his hair, then rubbed his forehead.

"Who do you suggest we tell?" Colin asked, knowing Brodie was right.

"I'll have to tell Da. The work here is greater than ever. He'll never let me go if he doesn't have a good reason."

Caleb stepped out from where he stood in the shadow of the loft. "We'll tell them we've gotten a lead on who stole the cattle and have decided to go after them before the bad weather hits. It's not a lie, just not the whole truth."

"Aye. It's a good idea, Caleb. What do you think, Colin?" Quinn asked, anxious to reach a decision.

"Agreed. We take a day to make sure the work is covered and ride out at sunrise the following morning. If we ride hard, we'll reach the outside of Crocker by the end of the second day. Brodie and Blaine ride in, locate Coffman, ride back to our camp, then we make plans to go after him."

"You make it sound simple, Colin, but we're dealing with experienced gunmen. People who kill for a living. We may all be good with weapons, but we aren't killers. We're ranchers." Blaine could always be counted on to be the devil's advocate, and with good reason. His family's enthusiasm would often outweigh their common sense.

"We won't be reckless, Blaine. We'll learn where Coffman holes up, keep watch on it, and take him when few of his men are around. If we're fortunate, there'll be no shooting."

"Oh, there'll be shooting," Blaine stated. "The question is...will all of us make it back home alive?"

"I forbid it, Brodie. None of you should be riding to Crocker to take out your vengeance. Let the law know where Coffman is and they'll arrest him." Ewan stormed around his desk, face hard. "It's too dangerous and it's not your job. They could arrest you for murder."

"We don't plan to kill them, Da." Brodie held his hands in front of him, palms out. "We'll do our best to bring them back to Conviction for trial."

"To watch them hang," Quinn interjected. He knew they'd have problems with Ewan. Ian, who leaned against a wall, had said nothing so far, his features stoic.

"I can't stop the rest of you, but I won't allow Brodie to go off on some dunderhead quest for revenge. The odds none of you will get shot, or killed, aren't good. We can't afford to lose any of you." Ewan looked at Colin and Quinn. "Have you told Kyla and Audrey?"

"Nae, and we don't intend to. There's no reason anyone except the two of you needs to know where we'll be riding and why." Colin held his ground. He had no intention of being dissuaded.

Ian pushed away from the wall, walking toward the desk, leaning his hip against it, glancing at the young men in front of him. "I want to make certain I understand. Your plan is for all of you to ride to Crocker, find Coffman—without raising suspicions in a town riddled with outlaws—ride to his hideout, capture him and any of his men who are there, then ride back with them in tow. Is that correct?"

Colin cleared his throat, speaking for all of them. "Aye, that about sums it up, Uncle Ian."

Ian glanced at Ewan. His situation was different. Sean, his oldest at eighteen, wasn't a part of the group of older cousins. He belonged in the next oldest set of MacLarens. It wouldn't be long before they'd insist on being included in these meetings.

"Like Ewan said, other than Brodie, we can't stop you from going, although I agree it should be left to the sheriff." He held up his hand when he saw Colin start to protest. "I understand you think Yost is incompetent, and I agree. But he's all we have unless we can get federal lawmen involved, and that hasn't happened so far."

"Have you contacted them?" Quinn asked.

"They've refused to send anyone." Ian shook his head in disgust.

"Da, I won't be left behind. I've given my word and I plan to keep it." Brodie's jaw worked as he thought through what he could say to persuade his father to step back and let him go. "I'm twenty-two. By rights, you can't stop me. More importantly, if it had been you or Uncle Ian who'd been killed, the others would ride with me to find your killers."

"He's right, Uncle Ewan. We've talked of this many times. Stealing our cattle and learning Coffman murdered the sheriff in River City just adds to the reasons we must go. Yost won't do anything and there's no law in Crocker. Unless we do something, he and his gang will continue to roam at will, stealing and murdering without conscience." He cast a quick look at the others. "This is our land, our home. We must protect it from men like Coffman or he'll see us as weak, unable to defend what's ours. I, for one, won't let that happen."

"I don't like it, Brodie. Taking the law into your own hands goes against everything we've taught you." His color had returned to normal, but the set of Ewan's jaw and cold tone of his voice conveyed his feelings. Letting his gaze move from his son to his nephews, he felt a surge of raw emotion at what fine men they'd turned out to be. He couldn't imagine losing any one of them. "I cannot give my consent," he said, holding up a hand when Brodie started to protest. "Nor will I stop you."

Brodie began to step forward, but came to a halt at his father's stern stare.

"If you weren't of age, I'd lock you in the cellar until the others were long away. As it is, you are a man and have the right to make your own decisions, no matter how wrong I believe them to be."

"I understand." Brodie hated to cause his father more worry than he already had, but he refused to let the others ride to Crocker without him.

"Nae, lad, I don't believe you do. But the decision is made and I see there'll be no changing your mind. Now, tell Ian and me the details, leaving nothing out."

Crocker, Nevada

"Taking the MacLaren cattle was a good decision, Lon." Deft sat on a chair outside their cabin. Located a few miles above Crocker, no one besides the men who rode with Coffman had ever been there. Not because it couldn't be found. No one seemed to have the nerve to confront him on his own land. "I say we ride in and take another hundred head before the weather turns bad."

Tipping his chair back on two legs, Coffman considered what Deft said. It had been easy and they'd made about as much money as they had from most bank robberies, without the high risk.

"Doesn't feel right. We'll find another ranch. It's too soon to hit the MacLarens again."

"Do you have a place in mind?" Deft took a draw from his cheroot. Over the years, he'd learned to heed Lon's instincts. His gut feelings had saved them from certain trouble on many occasions.

"A ranch south of MacLaren's. I heard about it from a couple cowhands at the saloon last night. Seems a new man has taken it over. He has five or six men working with him. They stopped by his place looking for work, but he told them he wasn't hiring anyone else for the winter."

"South would be a longer ride to the cattle, but would take less time driving them to Smith." Tossing the cheroot on the dirt, Deft laced his hands behind his head. "They give you the rancher's name?"

"Nope. Didn't ask." Standing, Coffman walked to the edge of the wooden porch, staring up into the star-filled sky. "I'm going to send some men to verify what those cowhands said. I don't want to ride there without knowing more about the size of the herd and the number of men he posts to watch them."

"That'll delay it at least a week. Right now, the weather's clear."

"Yep. It's a risk I'm willing to take. We're not riding in there blind. I'll send the men out tomorrow, then I'm riding into Crocker. I want to send a telegram to our friend in Sacramento."

Chapter Twenty-Two

"Don't try to lie to me, Colin MacLaren. You're going after them, aren't you?" Sarah stood in their bedroom, fists on her hips, eyes blazing.

Colin had climbed the stairs at a slow pace, sorting out his thoughts, trying to figure out how to tell Sarah he'd be leaving in the morning. He wouldn't lie to her, but he couldn't be completely honest. Entering their bedroom, he knew by looking at her something was wrong.

Tossing his hat on the bed, he leveled his gaze. "Going after who, Sarah?"

"Coffman."

"Where'd you hear something like that? Seems like a pretty foolhardy idea to me." He hoped she'd back away, but the tightening in his stomach warned him she wouldn't.

"Aye, it would be. And exactly something you, Quinn, and the others would try." Dropping her arms to her sides, she walked a few steps closer to him. "Tell me I'm wrong."

Turning away, he slipped out of his shirt and walked to the washstand, dipping his hands in the cool water, splashing it on his face. Picking up a sliver of soap, he scrubbed his hands, then rinsed them. Reaching for the towel, he saw Sarah holding it out to him, a scowl marring her normally cheerful face.

"Thanks." He took his time drying his hands while making a decision. Tossing the towel aside, he sat on the edge of the bed, reaching out his hands to her. "Come here, lass."

Hesitating, she swallowed the lump of fear in her throat, not sure she wanted to hear what he had to say. Stepping in front of him, she kept her hands clasped in front of her. "Just tell me, Colin."

Prying her hands apart, he engulfed them in his much larger ones, pulling her to him, settling her on his lap. Nuzzling her neck, he let his lips drift lower, hearing her sigh just before she pushed both hands against his bare chest and stood.

"You're not going to distract me. I want to know if you're going after Coffman." The way her brows furrowed, eyes narrowed, and lower lip trembled, he knew what she wanted to hear...but he couldn't lie to her.

"Aye."

"Why? It's not your job. You're a rancher, not a gunslinger or the law." Her voice held a pleading tone he'd never heard before.

Taking a clean shirt from the wardrobe, he slipped it on, buttoning it as he turned toward her. "Because the law won't do it. Coffman killed Da and Uncle Gillis...and Sheriff Walker. He's the one who took our cattle. There's every reason to believe he'll try to rustle from us again. He knows Yost won't do anything, and we can't get any help from federal law enforcement." Spreading his arms, he held his palms out. "We're the ones who must protect the ranch and our families from Coffman and men like him."

"It doesn't have to be you. You can hire others. Gunmen, bounty hunters, men who do it for a living. You don't have to risk your lives when you can hire someone to go after them." Sarah turned away, attempting to control the moisture building in her eyes. She didn't want him to see how afraid his decision made her, how she didn't know what she'd do if she lost him. Whirling back around, her glassy eyes beseeched him in a way that tore at his heart. "If you decide to leave, I don't know that I'll be here when you return."

Her words struck him as if she'd thrust a spear into his gut. The death of his father had been the one other calamity that had hit him this way. His jaw tightened as his mouth twisted into a thin line, eyes showing the pain her words caused.

"We will not handle troubles by walking out on each other, Sarah." His words were calm, hard, spoken with an unyielding certainty. "I'm sorry if you don't understand why I must do this. I hoped to have your support. If I don't, I *will* go anyway, and I expect you to be here when I come home." Grabbing his hat off the bed, he slammed it on his head. "If you aren't, I *will* find you and bring you back."

Colin hadn't expected his last night home to be this rough or this painful. He and the others spent considerable time preparing to leave the following morning

He'd been surprised Heather hadn't put up more of a fuss when he told her she wouldn't be riding with them. She'd argued, throwing out every reason she should be included. In the end, her shoulders sagging, she promised not to follow them and walked away. Quinn had also tried to talk to her, but she'd shut him up quickly, telling him Colin had already told her the decision. At least they didn't have to worry about her on the trip. Not so with Sarah.

"You know she'd never leave you, Colin." Blaine settled a hand on his shoulder and squeezed.

"You heard?"

"Our bedrooms are right next to each other and the walls are thin," he smirked. "If it gives you peace, I doubt Ma or anyone else heard."

"How can you be so certain she won't run when I don't even know it myself?" Colin closed his saddlebags, placing them over the saddle on a nearby stand.

"The woman's daft for you," Blaine chuckled. "Besides, she's not a fool. Once she thinks through our reasons for going, she'll understand why this must be done."

Colin hoped Blaine was right, but his chest still tightened at the thought she might not be waiting when he returned.

When he slipped into their bedroom close to midnight, he spotted the small bump under the covers. He sat on the edge of the bed, stroking her hair, watching her breathe. He loved her so much, yet he couldn't do what she wanted. He knew if she stayed, there'd be many times they'd disagree. She'd have to learn you don't solve differences by running.

Taking off his clothes, he slid into bed, wrapping his arms around her, and pulling her back into his chest. No other woman would ever feel this right. He prayed when she woke and found him gone, she'd think of all the reasons they were together—and be here when he came home.

Sarah woke with the sun streaming across the bed. Stretching, she reached behind her, sitting up when she felt the cold sheets. Her mind raced as she jumped out of bed, dressed, and hurried downstairs. She came to a halt in the kitchen door at the sight of

Kyla, Aunt Audrey, Geneen, and Heather sitting at the table, holding hot cups of coffee.

"Have they left?" she gasped, hoping she hadn't missed him.

"Aye, lass. About an hour ago. Colin said you looked so peaceful, he didn't want to wake you. He said he'd see you when they got back." Kyla filled a cup with coffee for Sarah, then indicated the chair next to her. "We were talking of the boys growing up and how little has changed. They are still stubborn and willful. It's the way of a MacLaren, I'm afraid."

Taking a seat, Sarah wrapped both hands around the cup, gripping it tight. Staring at the hot liquid, she glanced up, her gaze on Kyla. "I don't know if I can do this. The waiting, not knowing if he'll return."

"Ach, of course you can, lass," Kyla scolded. "You're much stronger than you know. Colin's always believed it. That's why he waited all those years for you." Her uncompromising gaze focused on Sarah. "You cannot be paying him back by being afraid or taking off like some weak female."

Sarah winced at the subtle rebuke, not knowing how to respond. She wasn't as certain about her strength as either Colin or her mother-in-law. Although her da had been stern with his daughters, he'd also protected them from many hard aspects of life.

"She's right, Sarah. If you're thinking of going, you need to push it from your mind. You've accepted this life, this family, and you'll not be leaving us." Audrey gave her a warm smile, resting her hand on the top of Sarah's. "Besides, I don't care to imagine what Colin will be like if you aren't here when he returns."

"You all talk as if you're certain they'll all come home safe." Sarah wished she had the same faith.

"We are. What good would it do to think otherwise?" Kyla walked to the sink, rinsing her empty cup. "Now, we all have chores."

"Geneen, if you're up to help, we could use an extra rider to keep watch on the herd."

Heather's comment surprised everyone, no one more so than Geneen. She jumped up, excitement on her face.

"Of course I'll help. Let me get my gloves and—"

"First, come with me. I have some pants and a shirt in my saddlebag that should fit you. They'll be better than your dress."

Geneen followed Heather, almost giddy with anticipation of being out with the herd.

"Well, I'll be..." Audrey's voice drifted as she hurried to the front window, watching the two young women talk, Heather gesturing toward the far pasture.

"You know what I think?" Kyla asked. "It's a sign all will be well."

"Crocker is a short distance ahead. We'll camp here." Colin had to raise his voice to carry over the pounding rain, which had started a mile back. They'd been prepared for it, already wearing their dusters.

"We should move off the trail. Down there." Quinn pointed toward a clearing hidden behind a thick stand of trees and brush.

The rain stopped as swift as it had started. As much as they wanted a fire, they didn't think it wise to draw attention to themselves this close to town. Besides, Coffman's place might be real close to where they stood.

"You still want Blaine and I to ride into town tomorrow, find out where Coffman lives?" Brodie crouched down next to the others, tearing off a piece of jerky and chewing.

"I don't see any reason to change," Colin answered. "No one's seen either of you. The rest of us were in the saloon a couple months ago, spoke with the bartender and the owner of the general store. I think you'll have a better chance of getting information for us."

"I'd start with the owner of the general store, maybe the blacksmith. Try to avoid talking to the bartender. He's real suspicious of newcomers. Don't mention you're from Conviction. Just say you're riding through on your way to Oregon. We don't want them connecting you to Da and Uncle Angus."

Quinn took a bite of hardtack, wishing he had coffee to wash it down with instead of tepid water.

"Do you think Coffman got a look at you two when he rode into our camp a couple weeks ago?" Colin wondered why it hadn't occurred to him before.

"Heather and I were crouched down behind some bushes, and Brodie was with the men scattered behind the boulders. Even if he noticed the number of horses, it's doubtful he would've spotted us." Blaine stood, stretching his arms above his head. "I'm going to get some shuteye."

Colin watched as Blaine grabbed his bedroll, placing it under a tall pine. He hoped they hadn't made a mistake deciding to come on their own. As he told Sarah, there wasn't anyone else. Everyone, including the law, feared Coffman. Sheltered in the small town, protected by other outlaws, he came and left at will, robbing banks and rustling cattle with no one to stop him. It would take at least thirty lawmen to get close to ridding the town of its outlaws.

"It'll be all right. We MacLarens are a lucky bunch." Quinn glanced at him as if he'd read his mind.

"And what about you almost dying in River City?" A slight smirk crossed Colin's face.

"Lucky shot, nothing more."

"Well, it has to be done. Caleb's taking first watch, then I'll relieve. You okay with the third watch, Quinn?" Colin stood, looking at the surrounding area, spotting nothing through the thick brush.

"I've got it. Get some sleep. We're all going to need it."

"What can I do for you gents?" The thin, elderly shopkeeper stroked his beard as he looked them up and down.

"Coffee, sugar, and bacon." Brodie glanced at the shelves behind the man. "And some of those dried apples."

"Anything else?"

"That's it." Brodie pulled out some money as the clerk scratched out the totals on a piece of paper. "You been here long?" He kept his voice casual, as if just making conversation.

"About ten years. Long enough to see it change."

"Change?"

"Used to be a quiet spot on the way west. Now, most wagons go around us, only sending in a few men to buy supplies." The old man glanced out the window, as if keeping watch.

"What happened?" Blaine asked, stepping forward.

"You men aren't from around here, are you?"

"Nae. We're from down south, heading to see friends in Oregon," Blaine answered, resting his hands on the counter.

"Well, you boys watch yourselves. We've got some bad elements in this town. Me and the missus been talking 'bout leaving, but don't know where to go. We got a small house a ways from the north end of town, so nobody much bothers us. Those on the east, well, let's say they're living too close to the devil to suit me."

"Sounds like that's an area for us to avoid," Brodie replied, crossing his arms.

"There's a man who lives out that way—"

"Hey, old man. The boss needs coffee, flour, sugar, and molasses. And make it quick."

Brodie and Blaine turned at the loud voice coming from just inside the door. A man of average build with a double set of pistols on his hips glared at them, daring them to start something.

"Nice talking to you boys. Have a safe journey." Turning, the old man got to work putting together the new order.

Taking the hint, Brodie and Blaine picked up their supplies, passing the gunfighter on the way out.

"Let's talk to the blacksmith before we head back." Brodie swung up on Hunter, glancing over his shoulder at the man who continued to glower at them. They rode toward the other end of town, dismounted, and walked their horses toward the smithy.

"Do you have time to check my horse?" Brodie asked, coming to a stop several feet from the forge.

The blacksmith looked up, then walked over to the horse, lifting his leg up. "Looks like it's loose. It'll take a couple minutes and you'll be on your way." The blacksmith set Hunter's leg down, then searched for the right nail.

"You been here long?" Brodie asked.

"Long enough. Thinking I'll head toward Conviction after the winter." Leaning against Hunter, he wrapped a large, brawny hand around his leg, lifting it so he could work on the shoe.

"Not enough business?"

He glanced up, a look Brodie couldn't decipher passing across his face. "Enough. Just time to move on."

"We're looking for a place east of here. Maybe you know where it may be." Blaine moved up closer, watching the man finish with Hunter.

"Got a name?"

"Coffman. We've got a message to deliver to him."

Not answering his question right away, the blacksmith quoted a price for the shoeing. Swiping a dirty sleeve across his forehead, he looked them over, then shrugged. "Take the road east out of town. When it forks, take the trail to the right. A friendly word of advice, though. Unless you're looking for trouble, I'd stay far away from there."

"Thanks for the information." Brodie paid the smithy, then took Hunter's reins and walked outside before turning to Blaine. "I think we have what we need. Let's head back."

Riding through town, no one seemed to spare them a glance as they disappeared out of sight.

Chapter Twenty-Three

"We agreed?" Colin asked, glancing up at the others, seeing each nod. "We'll move out late tonight, finding a place to camp close to Coffman's place. We'll keep watch until we're ready to take him."

Taking a trail around the town, they took the road heading east, Caleb keeping watch behind them, Blaine riding ahead to spot anyone coming their way. They never would've found the cutoff if there hadn't been a clear sky and partial moon. Within a few minutes of the fork, they heard the sounds of laughter, then spotted smoke drifting skyward. Riding closer, they saw a cabin nestled between dense pine trees in the distance.

"Let's backtrack and leave the horses. We'll go the rest of the way on foot." Colin reined Chieftain around, riding until he found a place well off the trail, but only a few hundred yards from the cabin.

Spreading out, they covered the distance in little time, the noise from the house covering their approach.

"I don't see any guards. Guess they're pretty certain no one will ever find them." Quinn hunkered down next to Colin.

"Or they don't believe anyone would have the guts to come after them."

"If that's the case, we'll have surprise on our side. I'm going to move up close, see if I can get a look in a window." Quinn moved toward one side of the house. Stretching up, he peered inside, his head shifting as he got a good look. Glancing back at Colin, he held up four fingers.

He flattened himself against the side of the house at the sound of approaching horses. Nodding to Colin, he bent low, dashing to the back where Caleb, Brodie, and Blaine had taken positions.

"I'll put the horses away, Lon, while you go inside." Deft grabbed the reins to both horses, walking to the stable along the side opposite Colin.

Glancing toward the back, Colin saw Quinn slip along the side, waiting under a window until Coffman had gone inside, followed by Deft several minutes later.

"You got news, Lon?" one of the men asked.

"We leave day after tomorrow. The boys confirmed there's enough of a herd to make it worth our while. I've heard back from Smith. He'll be waiting at the same place." Coffman set his hat on a hook, leaving his gun belt secured around his waist. "No drinking tomorrow night. I need everyone clearheaded."

"Guess tonight's our chance to go back to town for drinks. You got objections to that, boss?"

"Not as long as you're sober tomorrow night." Lon settled into a chair as all the men, except Deft, started to grab their gear.

Quinn had heard enough. He signaled Brodie, Caleb, and Blaine to circle around to meet Colin. Within minutes, he'd joined them. Waiting until they'd returned to their horses, he kept his voice low.

"Lon Coffman is there. He's the tall, hulking one that rode up last with the black hat. He told the others they got news about a herd large enough to take. They plan to ride out day after tomorrow."

"We only have tonight and tomorrow to take him then." Colin cursed their luck. They didn't have time to wait for the perfect opportunity, and he refused to ride back home without the outlaw. "Tomorrow night it is."

"No, Colin. We have to get them tonight," Quinn insisted. "Most of the men are riding to the saloon. Coffman and one other are staying behind. It will be our best chance to get him."

The sound of riders had them walking their horses as far off the trail as possible a minute before Coffman's men passed them on their way to town. Waiting until they were certain there were no stragglers, Colin signaled everyone to follow him. He found a secluded spot a mile from the cabin to discuss their plans.

"They're both still awake, an almost empty bottle of whiskey sitting between them. Their gun belts are hanging on a wall across the room. If we all rushed in, it would be hard for either to reach them." Quinn had just returned from checking on the two outlaws once more. "We should move now, before the other men return."

Colin nodded, glancing at his brother, cousins, and Caleb. "This is it, lads. Are you all ready?"

"Let's get the sonofabitches and take them to the Conviction jail," Brodie ground out, echoing the sentiments of everyone around the small circle.

"All right. Everyone get in place. Wait for my signal," Colin said. "And, lads, take no unnecessary chances. We'll all be going home—alive."

It didn't take long for them to get into place. Positioning himself at the front door, Colin looked at Quinn on his right, then Brodie on his left. Each glanced behind the cabin, then nodded, indicating Blaine and Caleb were ready to come through the back door. Drawing his gun from its holster, he held up one, two, three fingers. With a hardy kick, the door burst open. Colin dashed in, followed by Quinn and Brodie, as Blaine and Caleb did the same at the back.

"Get your hands up and don't move. There's nothing more we'd like than a reason to shoot each of you." Colin braced himself for the slightest move from either man. That's when he saw the smirk on the face of the one Quinn identified as Coffman. The next moment, his hand dropped, reaching under the table. A shot from behind Colin had Coffman cursing, holding up his now bleeding hand.

"He told you to stay still. Guess you don't listen too well." Brodie's gun still smoked.

"Nice shot," Colin said, never taking his gaze off the two men. "There are five guns trained on you. We don't care if you reach Conviction alive or dead. If we had a choice, dead is best."

"We need to get them out of here before the others return." Caleb held up a rope, moving behind Coffman. "Stand up and put your hands behind you."

"Don't do it, Lon," Deft snarled.

"Shut up, Deft. We both know they'll never get five miles outside of Crocker." He looked up at Colin. "Do your best. Truth is, you're all dead men."

"Go ahead, Blaine. Tie up the other one, then we'll get them on their horses."

Brodie disappeared outside, bringing two horses from the stable. Securing Coffman and Deft on the saddles, they bound their feet to the stirrups, encircling each man's waist before wrapping the rope around the saddle horns.

"We're ready, Colin."

"Good. Let's get out of here."

Instead of taking the road toward town, they took a trail north toward Mindell. Several miles past

Crocker, they veered west, then north, before riding southwest.

"Where the hell are you taking us?" Coffman demanded when they came to a brief stop.

"None of your business. Now, keep your mouth shut or we'll gag you." Colin pulled out his water canteen and took a swallow, offering none to Coffman or Deft. "Let's go, lads."

Three hours later, after changing direction several times, they came to a stop and slid off their horses as the sun rose in the east.

"We'll rest here a couple hours." Colin didn't want to stop, but the horses needed a rest.

"I'll watch our backs," Caleb offered.

"I'll keep you company." Blaine slapped him on the back, glad to be so close to home with no sign of the rest of Coffman's gang.

"Hey, you can't keep us on these saddles." Coffman looked around, his eyes panicked as Colin and the others walked off after securing the horses.

"Think we should give them water?" Quinn took a long draw from his canteen, handing it to Colin.

"You gonna share yours?" Colin took a swallow, handing it back.

"Nope."

"Neither am I. We'll be at the river soon. They can drink their fill there. By tonight, we'll be a short day's ride to the ranch and the jail in Conviction."

Circle M Ranch

"What will we do if they find him, Coral? I don't want him taking us again." Pearl clasped her hands in her lap, rocking back and forth, worry etched on her young face.

"Don't fret so, Pearl. They mean to take Coffman to jail, not bring him here." Coral couldn't allow herself to think of him by any other name.

"But if they do and he sees us, he'll take us away," Pearl pleaded.

Coral wrapped an arm around her youngest sister, trying to console her. "According to Mrs. MacLaren, they went to arrest him. He'll be tied up like the turkeys Ma used to make. You remember that, don't you, Pearl?"

"I remember."

"Well, he'll be just like that. I promise. He'll never be able to hurt us again."

"Not ever, Coral?"

"I give you my word. No matter what else, he'll never lay a hand on us ever again." Coral tightened her embrace once more before letting go. "Now, let's go help Heather and Geneen in the barn."

Pearl ran ahead, dashing past Heather's horse tied to the post outside and into the barn toward the two women.

"Can't it wait until tomorrow, Heather? It's been a full day and my backside's sore." Geneen rubbed it as if to emphasize the pain at being in the saddle several days straight.

"I'd at least like to meet them." Heather had heard about their newest neighbor. The last few weeks she'd done her best to change some of her ways. Blaine's honesty about her actions affected her enough to make her think hard about the way she treated others. She'd decided to start with Geneen, who'd made no secret about her desire to count Heather as a friend.

"You go ahead. I'll ride out in a few days, pay my respects."

"All right. Tell Aunt Kyla and Ma I'll be along for supper." Heather walked past Pearl, ruffling her hair before mounting her horse and riding south.

"Where's Heather going?" Coral had stayed back, thinking about her conversation with Pearl, trying to figure out what she could do to protect them from Coffman. Truth was, she'd thought of little else since the men left over a week ago. A part of her wanted to do as she'd dreamed night after night for as long as she could remember. Another part hoped to never see her kin again.

"She decided this afternoon was a good time to meet our new neighbors. I guess a foreman's been running the ranch south of here for a while. Now the owner's shown up and decided to stay."

"We should all go meet them." Pearl looked up at Coral and Geneen, hoping to take the pony she'd been allowed to ride.

"Why don't you, Coral, Opal, and I ride out there in a few days? We'll bake a pie and take it to them. They'd like that, don't you think?" Geneen put a hand to the small of her back, trying to ease the pain. She thought her soreness from riding in the saddle every day would have disappeared by now.

Pearl watched Geneen's motions, her face growing somber. "Ma used to rub gooey stuff on Pa's back when he worked too hard."

"You remember that?" Coral looked at her sister, astonished.

"I remember lots of stuff, Coral."

"Well, I'm headed into the house for a warm bath before helping Kyla with supper. Maybe the men will be back by nightfall." At least Geneen hoped they would. The mood around the ranch had deteriorated each day, worry turning to despair with each sunset.

"Smart decision, Colin. Coffman's men are probably still waiting for us on the trail near Thumb Butte." When they spoke of it, Quinn hadn't thought the idea of taking an extra day to ride home a good idea. He had a whole other opinion of it now that

334

they were almost at their ranch. "We'll be home for supper."

"We'll feed them, head to town, and hand them over to the sheriff." Colin pulled his collar up to ward off the chill. Fall had given way to early winter. It wouldn't be long before the first heavy snow fell. "I'll be glad to get them behind bars."

"I'll be glad when they hang." Quinn reined Warrior to a stop on a high peak overlooking their ranch. "Now isn't that a fine sight?"

Reining up next to him, Colin spotted the ranch house, wondering if Sarah would still be there, waiting for him. "That it is, lad. A real fine sight." Taking a quick glance over his shoulder, he saw Blaine, Brodie, and Caleb still at the back, keeping watch on Coffman and Deft.

Colin refused to let himself believe Sarah had left. In his mind, he pictured her running onto the porch to greet him, the same as she'd done every day since he'd brought her home. Then they'd go inside and talk of their day, deciding where to ride each evening. His heart told him there were still many more of those days. He took a deep breath, hoping his heart held the truth.

"Did you hear that?" Sarah's head shot up.

"What, lass?"

"Outside, Kyla. I thought I heard horses." Standing, she dashed to the front window, pulling back the curtains, letting out a shriek. "They're home!"

Geneen and the others came up beside her, looking out. "Who do they have with them?"

"Must be the men they went after," Sarah answered, hearing a gasp from behind her. Turning, she saw Coral race up the stairs, Opal and Pearl right behind her. "I wonder where they're going."

Geneen leaned toward her. "Remember, it's their father the men went after. I'll bet they're hiding."

"We'll make sure that man never gets near them again," Kyla interjected. "Come on. Let's greet the men."

Colin kept his gaze trained on the front porch as Kyla, Audrey, and Geneen came outside, followed by his younger siblings. The one person he didn't see was the one he needed most. When the hope began to fade, he saw the front door open. A moment later, Sarah stepped outside, her bright smile making up for all the worry he'd felt since leaving.

Jumping off Chieftain, he ran up the steps, gathering her into his arms, swinging her around. "Sarah, lass, you stayed," he whispered in her ear, placing kisses along her neck.

"Of course I stayed. Now put me down." Sarah laughed as her eyes glazed with unshed tears. She hugged him tighter as he set her feet on the ground. "Who are those men, Colin?"

His expression changed in an instant as his anger returned. He focused on the men tied to their saddles. "Lon Coffman and one of his men. We'll be taking them on into town this afternoon."

"They're the men who killed your da."

"Yes, they are." He looked over at his ma, who stood rooted in place. In all his years, he'd never seen hate cross her face—until today.

"Colin, we'll need to secure them in the barn until we're ready to leave." Quinn had followed him up the steps, giving Audrey a hug, telling her who the men were. Her expression matched that of Kyla's.

"I'll come with you." Dropping his arm from around Sarah's waist, he'd taken a few steps toward the prisoners when he heard a loud gasp from behind him. Turning, he saw Coral step outside, a rifle settled against her shoulder, pointed at Lon Coffman.

"Coral, no!" he yelled, a moment before a shot rang through the air and Coffman slumped in the saddle.

Dropping the rifle, she moved forward, her arms heavy, legs wooden as she walked down the steps, stopping a few feet from his horse. Staring up at his lifeless figure still tied to the saddle, her face showed no remorse.

"I told you I'd kill you one day."

For several long minutes, Coral stood without moving. Brodie walked up, gently turning her toward the house while Colin led Coffman's horse to the barn. They placed his body in the wagon, wasting no time taking it and Deft to Sheriff Yost, then returning to the ranch.

Kyla and Audrey took Coral to her room, waiting with her until she fell asleep. It took over an hour before anyone could coax anything out of Opal or Pearl. As they began to talk, the words tumbled out, creating a story none of the adults could imagine. When they'd told them all they knew, Sarah and Geneen took them upstairs, tucking them into bed.

"I'm so glad you boys brought the girls to live here." Kyla wiped a tear from her cheek, thinking of the cruelty of Lon Coffman.

Sarah sat next to Colin, holding his hand. "Who would've thought anyone could be so cold and brutal?"

"What should we do?" Kyla looked at Colin, her face ashen.

"Tell Yost the truth. Lon Coffman was their da's brother. He showed up at their place with Deft, worked for their da a while, then Coffman tried to force himself on the girls' ma. At least that's what I believe Opal and Pearl were trying to tell us."

"Sounded like it to me, Colin," Sarah said, the others nodding.

"Coffman shot his brother when he tried to stop him, then turned his gun on the girls' ma." Colin stared at the roaring fire in the living room.

"And the girls witnessed all of it." Sarah bowed her head, closing her eyes.

"According to Opal, he and Deft rode off with the girls, keeping them prisoners ever since, threatening them if they ever said a word to anyone about the killings. I can see why they ran." Colin scrubbed a hand down his face. "We'll have to speak with Coral before we say a word to anyone outside the family."

"I hope to God he didn't do anything else to them." Geneen stood, heading toward the stairs.

"Well, that's one sorry sonofabitch Yost won't have to waste jail space on," Colin murmured before taking Sarah's hand to lead her upstairs.

Three weeks later, everybody except Coral had moved on, letting Deft rot in jail as he awaited the arrival of the circuit judge. At first, Yost had hinted at charges being brought against her. His comments had been received with a great deal of contempt, as well as a groundswell of support for firing him in favor of someone who'd work harder to protect the citizens of Conviction.

Even with the MacLarens and the majority of townsfolk accepting her actions, Coral couldn't seem to move on. Each night, she'd thrash about, then awaken covered in perspiration, pushing those away who tried to help. Instead of receding as the days and weeks passed, her nightmares increased.

Coral refused to confide in anyone, tucking into herself as if holding all her emotions inside would solve the guilt she felt at taking a man's life—no matter how justified.

Pearl had been the one person to help the adults understand some of Coral's fear, believing her sister felt certain the MacLarens would send them away after what she'd done. No amount of assurances to the contrary could calm their fears, especially Coral's.

"I have a thought," Blaine offered one afternoon while the men were riding fences. "Why don't we adopt them? Maybe that will ease their minds and rid Coral of her nightmares."

"I think it's a great idea, Blaine." Quinn rode next to him, wondering why no one had thought of it before.

"Have you ever known a family to adopt someone? I sure don't know what needs to be done."

Colin liked the idea, too, and believed his ma and their uncles would approve.

"Do you think it's what the girls want? No matter how much they hated their uncle, it's still their family name." Brodie had no idea what would need to be done, but as long as the girls wanted it, he'd make it happen.

"Yes!" Opal's and Pearl's voices melded together when Colin and Sarah took them aside later that week and explained what the MacLarens proposed. Coral's face brightened for a moment at the news before slipping behind the mask she preferred to hide behind.

"What do you think, Coral? It isn't hard to do. We simply sign documents with our attorney stating you're taking the name MacLaren and relinquishing the name Coffman. We'd make you, Opal, and Pearl full members of the family, but only if it's what you want." Kyla sat next to her, reaching out a hand to touch Coral's arm. In truth, there wasn't any formal requirement for adopting them in California, but the uncles wanted to make it all official so no one could later claim they weren't legally MacLarens. It seemed the best course for everyone.

Coral caught her bottom lip between her teeth, glancing at her sisters, who nodded at her hesitancy.

"I want to be a MacLaren, Coral. Don't you?" Pearl stood before her oldest sister, her gaze solemn, her voice almost a whisper.

Looking up, Coral's mouth curved into a rare smile. "Yes, Pearl. I think I'd like that."

"All right everyone," Uncle Ewan interrupted the different conversations around the table, getting their attention. "We're here for our regular Sunday supper, except today we welcome three new MacLarens into the family. Coral, Opal, and Pearl are now officially part of our clan." He held up his glass, tilting it toward the girls. "Welcome, lassies. We're pleased to have you."

Following a few minutes of cheers and hugs, they settled into their normal Sunday banter, talking of chores for the following week until Ian mentioned the sudden resignation of Sheriff Yost.

"Ewan and I attended a meeting of the town leaders a few days ago. They made the decision to remove Yost and look for a new sheriff. I think it may have been the first decision having everyone's approval."

"What was Yost's reaction?" Colin asked, glad for the decision to rid the town of his incompetence.

"Strangely enough, he turned in his resignation the morning after our meeting. Seems someone must have warned him." Ian pushed his plate away and leaned back. "All I care about is he's gone."

"Any word on a replacement?" Quinn asked.

Ian shook his head. "Not that I've heard."

The table grew silent for a few moments before Brodie cleared his throat.

"I have one other announcement to make." He pushed away from the table, resting his hands on his thighs. "Seems a few of the town leaders *did* ask someone to take Yost's place. They offered him the position and he accepted."

"That so?" his father asked, his brows arching at the news. "Who is it?"

"Me."

Epilogue

Three weeks later...

"I doubt how you and Quinn feel about his decision will change his mind, Colin. Brodie is a grown man and he has his reasons for what he did."

Sarah and Colin had ridden into town the day before, taking a room at the Gold Dust Hotel for two nights to make up for the interruption the rustlers had caused in their honeymoon. So far, they hadn't seen Brodie. While Sarah shopped at the general store, Colin had stopped at the jail, leaving a message inviting Brodie to join them for supper tonight. So far, he hadn't responded.

"He shouldn't have done it the way he did. Uncle Ewan didn't have any idea of what he'd decided. I'll never forget the look on his face when Brodie made the announcement. In this family, we've always talked about decisions such as this first. It wasn't right." Colin had stated the same complaint since Brodie made his announcement, shocking the entire family. Sarah had grown used to his grumbling, figuring the reality of Brodie's new life would settle in after time.

"Let's go to breakfast, then see if we can find him," Sarah suggested as Colin escorted her downstairs to the dining room.

A small town by most standards, Conviction boasted two hotels. Both offered meals, although the quality had always been suspect in the one across the street. It had been added as an afterthought when the proprietor realized the Gold Dust made good money on the meals they served. A widowed rancher's wife had been hired to do the cooking, and her food had always been popular with the locals and visitors.

This morning, though, Colin found it hard to enjoy his eggs, bacon, and biscuits. His mind kept returning to Brodie and how much he missed him at the ranch. Perhaps his cousin would listen to reason after a while and return home. He couldn't imagine running the ranch without him.

"Look there." Sarah stared out the window at the jail.

Turning in his chair and following her gaze, he saw Brodie ride up on Hunter and swing to the ground. Looking around, he tipped his hat at a passing couple, then disappeared inside the jail.

"At least we know he's in town." Colin finished eating, pushing his plate away, noticing Sarah watching him. "What?"

"You don't plan to charge over there and demand he come home, do you?"

"As much as I'd like to, no. We'll invite him to supper, find out if he's met the new neighbor south of us, and that's all. No matter how much I don't like or understand it, I know it's his decision."

Walking across the street, Colin noticed a couple more stores than he'd seen on his last trip to town, and there was building going on at one end. The hotel clerk said another saloon and a couple more shops would be going up, as well as a newspaper. The growth made him realize how much Conviction needed a strong sheriff. As much as he didn't want to admit it, he knew Brodie would make an exceptional lawman, better than anyone Colin could think of.

Opening the door to the jail, they spotted Brodie walking from the back where the cells were located. "I wondered when you'd be coming to pay me a visit." Brodie set the keys on his desk, looking around Colin. "Quinn didn't come with you?"

"Not today. Sarah and I rode in alone. We're hoping you can take time to join us for supper tonight."

"Morning, Sarah." He sent her a broad smile, unlike the wary welcome he'd offered Colin. "I'd like to meet you for supper, as long as you don't try to change my mind about taking the sheriff's job." He nodded toward a couple chairs.

"You keeping busy?" Colin asked, pulling out a chair for Sarah.

"You'd be surprised—"

Brodie's head snapped around as the door burst open and a woman he'd never seen dashed inside. Taking deep breaths, she looked out the window, then turned toward Brodie, gasping for air.

"Can I help you, ma'am?"

"Are you the sheriff?" She turned to glance out the window once again.

"Aye."

Shifting back toward him, she wrapped her arms around her waist, eyes wide. "I hope you can help me. I think I killed my husband."

Thank you for taking the time to read Colin's Quest. If you enjoyed it, please consider telling your friends or posting a short review. Word of mouth is an author's best friend and much appreciated.

Please join my reader's group to be notified of my New Releases at:
http://www.shirleendavies.com/contact-me.html

I care about quality, so if you find something in error, please contact me via email at
shirleen@shirleendavies.com

About the Author

Shirleen Davies writes romance—historical, contemporary, and romantic suspense. She grew up in Southern California, attended Oregon State University, and has degrees from San Diego State University and the University of Maryland. During the day she provides consulting services to small and mid-sized businesses. But her real passion is writing emotionally charged stories of flawed people who find redemption through love and acceptance. She now lives with her husband in a beautiful town in northern Arizona.

Shirleen loves to hear from her readers.

Write to her at: shirleen@shirleendavies.com
Visit her website: http://www.shirleendavies.com
Sign up to be notified of New Releases:
http://www.shirleendavies.com/contact-me.html
Books by Shirleen:
http://www.shirleendavies.com/books.html
Comment on her blog:
http://www.shirleendavies.com/blog.html
Facebook Fan Page:
https://www.facebook.com/ShirleenDaviesAuthor
Twitter: http://twitter.com/shirleendavies

Google+: http://www.gplusid.com/shirleendavies

LinkedIn: http://www.linkedin.com/in/shirleendaviesauthor

Pinterest: http://www.pinterest.com/shirleendavies

Tsu: http://www.tsu.co/shirleendavies

Other Books by Shirleen Davies

Tougher than the Rest – Book One
MacLarens of Fire Mountain Historical Western Romance Series

"A passionate, fast-paced story set in the untamed western frontier by an exciting new voice in historical romance."

Niall MacLaren is the oldest of four brothers, and the undisputed leader of the family. A widower, and single father, his focus is on building the MacLaren ranch into the largest and most successful in northern Arizona. He is serious about two things—his responsibility to the family and his future marriage to the wealthy, well-connected widow who will secure his place in the territory's destiny.

Katherine is determined to live the life she's dreamed about. With a job waiting for her in the growing town of Los Angeles, California, the young teacher from Philadelphia begins a journey across the United States with only a couple of trunks and her spinster companion. Life is perfect for this adventurous, beautiful young woman, until an accident throws her into the arms of the one man who can destroy it all.

Fighting his growing attraction and strong desire for the beautiful stranger, Niall is more determined than ever to push emotions aside to focus on his goals of wealth and political gain. But looking into the clear, blue eyes of the woman who could ruin everything, Niall discovers he will have to harden his heart and be tougher than he's ever been in his life...Tougher than the Rest.

Faster than the Rest – Book Two
MacLarens of Fire Mountain Historical Western Romance Series

"Headstrong, brash, confident, and complex, the MacLarens of Fire Mountain will captivate you with strong characters set in the wild and rugged western frontier."

Handsome, ruthless, young U.S. Marshal Jamie MacLaren had lost everything—his parents, his family connections, and his childhood sweetheart—but now he's back in Fire Mountain and ready for another chance. Just as he successfully reconnects with his family and starts to rebuild his life, he gets the unexpected and unwanted assignment of rescuing the woman who broke his heart.

Beautiful, wealthy Victoria Wicklin chose money and power over love, but is now fighting for her life—or is she? Who has she become in the seven years since she left Fire Mountain to take up her life in San Francisco? Is she really as innocent as she says?

Marshal MacLaren struggles to learn the truth and do his job, but the past and present lead him in different directions as his heart and brain wage battle. Is Victoria a victim or a villain? Is life offering him another chance, or just another heartbreak?

As Jamie and Victoria struggle to uncover past secrets and come to grips with their shared passion, another danger arises. A life-altering danger that is out of their control and threatens to destroy any chance for a shared future.

Harder than the Rest – Book Three
MacLarens of Fire Mountain Historical Western Romance Series

"They are men you want on your side. Hard, confident, and loyal, the MacLarens of Fire Mountain will seize your attention from the first page."

Will MacLaren is a hardened, plain-speaking bounty hunter. His life centers on finding men guilty of horrendous crimes and making sure justice is done. There is no place in his world for the carefree attitude he carried years before when a tragic event destroyed his dreams.

Amanda is the daughter of a successful Colorado rancher. Determined and proud, she works hard to prove she is as capable as any man and worthy to be her father's heir. When a stranger arrives, her independent nature collides with the strong pull toward the handsome ranch hand. But is he what he seems and could his secrets endanger her as well as her family?

The last thing Will needs is to feel passion for another woman. But Amanda elicits feelings he thought were long buried. Can Will's desire for her change him? Or will the vengeance he seeks against the one man he wants to destroy—a dangerous opponent without a conscious—continue to control his life?

Stronger than the Rest – Book Four
MacLarens of Fire Mountain Historical Western Romance Series

"Smart, tough, and capable, the MacLarens protect their own no matter the odds. Set against America's rugged frontier, the stories of the men from Fire Mountain are complex, fast-paced, and a must read for anyone who enjoys non-stop action and romance."

Drew MacLaren is focused and strong. He has achieved all of his goals except one—to return to the

MacLaren ranch and build the best horse breeding program in the west. His successful career as an attorney is about to give way to his ranching roots when a bullet changes everything.

Tess Taylor is the quiet, serious daughter of a Colorado ranch family with dreams of her own. Her shy nature keeps her from developing friendships outside of her close-knit family until Drew enters her life. Their relationship grows. Then a bullet, meant for another, leaves him paralyzed and determined to distance himself from the one woman he's come to love.

Convinced he is no longer the man Tess needs, Drew focuses on regaining the use of his legs and recapturing a life he thought lost. But danger of another kind threatens those he cares about—including Tess—forcing him to rethink his future.

Can Drew overcome the barriers that stand between him, the safety of his friends and family, and a life with the woman he loves? To do it all, he has to be strong. Stronger than the Rest.

Deadlier than the Rest – Book Five
MacLarens of Fire Mountain Historical Western Romance Series

"A passionate, heartwarming story of the iconic MacLarens of Fire Mountain. This captivating historical western romance grabs your attention from the start with an engrossing story encompassing two romances set against the rugged backdrop of the burgeoning western frontier."

Connor MacLaren's search has already stolen eight years of his life. Now he is close to finding what he seeks—Meggie, his missing sister. His quest leads him to the growing city of Salt Lake and an encounter with the most captivating woman he has ever met.

Grace is the third wife of a Mormon farmer, forced into a life far different from what she'd have chosen. Her independent spirit longs for choices governed only by her own heart and mind. To achieve her dreams, she must hide behind secrets and half-truths, even as her heart pulls her towards the ruggedly handsome Connor.

Known as cool and uncompromising, Connor MacLaren lives by a few, firm rules that have served him well and kept him alive. However, danger stalks Connor, even to the front range of the beautiful Wasatch Mountains, threatening those he cares about and impacting his ability to find his sister.

Can Connor protect himself from those who seek his death? Will his eight-year search lead him to his sister while unlocking the secrets he knows are held tight within Grace, the woman who has captured his heart?

Read this heartening story of duty, honor, passion, and love in book five of the MacLarens of Fire Mountain series.

Second Summer – Book One
MacLarens of Fire Mountain Contemporary Romance Series

"In this passionate Contemporary Romance, author Shirleen Davies introduces her readers to the modern day MacLarens starting with Heath MacLaren, the head of the family."

The Chairman of both the MacLaren Cattle Co. and MacLaren Land Development, Heath MacLaren is a success professionally—his personal life is another matter.

Following a divorce after a long, loveless marriage, Heath spends his time with women who are beautiful and passionate, yet unable to provide what he longs for . . .

Heath has never experienced love even though he witnesses it every day between his younger brother, Jace, and wife, Caroline. He wants what they have, yet spends his time with women too young to understand what drives him and too focused on themselves to be true companions.

It's been two years since Annie's husband died, leaving her to build a new life. He was her soul mate and confidante. She has no desire to find a replacement, yet longs for male friendship.

Annie's closest friend in Fire Mountain, Caroline MacLaren, is determined to see Annie come out of her shell after almost two years of mourning. A chance meeting with Heath turns into an offer to be a part of the MacLaren Foundation Board and an opportunity for a life outside her home sanctuary which has also become her prison. The platonic friendship that builds between Annie and Heath points to a future where each may rely on the other without the bonds a romance would entail.

However, without consciously seeking it, each yearns for more . . .

The MacLaren Development Company is booming with Heath at the helm. His meetings at a partner company with the young, beautiful marketing director, who makes no secret of her desire for him, are a temptation. But is she the type of woman he truly wants?

Annie's acceptance of the deep, yet passionless, friendship with Heath sustains her, lulling her to believe it is all she needs. At least until Heath drops a bombshell, forcing Annie to realize that what she took for friendship is actually a deep, lasting love. One she doesn't want to lose.

Each must decide to settle—or fight for it all.

Hard Landing – Book Two
MacLarens of Fire Mountain Contemporary Romance Series

Trey MacLaren is a confident, poised Navy pilot. He's focused, loyal, ethical, and a natural leader. He is also on his way to what he hopes will be a lasting relationship and marriage with fellow pilot, Jesse Evans.

Jesse has always been driven. Her graduation from the Naval Academy and acceptance into the pilot training program are all she thought she wanted— until she discovered love with Trey MacLaren

Trey and Jesse's lives are filled with fast flying, friends, and the demands of their military careers. Lives each has settled into with a passion. At least until the day Trey receives a letter that could change his and Jesse's lives forever.

It's been over two years since Trey has seen the woman in Pensacola. Her unexpected letter stuns him and pushes Jesse into a tailspin from which she might not pull back.

Each must make a choice. Will the choice Trey makes cause him to lose Jesse forever? Will she follow her heart or her head as she fights for a chance to save the love she's found? Will their independent decisions collide, forcing them to give up on a life together?

One More Day – Book Three
MacLarens of Fire Mountain Contemporary Romance Series

Cameron "Cam" Sinclair is smart, driven, and dedicated, with an easygoing temperament that belies his strong will and the personal ambitions he holds close. Besides his family, his job as head of IT at the MacLaren Cattle Company and his position as a Search and Rescue volunteer are all he needs to make him happy. At least that's what he thinks until he meets, and is instantly drawn to, fellow SAR volunteer, Lainey Devlin.

Lainey is compassionate, independent, and ready to break away from her manipulative and controlling fiancé. Just as her decision is made, she's called into a major search and rescue effort, where once again, her path crosses with the intriguing, and much too handsome, Cam Sinclair. But Lainey's plans are set. An opportunity to buy a flourishing preschool in northern Arizona is her chance to make a fresh start, and nothing, not even her fierce attraction to Cam Sinclair, will impede her plans.

As Lainey begins to settle into her new life, an unexpected danger arises —threats from an unknown assailant—someone who doesn't believe she belongs in Fire Mountain. The more Lainey begins to love her new home, the greater the danger becomes. Can she accept the help and protection Cam offers while ignoring her consuming desire for him?

Even if Lainey accepts her attraction to Cam, will he ever be able to come to terms with his own driving ambition and allow himself to consider a different life than the one he's always pictured? A life with the one woman who offers more than he'd ever hoped to find?

All Your Nights – Book Four
MacLarens of Fire Mountain Contemporary Romance Series

Kade Taylor likes living on the edge. As an undercover agent for the DEA and a former Special Ops team member, his current assignment seems tame—keep tabs on a bookish Ph.D. candidate the agency believes is connected to a ruthless drug cartel.

Brooke Sinclair is weeks away from obtaining her goal of a doctoral degree. She spends time finalizing her presentation and relaxing with another student who seems to want nothing more than her friendship. That's fine with Brooke. Her last serious relationship ended in a broken engagement.

Her future is set, safe and peaceful, just as she's always planned—until Agent Taylor informs her she's under suspicion for illegal drug activities.

Kade and his DEA team obtain evidence which exonerates Brooke while placing her in danger from those who sought to use her. As Kade races to take down the drug cartel while protecting Brooke, he must also find common ground with the former suspect—a woman he desires with increasing intensity.

At odds with her better judgment, Brooke finds the more time she spends with Kade, the more she's attracted to the complex, multi-faceted agent. But Kade holds secrets he knows Brooke will never understand or accept.

Can Kade keep Brooke safe while coming to terms with his past, or will he stay silent, ruining any future with the woman his heart can't let go?

Always Love You– Book Five
MacLarens of Fire Mountain Contemporary Romance Series

"Romance, adventure, motorcycles, cowboys, suspense—everything you want in a contemporary western romance novel."

Eric Sinclair loves his bachelor status. His work at MacLaren Enterprises leaves him with plenty of time to ride his horse as well as his Harley...and date beautiful women without a thought to commitment.

Amber Anderson is the new person at MacLaren Enterprises. Her passion for marketing landed her what she believes to be the perfect job—until she steps into her first meeting to find the man she left, but still loves, sitting at the management table—his disdain for her clear.

Eric won't allow the past to taint his professional behavior, nor will he repeat his mistakes with

Amber, even though love for her pulses through him as strong as ever.

As they strive to mold a working relationship, unexpected danger confronts those close to them, pitting the MacLarens and Sinclairs against an evil who stalks one member but threatens them all.

Eric can't get the memories of their passionate past out of his mind, while Amber wrestles with feelings she thought long buried. Will they be able to put the past behind them to reclaim the love lost years before?

Hearts Don't Lie– Book Six
MacLarens of Fire Mountain Contemporary Romance Series

Mitch MacLaren has reasons for avoiding relationships, and in his opinion, they're pretty darn good. As the new president of RTC Bucking Bulls, difficult challenges occur daily. He certainly doesn't need another one in the form of a fiery, blue-eyed, redhead.

Dana Ballard's new job forces her to work with the one MacLaren who can't seem to get over himself and lighten up. Their verbal sparring is second nature and entertaining until the night of Mitch's departure when he surprises her with a dare she doesn't refuse.

With his assignment in Fire Mountain over, Mitch is free to return to Montana and run the business his father helped start. The glitch in his enthusiasm has to do with one irreversible mistake—the dare Dana didn't ignore. Now, for reasons that confound him, he just can't let it go.

Working together is a circumstance neither wants, but both must accept. As their attraction grows, so do the accidents and strange illnesses of the animals RTC depends on to stay in business. Mitch's total focus should be on finding the reasons and people behind the incidents. Instead, he finds himself torn between his unwanted desire for Dana and the business which is his life.

In his mind, a simple proposition can solve one problem. Will Dana make the smart move and walk away? Or take the gamble and expose her heart?

Redemption's Edge – Book One
Redemption Mountain – Historical Western Romance Series

"A heartwarming, passionate story of loss, forgiveness, and redemption set in the untamed frontier during the tumultuous years following the Civil War. Ms. Davies' engaging and complex characters draw you in from the start, creating an exciting introduction to this new historical western romance series."

"Redemption's Edge is a strong and engaging introduction to her new historical western romance series."

Dax Pelletier is ready for a new life, far away from the one he left behind in Savannah following the South's devastating defeat in the Civil War. The ex-Confederate general wants nothing more to do with commanding men and confronting the tough truths of leadership.

Rachel Davenport possesses skills unlike those of her Boston socialite peers—skills honed as a nurse in field hospitals during the Civil War. Eschewing her northeastern suitors and changed by the carnage she's seen, Rachel decides to accept her uncle's invitation to assist him at his clinic in the dangerous and wild frontier of Montana.

Now a Texas Ranger, a promise to a friend takes Dax and his brother, Luke, to the untamed territory of Montana. He'll fulfill his oath and return to Austin, at least that's what he believes.

The small town of Splendor is what Rachel needs after life in a large city. In a few short months, she's grown to love the people as well as the majestic beauty of the untamed frontier. She's settled into a life unlike any she has ever thought possible.

Thinking his battle days are over, he now faces dangers of a different kind—one by those from his past who seek vengeance, and another from Rachel, the woman who's captured his heart.

Wildfire Creek – Book Two
Redemption Mountain – Historical Western Romance Series

"A passionate story of rebuilding lives, working to find a place in the wild frontier, and building new lives in the years following the American Civil War. A rugged, heartwarming story of choices and love in the continuing saga of Redemption Mountain."

Luke Pelletier is settling into his new life as a rancher and occasional Pinkerton Agent, leaving his past as an ex-Confederate major and Texas Ranger far behind. He wants nothing more than to work the ranch, charm the ladies, and live a life of carefree bachelorhood.

Ginny Sorensen has accepted her responsibility as the sole provider for herself and her younger sister. The desire to continue their journey to Oregon is crushed when the need for food and shelter keeps them in the growing frontier town of Splendor, Montana, forcing Ginny to accept work as a server in the local saloon.

Luke has never met a woman as lovely and unspoiled as Ginny. He longs to know her, yet fears his wild ways and unsettled nature aren't what she deserves. She's a girl you marry, but that is nowhere in Luke's plans.

Complicating their tenuous friendship, a twist in circumstances forces Ginny closer to the man she most wants to avoid—the man who can destroy her dreams, and who's captured her heart.

Believing his bachelor status firm, Luke moves from danger to adventure, never dreaming each step he takes brings him closer to his true destiny and a life much different from what he imagines.

Sunrise Ridge – Book Three
Redemption Mountain – Historical Western Romance Series

"The author has a talent for bringing the historical west to life, realistically and vividly, and doesn't shy away from some of the harder aspects of frontier life, even though it's fiction. Recommended to readers who like sweeping western historical romances that are grounded with memorable, likeable characters and a strong sense of place."

Noah Brandt is a successful blacksmith and businessman in Splendor, Montana, with few ties to his past as an ex-Union Army major and sharpshooter. Quiet and hardworking, his biggest challenge is controlling his strong desire for a woman he believes is beyond his reach.

Abigail Tolbert is tired of being under her father's thumb while at the same time, being pushed away by the one man she desires. Determined to build a new life outside the control of her wealthy father, she finds work and sets out to shape a life on her own terms.

Noah has made too many mistakes with Abby to have any hope of getting her back. Even with the changes in her life, including the distance she's built with her father, he can't keep himself from believing he'll never be good enough to claim her.

Unexpected dangers, including a twist of fate for Abby, change both their lives, making the tentative steps they've taken to build a relationship a distant hope. As Noah battles his past as well as the threats to Abby, she fights for a future with the only man she will ever love.

Dixie Moon – Book Four
Redemption Mountain – Historical Western Romance Series

Gabe Evans is a man of his word with strong convictions and steadfast loyalty. As the sheriff of Splendor, Montana, the ex-Union Colonel and oldest of four boys from an affluent family, Gabe understands the meaning of responsibility. The last thing he wants is another commitment—especially of the female variety.

Until he meets Lena Campanel...

Lena's past is one she intends to keep buried. Overcoming a childhood of setbacks and obstacles, she and her friend, Nick, have succeeded in creating a life of financial success and devout loyalty to one another.

When an unexpected death leaves Gabe the sole heir of a considerable estate, partnering with Nick and Lena is a lucrative decision…forcing Gabe and Lena to work together. As their desire grows, Lena refuses to let down her guard, vowing to keep her past hidden—even from a perfect man like Gabe.

But secrets never stay buried…

When revealed, Gabe realizes Lena's secrets are deeper than he ever imagined. For a man of his character, deception and lies of omission aren't negotiable. Will he be able to forgive the deceit? Or is the damage too great to ever repair?

Reclaiming Love – Book One, A Novella
Peregrine Bay – Contemporary Romance Series

Adam Monroe has seen his share of setbacks. Now he's back in Peregrine Bay, looking for a new life and second chance.

Julia Kerrigan's life rebounded after the sudden betrayal of the one man she ever loved. As president of a success real estate company, she's built a new life and future, pushing the painful past behind her.

Adam's reason for accepting the job as the town's new Police Chief can be explained in one word—Julia. He wants her back and will do whatever is necessary to achieve his goal, even knowing his biggest hurdle is the woman he still loves.

As they begin to reconnect, a terrible scandal breaks loose with Julia and Adam at the center.

Will the threat to their lives and reputations destroy their fledgling romance? Can Adam identify and eliminate the danger to Julia before he's had a chance to reclaim her love?

Our Kind of Love – Book Two
Peregrine Bay – Contemporary Romance Series

Set in the beautiful lake country of Idaho, Peregrine Bay stories follow the lives of the five Kerrigan sisters and their family.

Read about Selena and Linc in book two. Releasing 2016

Colin's Quest – Book One
MacLarens of Boundary Mountain – Historical Western Romance Series

For An Undying Love...

When Colin MacLaren headed west on a wagon train, he hoped to find adventure and perhaps a little danger in untamed California. He never expected to meet the girl he would love forever. He also never expected her to be the daughter of his family's age-old enemy, but Sarah was a MacGregor and the anger he anticipated soon became a reality. Her father would not be swayed, vehemently refusing to allow marriage to a MacLaren.

Time Has No Effect...

Forced apart for five years, Sarah never forgot Colin—nor did she give up on his promise to come for her. Carrying the brooch he gave her as proof of their secret betrothal, she scans the trail from California, waiting for Colin to claim her. Unfortunately, her father has other plans.

And Enemies Hold No Power.

Nothing can stop Colin from locating Sarah. Not outlaws, runaways, or miles of difficult trails. However, reuniting is only the beginning. Together they must find the courage to fight the men who would keep them apart— and conquer the challenge of uniting two independent hearts.

http://www.shirleendavies.com/books.html

Colin's Quest is a work of fiction. Names, characters, places, and incidents are either products of the author's imagination or used facetiously. Any resemblance to actual events, locales, or persons, living or dead, is wholly coincidental.

www.ingramcontent.com/pod-product-compliance
Lightning Source LLC
Chambersburg PA
CBHW070418170726
48291CB00002B/257